CW00687968

Somebody Told Me

Stephen Puleston

ABOUT THE AUTHOR

Stephen Puleston was born and educated in Anglesey, North Wales. He graduated in theology before training as a lawyer. Somebody Told me is his third novel in the Inspector Marco series

www.stephenpuleston.co.uk
Facebook:stephenpulestoncrimewriter

OTHER NOVELS

Inspector Marco Novels

Prequel Novella– Ebook only
Dead Smart
Novels
Speechless
Another Good Killing
Somebody Told Me

Inspector Drake Mysteries

Prequel Novella– Ebook only
Devil's Kitchen
Novels
Brass in Pocket
Worse than Dead
Against the Tide

Copyright © 2016 Stephen Puleston
All rights reserved.
ISBN-13: 978-1534746886
ISBN-10: 1534746889:

In memory of my mother
Gwenno Puleston

Chapter 1

In a puddle of Diet Coke and piss is an unedifying place to die. I counted a single bullet wound to the centre of the man's forehead and several to his chest. His sweatshirt was a neutral grey, frayed around the collar. His jeans looked clean, at least the parts I could see. The oblong storeroom stank of the urine that had pooled by his feet on the concrete floor.

And there was blood. Thick pools of the stuff.

Against one wall were towers of various coloured soft drink cans, and lining another were boxes of crisps and snacks and chocolate bars. A wooden chair lay on its side a few feet away from the corpse. He looked mid-forties, clean-shaven, blonde hair. He lay on his side, one leg neatly on top of the other, facing towards me. I could see the outline of a wallet in his rear right hip pocket. Outside I heard a man's voice raised in disbelief, then a woman answering back in a thick Cardiff accent. I opened the door and walked into the kitchen of the café and then through into the main seating area. It was a bright warm September morning and I looked over Roath Park lake; two boats were already bobbing along on the surface of the water.

A uniformed officer, his face flushed and harassed, was talking to a stocky woman with a pale complexion, who I had seen dragging heavily on a cigarette outside the café earlier. She was sitting by one of the tables snivelling into a handkerchief. The officer left us and joined a colleague in talks with customers who kept pointing at the café as though they expected the place to open without more delay.

'This is Mary Peters, sir. She found the body first thing this morning.'

Mary made another blubbing sound and then blew her nose.

'It's terrible. I should be open now. I don't know what my boss will say.'

'Do you know who the dead man is?'

She gazed up at me in disbelief. Then she blew her nose again and shook her head at the same time.

'When did you arrive?' I said.

'It was the usual time.'

'And what time is that?' I would be here all morning at this rate.

'Half-seven.'

'What time do you open normally?'

She blew her nose yet again. 'Half past eight.'

'Did you notice anything out of the ordinary this morning?'

She opened her eyes wide, the shock evident. Then she shook her head slowly. After a halting explanation that everything was normal when she arrived at work I heard a voice raised in temper by the front door before a man barged in. He was swarthy, with thick black hair. In the distance, I could hear the siren of an approaching police car.

'What the hell has happened?'

I pushed my warrant card towards him. 'Detective Inspector John Marco. Who are you?'

'Steve Tucker. I'm the manager here.'

'Mary discovered a body in the storeroom when she arrived at work.'

He glanced at the door to the kitchen.

'Who is it? I mean, is it one of the girls who work here?'

'It's a man. This is a crime scene so I'm afraid you'll need to leave.'

I ushered them towards the door and gestured at

one of the uniformed officers.

'When can we open?' Tucker said, hovering by the door. 'I can't afford to lose all this business. It's my livelihood and our busy period's starting.' He stood quite still, hands on hips. 'I need to know when I'll be able to open. I've got staff to pay. This could be a disaster for my business – people talk, soon everyone will know that someone was killed here.'

'A man was murdered in your café: which was a *disaster* for him. And his family. You'll be notified once we've finished.'

The uniformed officer stood by my side now. 'Give your personal details to this officer. We'll be in touch with you shortly.'

Tucker stared at me defiantly as though he was thinking how he could challenge me further. Common sense prevailed, and he left. After a few seconds I followed him outside where I dragged a packet of cigarettes from my pocket. It was the second of my five-a-day habit and I sparked my Zippo into life and drew deeply.

It was my first day back after a three-week holiday. Hundreds of emails needing my attention swamped my inbox that morning making my vacation a distant memory. I had heard the reluctance in my voice when area control rang to tell me that as the nearest senior officer the case had been allocated to me. And, surprise, too, as normally I preferred the day-to-day work of real policing to the grind of paperwork.

There was a commotion as more uniformed police officers arrived, followed quickly by Alvine Dix, a crime scene manager, with two of her regular investigators in tow. Alvine had been a fixture at Queen Street police station longer than I had been there. She liked walking in the Brecon Beacons, I knew that much, and she'd had an unsuccessful marriage to a librarian she had met online, but after she caught him wearing her clothes one evening when she returned home early things hadn't worked out between them.

'Good morning, John,' Alvine said.

I crushed the butt under my shoe. 'Alvine.'

I gave her colleagues brief nods. She dictated instructions for the CSIs to establish a perimeter and then we walked through the café to the storeroom. It felt hotter now and the smell stronger.

'Who found the body?'

'One of the staff when she arrived for work.'

Alvine scanned the room taking in the stacks of cans shrouded in thin plastic. 'We'll get started.' There was a purposeful tone to her voice, almost contented.

'I'll need the wallet in his pocket. There might be identification.'

She shouted for the photographer who appeared in the doorway moments later. He was finished in seconds and she fished out the wallet into an evidence pouch and handed it to me. I snapped on a pair of latex gloves and counted forty pounds in well-thumbed five-pound notes and some loose change in a pouch. But no credit card or debit card or driving licence and nothing to tell me who the man might be so any family would have to wait.

Back in the café I stopped to look out over the lake again. The sunshine glistened on the water now and onlookers had gathered on the opposite bank, craning to get a view of the café. Soon the reporters would arrive with cameras and lights and notebooks at the ready.

In the meantime, I had to find out who the mystery man might be.

Then I heard the familiar sound of Lydia's voice. I turned and noticed her nodding to one of the officers by the door. I followed her purposeful and determined walk through the café: she had the ability to make calmness seem natural.

'Good morning, boss.' Her black jacket looked new and flecks of her auburn hair already coloured its shoulders. In profile her nose was bold but face-on it complemented her wide mouth and strong dark eyes perfectly. 'How was your holiday?'

'Great thanks.'

'Glad to be back?' She grinned, knowing I need not answer. 'Did Dean enjoy himself?'

Spending time with my son had been the big bonus of my holiday. I wanted to be a real father, not like the semi-detached version I had been over the past few years. Dean had picked up a few words of Italian and my mother's family had spoilt him continuously for the three weeks we had been staying with them. Even my vocabulary had improved.

'We had a great time. And what a welcome back.'

Her face hardened. 'There's a body?'

I jerked my head behind me. 'A member of staff found the corpse in the storeroom behind the kitchen when she arrived this morning.'

'Any ID?'

I wandered over to the window. 'Only an empty wallet.'

I read the time. The pathologist was late. A hearse might even arrive before him.

'I'll call central operations.' Lydia dialled the number, and I heard her asking for details of all missing persons for the last forty-eight hours. I caught a glimpse of the uniformed officers outside marshalling the perimeter of the crime scene and talking to the public. Then I noticed the small figure of Dr Paddy McVeigh walking down the path towards the café entrance. He spoke a few words with one of the officers and then disappeared from view only to re-emerge through the main entrance.

'Inspector Marco. Sorry I'm late. Traffic was terrible.'

'Paddy. How are you?'

'Fair to middling. Can't complain. So where is ...'

I nodded to the kitchen door. 'In a storeroom at the back.'

Paddy strode into the kitchen, past the stainless steel worktops and microwaves to the door at the rear. I followed and listened as he exchanged pleasantries with Alvine who then stepped out into the kitchen. He knelt by the body and started his examination.

I gazed around the storeroom. In the far corner a double door was barred. A single fluorescent tube hummed loudly. I struck me as odd that there was only one chair. If the dead man had been sitting on it had the killer stood up, I wondered. Or had he been the one sitting down?

I looked over at Alvine. 'I want all the chairs in the café dusted and examined.'

She frowned and opened her mouth to reproach me, no doubt. I didn't give her an explanation because Paddy stood up and turned to me.

'Gunshot wounds. Small bore hand gun, I'd say and ...' He looked around the storeroom. 'The body hasn't been moved so he was killed here. I'll get more from the post mortem report but it looks like he drank some Coke before he was killed. It must have gone all over him.'

Once Paddy had left I looked down at our mystery man, who was lying on his back now, when Lydia came in to stand by my side. She peered down and then turned to me.

'I know that face.'

'What?'

'That's Felix Bevard.'

Chapter 2

The house had well-maintained hedges in a crescent-shaped rockery that edged the drive. Small ornamental trees stood in wooden tubs near the front door. It looked like an ordinary suburban house with a double garage and vertical blinds on the downstairs windows. Lydia drove past and then turned round to park. After reading the intelligence report on Felix Bevard sent to my mobile I realised that he was far from ordinary. His minicab business was suspected of being implicated in drug trafficking and prostitution and his pub, the Lemon Grove, was the ideal venue to launder significant amounts of ready cash. I wondered what his neighbours thought of him.

Three unsolved murders in Cardiff were linked to Bevard and known organised crime groups. A flag on the file warned of significant intelligence on Bevard being available in other police force areas. When her husband hadn't arrived home the night before Mrs Bevard had reported him missing. The details were unremarkable, standard phrases taken from the computer system that never reflected the worry of a wife or husband. The usual reassurance had been given that everything would be done to find him. A family liaison officer was due to arrive later.

I stood by the front door and pressed the bell. It had a nice middle-class chime to it and I imagined Gloria Bevard in happier circumstances making pastry in the kitchen listening to Radio 4.

She yanked the door open and stared at us. 'Have you found him?'

Gloria Bevard had blazing red hair, a long chin and one eye that looked slightly off centre, making it difficult to judge how to look at her. No amount of make-up could disguise the crow's feet gripping the side of each eye under which there were deep bags. A silver pendant hung around her neck with the word Gloria engraved on it.

She lowered her head hoping, I guessed, for some positive response.

I had my warrant card ready. 'Detective Inspector Marco and Detective Sergeant Flint. May we come in?'

Gloria led us into an enormous sitting room. Prints and photographs of family adorned one wall. Heavy curtains with extravagant swags and swirls hung at each end of the windows. Gloria stood by a sofa fidgeting with her hands until she started chewing a nail. Breaking bad news was never easy.

'May we sit down?' I used a warm get-to-know-you tone.

She nodded and fell into one of the sofas that almost engulfed her thin figure.

'Do you have anyone at home with you?'

She shook her head. 'Kids are at school.'

'I'm afraid we have bad news. We found a body this morning that we believe is your husband.'

Her lips quivered, she clutched her hands to her mouth, and sobbed.

'Can I get you some water?' Lydia said.

Gloria mumbled confirmation before reaching for a box of tissues on the coffee table.

'I knew something was wrong. He's never late home.' Then the tears started.

Lydia returned with a glass of water that Gloria grasped tightly.

'We've arranged for a family liaison officer to be with you later today.'

She looked over at me wide-eyed and shell-shocked.

Lydia continued. 'They are specially trained officers that will help you.'

I hesitated. 'I know this is a difficult time but I need to establish where your husband was last night.'

She sipped on her water before speaking. 'He's never late ... And I know he wasn't the best of people ... But we loved each other. What am I going to do now?' She put down her glass and reached for fresh tissues to wipe her eyelids.

'When did you see him last?'

She looked down at her hands. 'Yesterday. I can't think ... breakfast. I don't ...'

'Where was he going yesterday?'

She wrapped her arms around her knees and rocked back and forth. 'He was going to play golf. He should have been ...'

'When were you expecting him home?'

'Last night. He should have been here when I got back.'

'You were out too?' Lydia asked.

'I should have been here.' She scrunched up a handful of tissues. 'I was out with friends for a birthday party.'

'Who was your husband playing golf with yesterday? I'll need their names.'

The doorbell rang. Lydia stood up and left as Gloria found the contact telephone numbers of Bevard's playing partners, which I jotted down in my pocketbook. A family liaison officer appeared at the sitting room door with Lydia and we made the introductions.

'Do you know of anyone who might want to hurt your husband?' I asked.

Gloria glanced over at Lydia and then at the family liaison officer before she crumpled her face into an agonising frown. Then she looked up. 'It must have been that scumbag Walsh.'

Lydia glanced over at me, puzzled.

'Who do you mean?' I said.

'Jimmy Walsh. This has got his name all over it.'

I stood by the hastily erected board in the Incident Room and stared over at the rest of my team. Wyn Nuttall looked thinner than usual: his neck longer than I remembered, his head high above his shoulders. His shirt was a size too large and that made the neatly knotted tie look untidy. He stared over at me intently. Everything seemed exciting for Wyn, more adventurous than policing in his native North Wales no doubt.

A photograph of Bevard taken by the CSIs had been pinned to the board.

'Who was he, boss?' Wyn said.

'Felix Bevard owns a minicab business and a pub, which are perfect ways to launder money. He was killed in a storeroom in the café at Roath Park. He was shot in the head and the chest – several times. Mrs Bevard will make the formal identification later today. Lydia identified Bevard at the scene.'

Lydia cleared her throat. 'I was a detective constable on a case where we suspected he was involved in a string of burglaries. We couldn't prove anything and in the last few years he has kept out of trouble.'

Jane Thorne, sitting alongside Lydia, piped up. 'Any forensics yet on the gun used?'

I shook my head.

Jane had been languishing as a detective constable for too long to have any realistic expectation of promotion. Her last attempt at the sergeant's exams had been unsuccessful, so she had settled into her role with a seriousness that made her boring. Steely grey streaks in her centre-parted hair reinforced the impression she was the oldest in the room.

I shared a glance between Jane and Wyn. 'We've got the names of two men he was playing golf with yesterday afternoon. And the names of the staff at the café. I need you to contact them and get preliminary statements. And we find out from the widow where she was last night and get the names of her friends etc... You know the drill. We piece together Bevard's last known movements.'

I reached for a photograph from the desk in front of me. 'This is a picture of Jimmy Walsh, who the widow named as being responsible for his death.'

'Who's Walsh?' Jane said.

I replaced the image before replying. 'Mrs Bevard told us that Felix and Walsh had a falling-out over a property in Newport. Before that they were best mates. Walsh was implicated in an unsolved murder of a man called Robin Oakley, who was allegedly killed because he wouldn't agree to sell a property to one of Jimmy Walsh's companies.' Stillness fell on the Incident Room. 'His body was found in a boat floating on Roath Park lake early one morning. He was a nice bloke apparently, well known in the community, supported local charities. We couldn't prove anything. Not a bloody thing.'

Lydia interjected. 'Walsh's reputation is for random violence.'

I continued. 'So I need a full analysis on Bevard's mobile telephone. And we need to go through all his bank accounts, credit cards. I need to know everything about him.'

'Do we start on Walsh too, boss?' Jane said.

Lydia responded. 'That will prove difficult.'

'He's in prison,' I said.

Chapter 3

The call to visit Superintendent Cornock wasn't a request, but more of a summons. His normally pallid complexion had greyed more than just a shade or two. Now he was looking positively unhealthy. Years of working ridiculous hours had taken their toll and he sat unselfconsciously fingering a packet of painkillers, a glass of water on the desk in front of him. The tropical fish tank in the corner made a gurgling sound.

'Felix Bevard,' Cornock announced as though the dead man were the first minister of Wales.

'His body was found this morning.'

Cornock nodded, 'I know.'

'I've spoken to Mrs Bevard. She was pretty cut up and she pointed the finger at Jimmy Walsh.'

More nodding. It was unlike Cornock not to respond.

'But as you know, sir, he's inside. I haven't checked his release date but it can't be long.'

'Sixteen days.'

The precision of Cornock's reply rattled me. Realising that he had more to tell me, I stopped. He slowly turned the packet of paracetamol through his fingers. 'I've arranged for you to be briefed by an inspector from one of the dedicated source units.'

I moved forward slightly in my chair.

'Felix Bevard was about to sign a deal to make him a supergrass. He would give evidence against Jimmy Walsh in exchange for being taken into witness protection.'

'Bloody hell. Walsh must have got to him first.'

Cornock leant forward over the desk. 'Walsh is a sociopath that we've been trying to lock up permanently for years.'

'But he's got the perfect alibi.'

'It must have been someone with links to Walsh. So you had better be careful.'

I didn't need to find obstacles; Cornock had thrown them into the investigation like an unexploded grenade. A dedicated source unit handled human intelligence, not something from a sci-fi movie, but in fact a team of officers that specialised in handling informants. And this DSU had the task of handling Bevard. I groaned to myself at the prospect that poking into their little empire would be unwelcome.

But we had a suspect. Jimmy Walsh. He had a motive.

Walsh would have friends and fixers – people who did things for him, solved his problems so he wouldn't have to get his hands dirty. Or dirty enough for him to be caught.

'There's one more thing, John.' Cornock looked up at me. 'I'm taking a sabbatical for a few weeks – doctor's orders.' His eye contact drifted away. 'My wife hasn't been too good recently and perhaps you weren't aware but my daughter is back home with us now.'

I nodded. Cornock's daughter's drug addiction had been the subject of gossip around Queen Street but I hadn't heard that she was back in Cardiff. I realised that I had no idea how old Cornock was – probably older than I thought. Then I wondered about his replacement – most likely a DCI from one of the other teams. Mentally I ticked off various names.

'I'm sure you're interested in who might take over from me.'

I smiled wanly. 'Of course.'

'This is your first day back?'

'Yes, sir.'

'Then you possibly haven't heard about Dave

Hobbs' promotion.'

My body froze. Rigid to the spot. I couldn't move. And I definitely couldn't find anything to say.

'While you were away DCI Webster died of a heart attack.'

I hadn't heard and I should have felt sad. I knew Webster, and he had always been a decent officer. And now Dave Hobbs would be his replacement.

'With you on holiday in Lucca a decision had to be made quickly. I know that you and Inspector Hobbs have had your differences in the past but I hope you can put all of that behind you now?'

Not a chance. Hobbs hates my guts.

Dave Hobbs had never hidden his dislike for my methods or his contempt for my past when the booze had its claws into me, even though I had put my drinking days behind me. And his naked ambition made working with him difficult when I never knew what was going on in his mind.

'His promotion to Acting Detective Chief Inspector was confirmed this morning.'

I wanted to offer my resignation on the spot but I was too surprised to say anything.

'You'll be answering to him during this investigation while I am on sabbatical until the correct command structure can be put in place.'

I left Cornock's office and dragged myself back to the Incident Room, my head a mass of conflicting emotions. My shoulders wanted to sag. I desperately wanted to be back in Lucca, walking along the city walls with Dean or drinking coffee in one of the small cafés off the main square. Anywhere but Queen Street police station being answerable to *Acting* Detective *Chief* Inspector Hobbs. The image of his small piggy eyes came to mind and then I heard his grating accent, from Caernarfon or one of those places in the mountains of the north that had a castle. I ignored Lydia, who was saying something, and after slamming the door to my office shut, I slumped into my chair.

The telephone rang in the Incident Room beyond my door. And it didn't seem to stop.

Then it rang in my office and I snatched the handset off the cradle. It was Lydia. 'I've got an Inspector Ackroyd from a DSU wanting to fix a meeting with you. He says it's urgent.'

'Tell him … We need to go … Later, tell him later this afternoon.'

I slammed the telephone down.

I drew a hand over my face. Then I stood up and headed for the door. Lydia and the others didn't look up and nobody asked what was wrong. And what could I tell them? That my senior officer was a north Walian who had scrambled eggs for brains.

I left the station intending to walk around the block, clear my thoughts, restore some equilibrium to my mind but I kept picturing Hobbs sitting in Cornock's office and each time the stress returned. I marched down Queen Street and into one of the main shopping arcades. The shops didn't register and eventually I found myself on the Hays where I stopped and ordered a coffee. I sat watching the mid-week shoppers passing me. The words of the resignation letter I had been drafting lost their urgency as my mind turned to the tasks in hand. Hobbs' promotion was only temporary after all and I was still the senior investigating officer. I had a killer to find so I threw off my frustration and made my way back to Queen Street.

Lydia stood up as I entered the Incident Room and followed me through to my office. 'Inspector Ackroyd has called again.'

I sat down by my desk.

'What does he want, boss?' She said it slowly as though she was measuring every syllable.

It took me five minutes to summarise the position.

'So we'll have to investigate the DSU officers,' I added.

She creased her mouth. 'Jesus. They won't like that.'

Detective Inspector Malcolm Ackroyd had restless eyes that darted around. He wore a three-piece navy pinstripe suit, a rarity in plain clothes these days. He turned up his nose as he scanned my navy trousers and my battered herringbone jacket. He sat down on one of the visitor chairs.

'John. I need to brief you on this Bevard case.' Ackroyd had a dense, deep voice.

Lydia closed the door to my office and Ackroyd gave her a truculent glance but said nothing. I was ready to tell him that briefing me included Lydia no matter what he thought.

Ackroyd pulled out a sheaf of papers from the briefcase on his lap. 'Bevard and Walsh were implicated in a murder two years ago in Roath Park.'

He glanced at me before continuing.

'Detective Chief Inspector Webster was the SIO for that inquiry and he made absolutely no headway with the case.'

At the time, I was a sergeant in plain clothes in Merthyr Tydfil but I recalled the publicity surrounding the inquiry.

'Mr Oakley was shot and then his body dumped in a boat on the lake. There was no forensics although we were certain he wasn't killed in the park.'

'Does Walsh have a thing for Roath Park?'

'He was brought up in Roath. He met his wife there

apparently and he loves the place. His Facebook page is full of images of him and his family walking in the park.'

Lydia snorted her surprise. 'He's in prison and he's got a Facebook page?'

'His wife runs it.'

'So what changed?' Something had made Bevard a candidate for a supergrass deal – he must have had new information about the Oakley murder that implicated Walsh.

Ackroyd put the briefcase down by his feet and settled back into his chair. 'A routine CSI search of one of Bevard's minicabs, part of another investigation unrelated to the Oakley case, discovered blood residue in the boot. It came back as a match to Oakley.'

I whistled under my breath. 'That's a result.'

Ackroyd nodded. 'But although we had Bevard implicated, we wanted Walsh too. More than anything the senior officers wanted Walsh convicted of murder. It was like an obsession. He had to be put away at all costs. So we looked at the supergrass option. Then we planned Bevard's arrest carefully to avoid any possibility that anyone, including his wife, would get to know.'

'So what was the deal?'

'He had been promised immunity from prosecution in exchange for enough evidence to convict Walsh of Oakley's murder.'

I sat back in my chair stunned. A troubled look appeared on Lydia's face.

'But Bevard was involved in the Oakley murder,' I said.

'On the basis of his evidence the most we could prove against him would have been a secondary role. The senior officers were salivating at the prospect of a clear-cut case against Walsh – something to put him behind bars for years.'

The supergrass deals had a bad reputation. It meant dishonest, disreputable men giving evidence against equally dishonest, disreputable men where the motives of everyone were dubious. Prosecutors hoped for minimal publicity whenever there were trials that relied on such evidence because the whole process stank. I was getting a very bad feeling the more I listened to Ackroyd.

'Who knew about the agreement?'

Ackroyd sighed. 'It was my team that led the process.' He pointed to the file. 'The names of everyone involved are in the papers. All the officers have been with my unit for years and all fully cleared.'

I had never worked in professional standards, the department that policed the police officers, and I had no interest in doing so but now I'd have no choice.

Ackroyd continued. 'The whole purpose of a dedicated source unit is to make certain that we have a *sterile corridor* to all of our informants.' He paused and drew a hand in the air. 'But you know that of course.'

'There must have been prosecutors involved.' Until her intervention, Lydia had sat silently staring at Ackroyd.

He started to nod. 'Of course. Everyone linked to the supergrass deal is mentioned in the file.

'We'll need—'

Ackroyd finished my sentence in a neutral tone. 'Full financial checks on everyone associated with the case and full background checks. I can tell you now, John. It wasn't anybody in my team. They are *one hundred per cent* safe. Nobody would sell Bevard out. Nobody.'

I drew a hand over the buff folder on the table. But somebody *had* sold him out. As well as investigating fellow officers there would be lawyers too.

'I'll need the original file from the investigation into

Oakley's murder.'

'Why?'

Ackroyd's reply annoyed me. He had promised complete cooperation and yet in the same conversation challenged me.

'I'll run this investigation the way I please. We'll collect the file this afternoon.'

'You know full well I can't tell you where the DSU is based.'

I leant forward on the desk. 'Your unit is compromised from top to bottom. So you can forget the petty protocols about keeping your address secret from the rest of us ordinary plain clothes officers.'

Ackroyd glared at me and paused. 'I'll deliver the papers personally.'

'I need to explain this to my team and you're staying.' I stood up and paced out into the Incident Room.

'I really don't think ...' Ackroyd protested.

A photograph of Bevard was already pinned to the middle of the board. I turned to face Wyn and Jane, unease creasing their faces. Lydia stood behind them alongside Ackroyd who had his arms folded. I could see the incredulity on the faces of Wyn and Jane when I explained that we'd have to investigate the DSU. And Crown Prosecution lawyers. 'Detective Inspector Ackroyd here has given us his assurance that there will be full cooperation from his team.'

Ackroyd mumbled his agreement.

'Where do we start, boss?' Wyn said.

'At the beginning. All the usual checks, bank accounts, family etc... Any links to Walsh or anyone who may have worked other cases involved with him and his family.'

Ackroyd made to leave. I turned to him. 'Malcolm. One more thing. Who was the sergeant on the Oakley case?'

He stopped by the door and turned to face me. 'Dave Hobbs.'

Chapter 4

A single red horizontal barrier guarded the main entrance to HMP Grange Hall. Adapted as an open prison after the end of the Second World War from an RAF base, it had no fences or guards patrolling the perimeter. Occasionally a prisoner found the temptation to abscond too great and publicity would follow. After identifying ourselves to a guard engrossed in the morning's newspaper we walked over to the administration block. I pressed the intercom and stood waiting. It reminded me of the black-and-white war films featuring men with clipped accents flying off into the sunset in Spitfires and Hurricanes.

The intercom crackled and I introduced Lydia and myself. There was a bleeping sound and I pushed open the door. A woman with an intense stare and clothes that my mother would have thought fashionable led us through corridors covered with lino that sparkled from recent cleaning.

Outside a door with *Governor* printed on a large metal plaque, she stopped and knocked. After a shout from inside she pushed open the door and led us inside. Governor James stood in front of her desk, and reached out a hand. 'Amanda James, governor.' We shook hands and she waved us to a round table in one corner of the room. I had expected the woman who'd met us to leave but she sat down and dragged a folder on the table towards her.

'You've already met Sandra,' James said.

'I don't believe we were properly introduced,' I said.

Sandra didn't raise her eyes from the sheets of paper open in front of her. 'Sandra Green. Jimmy Walsh's probation officer.' She managed an indifferent tone that matched her colourless complexion.

'I'm not certain how we can help,' James said once

she had sat down.

I leant over the table. 'Walsh is a prime suspect in relation to the murder of Felix Bevard.'

James nodded; Green cast me an intense frown.

'You're not seriously suggesting that Walsh was personally responsible?' James didn't give me an opportunity to reply. 'Because I've been through our roll call for the past three days and Jimmy Walsh was present and accounted for on each occasion.'

'Don't some of your prisoners work outside in the community?'

'Yes, but not Walsh. And before you ask, he could not have *slipped out* on the evening in question.'

'How many times are the prisoners checked each day?'

James let out a brief sigh. 'The first roll call is at midday before they have lunch. The second is in the afternoon. And the final roll call is in the evening. An officer will go around the billet and check on each prisoner – there are spy holes in the door, the sort you get in hotels.'

'Have you spoken to the officers who conducted the roll call check?'

James gave me a puzzled look. 'Whatever for? If a prisoner is absent from the roll call then we have a system for instigating a search. Inspector, Jimmy Walsh was here on the night Bevard was killed.'

'Of course, but he might be responsible for directing the murder.' I paused. 'Presumably you keep a record of Walsh's visitors?'

'Of course.'

'I'll need to see a complete list.'

James pushed over a folder.

'Do you have details of the telephone calls he made?'

'We can do better than that. All the calls are recorded digitally. I'll send you the voice file of all his recent conversations.'

Lydia made her first contribution. 'How long has Walsh been in Grange Hall?'

James played with a ballpoint, failing to hide her irritation. 'He was transferred here six months ago for the last part of his sentence. He was allocated work in one of the greenhouses supervised by the gardening staff. We grow vegetables for the prison estate. So he spends his days cutting tomatoes, weeding, general gardening chores. Sandra can tell you more about him.'

We turned to look at Sandra Green. She had thin colourless lips and untidy hair. She squinted, first at me then Lydia, before putting both hands on top of the papers in front of her as though she were preparing to make an announcement.

'Walsh has always been civil to me and my staff.'

'We were hoping you could give us more background into his family,' Lydia said.

'He was brought up by a single mother, and she had a string of failed relationships often with violent men. All of which contributed to his behaviour and personality. And she was an older mother – late thirties.'

'Were there siblings?'

'I believe there was mention of a twin having died at birth. Multiple births are more common in older mothers.'

James butted in. 'He had a difficult upbringing. That doesn't excuse his criminality.'

I doubted that the family of Mr Oakley would take such a sympathetic view of Jimmy Walsh.

'Do you check his mail?'

'All the mail is opened and given a cursory check. But letters aren't read. We don't have the resources to undertake that sort of task.'

'Did Walsh share a cell?'

James shook her head. 'He had his own cell on a billet with sixteen other men of his own age. All very quiet, no trouble.'

'We'll need a list of all the other prisoners on the same billet as Walsh.'

James made an exaggerated motion of reading the time. 'I *hope* this will not be a waste of your time, Inspector.'

I hoped so too. Walsh was our only suspect. He might not have killed Bevard, but he had directed the murder. All I had to do was find out who had pulled the trigger. 'If Walsh conspired with somebody else to kill Bevard, then that somebody could have been on the same billet as Walsh. So I'll need a list of all the prisoners released in the last month.'

'But there are other billets, and prisoners are released every day,' James sounded sceptical. 'Where are you going to stop?'

'When I've secured a conviction.'

It earned me a dull glare. And when I asked to see Walsh's cell James's forehead creased with incredulity. I wanted to see his personal space and grudgingly James agreed to accompany us.

'How many prisoners have you got?' Lydia asked as we skirted round a collection of single-storey buildings set out on each side of a quadrangle.

'It varies but usually just over six hundred.'

James led us to the far end of the prison. Eventually we stopped by the gable end of a billet. A uniformed prison officer that James introduced as Prison Officer Yelland joined us. I caught the smell of stale alcohol on his breath as we exchanged a few words. Then he paced over to the entrance and moments later a prisoner emerged looking puzzled.

We followed James into the billet and Yelland locked the door.

'He was the billet cleaner,' Yelland announced. 'All the other prisoners will be at work.'

The floors looked clean, more sparkling lino and smooth plastered walls. In front of us was a small makeshift kitchen, two microwaves and a sink. I walked down the corridor, each door numbered. Tucked into one corner of the ceiling was a CCTV camera.

'How long do you keep the CCTV tapes?' I said.

James sounded hesitant. 'I'm not certain. One of the staff—'

'Send us all the coverage for two weeks before the murder of Bevard.'

'I can't see how that will help.'

'Everything we know about Walsh will help.'

At the end was a toilet and shower block and two telephones screwed to a wall. I stared at them, conjuring up images of Walsh speaking to his family: exchanging small talk, asking about the weather.

Lydia was behind me. She pushed open the door to the bathroom. A half-empty bucket of water with a mop stood in the middle of the floor. The adjacent shower block smelt of disinfectant.

I turned back and joined James and Yelland outside a door marked sixteen.

Yelland found the master key and a second later the door was open.

I stood for a moment staring at the small cell that Walsh occupied. He had planned Bevard's murder here. I stepped in, Lydia following behind me. A small television sat on a shelf above a table. A duvet lay in untidy lumps over the bed. Walsh had few personal possessions; a biography of a well-known footballer sat alongside a book that accompanied a TV series about tracing your family. At the end of the narrow shelf were six CDs: Michael Bublé, a Rod Stewart Christmas special and four different compilations.

'I've never been inside a prison cell before,' Lydia said.

I walked over to the window. It opened a few inches only, dispelling any notion that Walsh could have slipped out in the middle of the night, killed Bevard and then returned unnoticed.

'Have you seen enough, Inspector?' James said.

I stared around the cell. I had moved nothing. Walsh would be none the wiser. I turned and left, letting Yelland pull the door closed. The billet cleaner sat on a wooden bench drawing heavily on a roll-up cigarette when we walked past him.

Twenty minutes later we were heading back for Cardiff and our second appointment with Mrs Bevard.

Chapter 5

Gloria Bevard had her mobile telephone pinned to her ear, obviously deeply engrossed in some conversation as I parked next to her Ford Focus in the car park of the Lemon Grove pub. She gave us an intense stare. Earlier that morning I had spoken with the family liaison officer who had stayed with Gloria the previous day. Her parents had arrived, then her sister and gradually Gloria's extended family were providing the sort of support that only a closely knit family could do. I had suggested that the family liaison officer keep regular contact with Gloria; after all, widows could appear resilient in the first few days after a bereavement only to find their world collapsing when they truly realised what had happened.

Looking over at Gloria sitting in her car, talking calmly on the telephone, make-up seemingly perfect, not a hair out of place, I wondered what sort of relationship she really had with Felix Bevard.

'What did you make of Mrs Bevard?' I said.

'She was genuine enough.' Lydia gave me a sharp glance. 'Why?'

'She must have known all about her husband.'

'That doesn't mean she's involved.' Lydia opened the door and I did the same. Gloria Bevard was still talking animatedly to someone as we stood self-consciously waiting for her to finish.

'Sorry about that,' Gloria said, emerging from the car. Seeing her outside didn't change the impression she had created in my mind earlier. She wore a black trouser suit and modest heels. She sounded businesslike when she looked over at the main entrance. 'Shall we go in?'

Since I had stopped drinking, entering a public house created a certain apprehension, revisiting part of my life that I had wanted to close off. I shrugged off my uneasiness; nobody was forcing me to have a drink – this visit was all part of work. The Lemon Grove was rediscovering itself as a bistro pub. Gloria led the way past a collection of leather sofas and healthy-looking indoor plants. A board with the daily specials menu written up in white chalk had a prominent place above the bar area.

Felix Bevard's office was on the first floor so we followed Gloria up the narrow staircase.

She sat down on a cream leather executive chair and sighed. 'He loved this chair. It cost him a fortune. I told him he was mad to spend so much money.'

She gazed over all the paperwork on the desk. And then she scanned the room as though it seemed unfamiliar.

'We'll need a list of all his employees,' I said.

'He kept all his paperwork neat and tidy.' She tipped her head towards two grey filing cabinets.

'Did he have anyone who helped him?' Lydia said.

Gloria frowned. 'What, like a secretary you mean?' She answered her own question. 'The accountants came in once a month and did all the paperwork, the payroll, kept everything legit.'

I wanted to guffaw but she continued. 'There's a woman who runs the minicab business. She does the rosters for the lads. She makes sure all the cars are serviced. We've had complaints made to trading standards in the past so we always keep all the cars bang up-to-date.'

I scanned the framed photographs on the walls that contained images of various footballers. Lydia turned to Gloria. 'How many people are employed here?'

I looked over at Gloria who shrugged. 'A dozen maybe. You need to talk to Harry.'

'Harry?' I said.

'He's the manager here.'

'So there *is* someone who helped Felix with running the place.'

'Yeah, of course.'

'Was he on good terms with Harry? Anybody been fired recently?'

'What do you mean? I told you, it was that scumbag Jimmy Walsh who killed my Felix. I'd swear on a stack of bibles that there was nobody else involved. He didn't have any other enemies.'

'Has there been anybody making any threats against Felix?' Lydia said.

Gloria shook her head. I stood up and walked around the office. I tugged open the top drawer of one of the filing cabinets and found three half-empty bottles of Scotch, varying in age and quality – so much for Felix Bevard's paperwork. Above the cabinets were photographs of Felix smiling with a group of men of a similar age in football gear and trainers at one of the artificial football pitches in the city. Underneath the images was a reference to a seven-a-side football competition. I could hear Lydia probing with some more questions, getting equally bland and noncommittal replies.

'Was he a keen football player?' I said.

'He played a couple of times a week during the season. Waste of time if you ask me. It was an excuse to keep fit but then he'd go to the pub afterwards.'

'We'll need details of the men in the football club.'

'It was Jack Ledley that organised the club. Felix knew him from way back. But you're wasting your time there.'

Gloria organised coffee and some fancy chocolate biscuits. We jotted down the contact details for every present member of staff, as well as those who had left recently, together with the mobile telephone number for

Jack Ledley. We scoured through the filing cabinets but reading back issues of various magazines for licensees and health and safety policies wasn't going to get us any nearer Felix Bevard's killer.

Harry arrived but before he settled down to his shift he spent an hour answering our questions, occasionally glancing for reassurance from Gloria. He was a thin, surly man in his forties who had little interest in cooperating with us. It was late afternoon by the time Lydia and I left. We retraced our steps to the car park which was now filling with customers.

'She's convinced that Jimmy Walsh was behind Bevard's murder,' Lydia said.

'I don't trust anyone who says that she has to swear on a stack of bibles.'

'Lots of people say that. It's a turn of phrase.'

I didn't reply. Lydia hadn't convinced me. Felix Bevard had been a crook and maybe I was unfair to distrust Gloria. But years of seeing families of innocent men grieving gave me an unsettling feeling about the Bevard family.

Sitting in Superintendent Cornock's room looking at Dave Hobbs was a disconcerting experience. The benefits of my three-week holiday in Lucca – walking in the sunshine, enjoying being with my son – seeped away as I sat there, as though like an invisible leach Dave Hobbs could suck the benefit from my body. Listening to him droning on set my nerves on edge. He said something but I didn't hear him.

'Bring me up to date,' he repeated, more loudly this time.

Mentally I refocused; even the chair felt more uncomfortable now than when it was Superintendent Cornock's office. I concentrated on his face as if it might help me. He had small piggy eyes and oversized cheeks that made him look chubby even though the rest of his body was averaged-sized. It was his accent I hated the most. Especially, the way he rolled his 'r's and warmed every vowel. There were newsreaders on the television and weather forecasters all with the same north Walian accent. And underneath it all he had that remarkable ability to make mediocrity a virtue. I had never been able to talk the talk as Dave could. I wondered if there was a Mrs Hobbs. She probably taught Geography or Home Economics in one of the Welsh language schools in the city and they went for pleasant Sunday afternoon walks in Roath Park.

'We're building a picture of Jimmy Walsh at the moment. All his known associates, family and friends. He had a motive to kill Bevard so we believe he was behind the murder.'

'I hope you will be using the HOLMES system.' He gave me a sly smile as he referenced the Home Office system for conducting a murder inquiry.

'Of course. Lydia and I are well acquainted with it.'

'I'm so glad to hear that. If you have any problems then all you have to do is ask. I've had the benefit of extensive training on the system.'

Extensive training.

Hobbs sat quite upright to the desk, placed his hands on the paperwork in front of him. A supercilious menace permeated every pore of his being. There was even a supercilious smell hanging in the air.

'Dave, I was wondering if you could give me some background on the Oakley murder? I understand that you were the sergeant on that case.'

I was certain that a grain of worry crossed his eyes. He fidgeted with his hands and he let his eyes drift off towards Cornock's fish tank in one corner of the room.

'It was a terrible case. My first major murder inquiry. I didn't always agree with the SIO. Things that could have been handled rather differently. But ... You know how it is.' He fluttered a hand in the air. 'Mr and Mrs Oakley owned a property in Bridgend. The Walsh family owned several adjacent properties. The Oakleys' premises prevented Jimmy Walsh from maximising his investments. He tried to persuade Mr and Mrs Oakley to move and he made them a generous offer, allegedly. When they refused he ran out of patience and decided that more *direct action* was needed.'

He paused. I waited for him to continue.

'The only suspect we had was Walsh. But he had a cast iron alibi. He was at a family party with lots of eyewitnesses. We suspected that Bevard was involved. At the time he and Walsh were very close.'

'Did you know that Bevard was on the verge of signing a supergrass deal?' The surprised look on his face gave me the answer. 'Apparently he would provide enough evidence to convict Walsh of the Oakley murder.'

'Interesting. And I suppose all of that goes down the drain now?'

I gave my face a serious expression as I nodded.

Hobbs continued. 'Well, if you need any assistance please ask.' He scanned the papers on his desk, Cornock's desk, with glee.

'Thanks for the insight, Dave.' I stood up and made for the door.

'One more thing, John. If we are in the company of other officers I would much prefer it if you respected my rank and used 'sir' to address me.'

I gazed over at him. His eyes had been set into a haughty self-righteous, smug look that annoyed me intensely. It was only the remnants of my post-holiday exuberance that stopped me from telling him in explicit terms what I really felt.

I walked back to the Incident Room, very slowly. I had to call Dave Hobbs 'sir'. I didn't want to think about it. I had a comfortable established routine with Superintendent Cornock who knew how I worked. From other cases where Hobbs and I had worked together I knew he resented me. The feeling was mutual of course.

The memory of my holiday was receding into a deep and distant corner of my mind and now after only a few days back in Cardiff I felt stale and dull.

I arrived back in the Incident Room and glancing at the board I noticed new faces pinned to it: a man, mid-forties and a woman heavily made up about the same age although it was difficult to be certain.

Lydia walked over to the board. 'It's Martin Kendall. He's Jimmy Walsh's right-hand man. He's visited Walsh regularly in Grange Hall. And he was implicated in Oakley's murder with Walsh and Bevard.'

I joined her and stared at Kendall. His nose was bent as though it had argued with a Japanese wrestler. 'Do we have an address?'

'Sure thing, boss.'

'And the woman?'

'Mrs Walsh. Bernie, short for Bernadette. She's quite the player. Always been the one to support Jimmy in his life of crime. She protects the family and her lifestyle. And she's another regular visitor to Grange Hall.'

'I need a full analysis of when Kendall and Bernie met Walsh. Go back through the prison records and find out how often they've been to see him and then contact the governors of all the prisons he was in before he got transferred to Grange Hall.' I turned to face the team. Jane sipped on her coffee. Wyn lifted his head and stared at me intently. 'I want to know who he shared a cell with, who was on the same prison wing as him. And then cross-reference everyone and anyone with a criminal record for violence. Ignore the fraudsters and drug dealers; we're looking for someone capable of murder.' I looked at Lydia. 'Anything from the recordings of the telephone calls Walsh made in prison?'

'Nothing yet. We've only just started. It's all mundane stuff. They talk about his family and hers. Who had fallen out with who. Who is cheating on their spouses and then they talk about what they will be doing once he's out. One of the calls is quite explicit. It all sounded staged.'

'I want a transcript of all their telephone calls. There might be some aside or comment to suggest they were planning something.'

Lydia nodded.

'Don't these prisoners have weekend releases before they reach the end of their sentence?' Wyn said.

'Check that too. If he was released, we need to know the times and his address. Everything. If he went out for a meal I want to know which restaurant and if he went to the pub I need to know which one. I want every single detail on Jimmy Walsh.'

Wyn and Jane had been uncharacteristically quiet, both listening.

'And then,' I continued, 'we take his life apart until we find something.'

I turned to Lydia. 'We'll pay Kendall and Bernie a visit in the morning.'

Chapter 6

Lydia and I left the rest of the team huddled over their monitors the following morning and headed down to the car park. Her Ford was neat and clean and I stared at the litter-free foot well in surprise. She paid me no attention as she rummaged through the storage compartment in the driver's side door until she found a CD of Pavarotti's greatest tracks. After choosing a disc she pushed it gently into the player. Then she pressed the forward button until she found track fourteen.

'This is my favourite track "O soave fanciulla". Excuse the pronunciation.'

'*La Bohème.*'

Lydia turned and gave me a surprised look. I shrugged. 'It's an Italian opera.'

She started the car as Pavarotti's voice filled the cabin.

The music took me back to my childhood of listening to my Nonno on a Sunday afternoon humming along to the opera in his sitting room, insisting I sit with him. If I became restless Nonna scolded him but he would tell her how important it was for me to get a grounding in Italian music.

Lydia interrupted me as I hummed along. 'I thought you weren't a fan of opera.'

'I know all the important arias. Every Italian does, even one from Aberdare.'

Lydia rolled her eyes.

'How long have you enjoyed Italian opera?'

'I had a boyfriend when I was at university. He studied music and he'd memorised all the words for most of the famous arias. I got to like the same music.'

Sunshine caught against the surface of Lydia's

purple fingernails; her hands complemented her slim figure. Almost a year had passed since she'd been assigned to work with me.

'Are you still together?' I made it sound innocent enough. Lydia wasn't my type, too serious, and there were protocols about officers having relationships with each other.

'No, it was one of those university romances that didn't last.'

Not having been to university I couldn't really comment.

She parked about two hundred metres from the restaurant and takeaway owned by Mrs Walsh. In fact most of the businesses owned by Jimmy Walsh were in his wife's name. And that made her a person of special interest. A few metal tables and chairs were set out on the pavement either side of the door like a scene from *The Sopranos*. I could imagine broad-shouldered Italian-looking thugs puffing on large cigars sitting around a table in a back room playing cards.

But this was Grangetown, in Cardiff, and the restaurant sold fish and chips.

There had been a collective sigh of relief audible throughout the police stations of Cardiff when Jimmy Walsh had been stopped in his Range Rover Sport in possession of enough class B drugs to make contesting a possession with intent to supply charge impossible. Relief had turned to despair when the expected five years in prison became three. Walsh had deep enough pockets to afford the best lawyers that money could buy.

I left the car and walked over the road. Lydia was ahead of me; the discreet heels on her shoes and her well-pressed denims made the most of her legs that morning. I got distracted and a cyclist swore at me as he narrowly missed a collision.

A smell of disinfectant and cleaning fluid and then stale chip-fat made an odd combination as we entered the café. A radio competed unsuccessfully with the sound of vacuuming from the rear so we wandered through and found a woman pushing a machine through the legs of plastic-topped tables. When she saw us she turned the machine off.

'We're looking for Mrs Walsh,' I said.

'In the office round the back, love.' She nodded towards a door with a lopsided sign saying *Office*.

Behind it a staircase led to the first floor and at the top I heard the sound of voices at the end of a corridor. I glanced over at Lydia before heading past a window. Outside in the car park were a Porsche Carrera and a gleaming Range Rover Evoque. I'd heard the Walsh family were good customers of the Range Rover dealers in Cardiff and realised then that the Porsche dealers must be doing okay too.

The voices became louder as we reached a door at the end. I didn't knock: we weren't calling on civilised society where politeness and manners were valued. So I barged in despite the feeling that Lydia had been about to say something. Sunshine streamed through large windows. Sitting at a table was a woman in her mid-forties, tanned and slim, with perfect hair and so much bling on her fingers she must have been tired at the end of each day from the weight of hauling the stuff around.

'Mrs Walsh?' I said.

She didn't answer. But the man by her side did. 'And who the fuck are you?'

He stood up and drew himself up to his full height. He looked exactly like the photograph pinned to the Incident Room board. His powder-blue shirt followed the contours of his frame like a blanket covering a racehorse. A braided leather belt held up dark grey trousers. The thick neck and broad shoulders indicated a regular gym subscription.

I pushed my warrant card towards him before moving it slowly so that Mrs Walsh could read it. 'I'm Detective Inspector John Marco, Wales Police Service, and this is Detective Sergeant Flint.' I kept my eye contact direct. Martin Kendall did the same. In fact he never even blinked. He had deep-set eyes, black and unreadable.

On the table were two coffee cups, their tide marks evidence of recent refills. The smell of fish and chips had disappeared but now there was something else hanging in the air: expensive aftershave and perfume, no doubt.

'What do you want?' Kendall said.

'Who are you?' I said.

He scowled.

'Simple question,' I added. 'What's so difficult about telling me your name Mr Kendall?'

Now he glared at me. I sat down at the table, nodding for Lydia to do the same.

'What do you want?' Kendall said again. I took against him as soon as I heard the Scottish accent.

'We're investigating the murder of Felix Bevard.' Kendall glanced at Bernie Walsh who told him with a raise of an eyebrow to sit down.

'How can we help, Inspector?' Bernie managed a narrow smile.

'Felix was a business associate of your husband. So I was wondering if you had any recent contact with him?' Bernie looked away and she feigned disinterest with a lazy shrug.

'Felix Bevard was found killed in Roath Park café.' Lydia had an irritated edge to her voice.

'I'd heard. Very sad,' Kendall said, making an effort to keep his voice flat.

'When was the last time you saw Felix Bevard?'

'I can't recall.' Bernie leant over to Kendall. 'Can you remember Martin?'

He shook his head while staring at me.

'It must have been several years ago. But come to think of it I saw him going into that flash Indonesian restaurant in the Bay, *a week* after Jimmy went down.'

There was more nodding now from Kendall's direction.

'What makes you think he was a *business associate* of Jimmy's?' Bernie asked.

I was prepared for that one. 'I thought they'd been involved in that night club in Newport.'

'Of course,' Bernie said as though it had slipped her mind.

'And I understand they were involved in a property development in Bridgend. The one involving Mr Oakley.'

'Ah, yes, Mr Oakley,' Bernie said as though he were a long lost friend instead of a dead adversary.

'The original complaint states that Bevard and Jimmy had bullied and harassed Mr Oakley.'

Bernie purred. 'My Jimmy would never bully anyone.'

I wanted to snort out loud. Jimmy probably thought that harassment and bullying should be included in the national curriculum and taught in schools.

'Where were you on the night Felix Bevard was killed?' I said.

The atmosphere changed: silence invaded the space between us. Was she thinking how to respond? I half expected some righteous indignation. I guessed wrong.

'I was with a crowd of girls that night. We went out

to the cinema: and before you ask we watched *Fifty Shades of Grey*. Then we went out to that new French restaurant in the brewery quarter. It was after midnight when we left. Then we went to the nightclub near the Boulevard de Nantes. We stayed there until after three. I'd drunk far too much by then, and I got a taxi home.'

'I'll need the names of your friends and their contact details.'

'Of course.' She reached for her handbag and fished out her mobile.

I turned to Kendall. 'And—'

'I played golf in the afternoon and then we all had a few drinks in the club.'

Lydia jotted down the details in her notebook as he talked.

'Once we'd finished – don't ask me the time – we left and got a taxi into town where we started a pub crawl. We have this challenge, me and my mates in the golf club, to visit sixteen pubs in the middle of the city and have a pint in each one. And our last is in one of the clubs in the Bay.'

He leant over the table. 'So by the end of the night I was shit-faced.' I could almost smell Brains best bitter on his breath.

'We'll need the names of all your friends, too.'

'No problem,' he grinned.

'To eliminate you from the inquiry, of course.'

He couldn't hide the smirk on his face.

Kendall made an exaggerated gesture of checking his mobile for the names and contact details of the men who were with him. Again Lydia jotted down the details.

'Was there anything else, Inspector?' Bernie said casually.

'You must be looking forward to Jimmy's release from prison?'

'Of course.' A broader smile this time.

She pushed over a card with her name and title printed in large letters: 'Bernie Walsh Director' – below the name of a limited company.

I stared at the business card for a good couple of seconds, imagining Bernie Walsh in a business meeting with her bank manager.

So, Mrs Walsh, how is business?

Good thanks, we've just killed a competitor who wanted to grass up my Jimmy.

That's grand. Tell me about the latest turnover figures.

I clutched the card in my right hand and beamed at her and then at Kendall. 'I'll be in touch.'

We drew the door closed behind us and I memorised the number plates of both cars as I passed the window.

The woman in the café gave us a tired look as we walked out. I sat down in the passenger seat and thumped the dashboard.

'Ever had the feeling that you've been set up and taken as a complete fool?'

'Sorry, boss?'

'They knew we were coming.'

'I don't—'

'They had all their alibis ready and rehearsed.'

Lydia scanned the names in her pocketbook.

'They knew we were coming,' I repeated. 'And now we've got to spend hours and hours checking out all the details of their alibis and you know what, they'll prove absolutely bullet proof.'

Just then Kendall drove out of the car park in the Porsche. He looked over and I could have sworn he grinned. I yanked at the safety belt and clicked it into place.

Now I *knew* that Jimmy Walsh was responsible for Bevard's death.

All I had to do was prove it.

Chapter 7

I stood by the entrance to Roath Park and looked up and down Lake Road West. The properties were comfortable, semi-detached homes in a desirable part of Cardiff. I stared down towards the middle of the city towards the side street where Felix Bevard's car had been discovered, neatly parked. Had the killer arranged to meet Bevard, I pondered? If he had, Bevard must have known him and even agreed willingly to see him.

I tried to picture in my mind the circumstances that led to Bevard's killing. It helped me dispel the image of Bernie Walsh and Martin Kendall smugly telling me the precise details of their movements on the night Felix Bevard was killed. I knew it was pointless even contemplating asking Jimmy Walsh about his movements. I left Lydia talking to the uniformed officers staffing the mobile incident room and walked to the other entrance on the eastern side passing the Captain Scott Memorial. On the lake itself there were couples boating leisurely, the sound of muffled laughter and conversation floating to the shore. The killer must have parked somewhere close by. I retraced my steps to the café wondering if Bevard had been dragged unconscious into the storeroom or if he had walked there unaided. The preliminary reports from the crime scene investigators had described how the storeroom doors had been forced, suggesting perpetrators with a specific reason for wanting to kill Bevard in the café storeroom.

I joined Lydia as she finished her conversation with a tall, gangly officer who looked as though he should still be in school.

'There have been lots of people complaining at the lack of policing in the neighbourhood,' Lydia said.

'Is there anything significant?'

She shook her head.

It was still early in the investigation and the presence of the mobile incident room would reassure the local population.

'Let's go and find Jack Ledley,' I said, heading for my Mondeo.

Lydia gave the pebbles and assorted grit in the foot well of my car a quizzical look as though she were examining some rare fossil as an extra in a David Attenborough documentary. Then she gave me a weak smile. I made a mental note to clean the car – next week maybe.

Jack Ledley was a self-employed property consultant but Gloria Bevard had been hazy about what he did exactly. And all she had was a mobile telephone number with no address so we had to rely on one of the staff in the Lemon Grove giving us an address in Birchgrove, a suburb to the north of the city.

After ringing the bell of his property, peering into the living room through the front window and then talking to various neighbours, all we had established was that Jack Ledley hadn't been home for at least a week. None of his neighbours even knew if he was married or not.

We returned to Queen Street as Wyn returned to the Incident Room carrying a tray of coffee mugs. I took one and headed for my office where I booted up my computer. Alvine had sent me another forensics report that confirmed the details of various fingerprint samples taken from the café. She had checked each against the Police National Computer and I scanned the results. Most had no criminal records but half a dozen stood out. Each would have to be checked in turn. I left my office and sat at one of the desks in the Incident Room.

'So how did Jimmy Walsh discover that Bevard was

about to sign a supergrass deal?'

Lydia made the question sound routine. Wyn stopped munching his way through a chocolate bar and exchanged a worried glance with Jane, neither able to decide whether they should reply.

'And who did Jimmy Walsh get to kill him?' I paused. 'I'll chase Inspector Ackroyd for the dedicated source unit file. I know that it's unpalatable to contemplate that police officers or Crown prosecutors may have leaked the information, but our task is to find who killed Bevard. And our number one suspect was safely locked up in jail. Which means we look elsewhere.'

I stood up and walked towards the board.

'Wyn.' He looked startled again. 'We need to check out Kendall's and Bernie Walsh's alibis.'

He nodded. 'We've already started, boss. I'm checking out Kendall's alibi tomorrow morning.'

'And I'm doing the same for Bernie Walsh,' Jane added.

Lydia distributed a single sheet of A4 paper. 'We've had a list of Jimmy Walsh's known associates. People that were connected to him through various businesses implicated in criminal activity.'

I read through the list. My eyes focused on one name in particular.

'Owen Norcross,' I said. 'I've read his name in a list that Alvine sent me of people who match fingerprint samples from the café at Roath Park.'

I sensed three sets of eyes boring into me.

'Let's get a full PNC check done on him immediately.'

It took Wyn no more than twenty minutes to get all the details displayed on his screen.

'Get his photograph up,' I said.

Wyn hit the print button without me asking him. The machine hummed and then spewed out a single colour image which filled the page. Lydia pinned it under the faces of Kendall and Bernie Walsh.

'I wonder whether he has an alibi?' Lydia said.

'Tomorrow morning we find out,' I said.

Tracy was pottering in the kitchen of my flat when I got home that evening. In the weeks before I had left for my holiday in Lucca I had sensed that our relationship had lost its initial intensity and I wasn't certain how things would develop. It must have been awkward for her working as a crime scene investigator knowing that her colleagues and the officers in the Wales Police Service all knew about her brother's conviction for abducting a police officer, an offence linked to various high profile murders. At the height of the publicity reporters had been camped outside Tracy's parents' home in Bournemouth until they became yesterday's news but the impact still lingered and since the court case Tracy visited her parents regularly.

The averted glances and muffled remarks were taking its toll on Tracy and our relationship. She had kept her own flat, making clear she wanted her own space. And my holiday with Dean had made me realise that perhaps I wasn't ready to make a commitment that might disrupt my relationship with him.

She smiled but her face didn't light up. Her lips grazed mine.

'Making progress?'

I shrugged, pulled a carton of juice from the fridge and filled two glasses. Tracy continued. 'The murder of Felix Bevard has been all over the newspapers.'

'I know. And with Superintendent Cornock on

sabbatical I've got Dave Hobbs breathing down my neck.'

'Nobody seems to like him.'

I shrugged. 'He makes you think that he doesn't trust you. And he is very ambitious.'

'I don't think Alvine likes him very much either.'

We sat at opposite ends of the sofa and Tracy curled her legs up taking a mouthful from her glass. My shoulders ached and tomorrow, instead of a leisurely Saturday morning, I would be back at Queen Street aiming to make progress. I heard about Tracy's week; there was a tinge of regret in her voice that she hadn't been on Alvine's team on the morning Bevard's body had been found. A burglary in a house near Bridgend meant she had spent two days dusting and gathering evidence.

'The place was disgusting. It stank to high heaven. I had to stand in the shower for half an hour when I got home.'

After an hour, we decided to get a Chinese so we ambled down into the Bay. It was bustling; couples hand-in-hand jostled with families choosing a restaurant and older couples out for an evening stroll. We managed more small talk but Tracy's mind was far away.

'Are you going to come with me to see my parents tomorrow night?'

She shook her head. 'I'm going to go down to Bournemouth in the morning. Dad isn't well.'

We found a restaurant and spent a couple of hours eating and talking about nothing of importance. After paying, I took her hand as we walked back to my flat but she was uncharacteristically silent. She stopped by the entrance to my apartment block.

'Are you ...?'

'Not tonight John. I'm exhausted and I want to get an early start. I'll call you over the weekend.'

She grazed my lips again and, head bowed, walked over to her car.

She gave me an insipid wave as she drove out of the car park. I returned to my flat, apprehensive that I might not sleep. Not wanting Tracy to dominate my thoughts, I watched some mindless television until a yawn gripped my jaw. Then I went to bed and tossed and turned until I woke the following morning.

Chapter 8

The morning traffic had thinned by the time we left Queen Street but we still got snarled up along Dumfries Place heading for the turning north towards Whitchurch. The city's civic centre on our right, including the Crown court building and the national gallery, had a classical feel from the Edwardian era. Lydia powered the car out along Northern Avenue, which would eventually lead to the A470 north up towards Merthyr Tydfil and North Wales. Whitchurch was one of those suburbs that was trying to be posher than it was and it wasn't helped by the likes of Owen Norcross living in a semi-detached property just off the main street.

We parked right opposite his house and I noticed activity in the first floor bedroom as a woman moved back and forth. Cracked slabs covered the paved area outside that had once been a garden.

Norcross had a list of previous convictions that made him the possible muscle to Walsh's brains. He had worked for Jimmy Walsh for several years, an employment record interrupted only by a stretch inside Newport jail for an aggravated assault. The intelligence reports on Norcross all focused on his connections to the Walsh property business.

Lydia scanned Norcross's record of convictions. 'His history of violence certainly makes him a person of interest.'

'Let's see what he has to say for himself.' We left the car and headed over to the house.

The door opened and Norcross stood in the doorway wearing a pair of shorts and a thin short-sleeved summer shirt. I thrust my warrant card towards him and he gave it a grudging acknowledgement before looking over my shoulder, surveying the street. 'You'd better come in.'

Two suitcases on wheels stood in the hallway with another pair of airline cabin-sized bags.

'Are you going on holiday?' I said as we reached the kitchen.

Norcross stood and checked his watch. 'What's this about?'

'We're investigating the death of Felix Bevard.' The prospect that our only suspect was leaving the country left only one option. 'And we need you to answer some questions at the police station.'

'You cannot be serious.'

'Find a coat.'

Twenty minutes later Owen Norcross had been booked into the custody suite by a sergeant who knew him well and even asked after his kids. We settled Norcross into one of the interview rooms with a plastic cup filled with rancid-looking coffee. We let him stew as we reviewed our hastily assembled list of questions.

A thin skin of some unidentifiable substance had formed on the top of the coffee that Norcross had ignored. His holiday apparel made him look completely out of place although being interviewed was something he was accustomed to. I sat down and looked over at him. I dropped onto the desk a buff folder with the forensics report and the record of his visits to HMP Grange Hall that Wyn had provided.

'We are investigating the murder of Felix Bevard. Did you know him?' I said.

'Can't say I did.' Norcross folded his arms.

'Bevard ran the Lemon Grove public house and he had a minicab business.'

Norcross stared at me blankly.

'He was killed in the café in Roath Park last Wednesday night.'

'What has that got to do with me?'

Lydia spoke up. 'We have reason to believe Jimmy Walsh was involved with Bevard.'

Norcross looked down at Lydia through hooded eyes already into a I'm-not-going-to-tell-you-anything mode. 'Sorry, love. Don't know what you're talking about.'

'It's Detective Sergeant Flint.'

Norcross managed a sly grin. Lydia narrowed her eyes and let out a snort. 'Where were you last Wednesday evening?'

'In the cinema.' Norcross didn't flinch or hesitate.

'Really.' He was getting under Lydia's skin so I decided to intervene.

'And Wednesday afternoon? I want an account of your movements that day.'

'Am I a suspect?'

'Answer the question.'

'I can't remember. I'd need to check my diary.'

I paused and read the time. By now the search warrant we had obtained to search Norcross's house would be in the hands of a sergeant and a team of officers authorised to undertake a search. They had instructions to bag up every item of clothing, remove his holiday luggage and impound his car. I had to hope there'd be gunshot residue on his clothes or some fragment the forensics could use to link him to the café and the murder of Bevard.

'Look, is this going to take all morning? I'm going on holiday tonight.'

I glanced over at Lydia who raised an eyebrow. The only stay away from home that Norcross was going to enjoy was an extended weekend in Queen Street police station.

'You know Jimmy Walsh very well,' I said.

'Yeah, of course. We go back a long time.'

'And you've been to visit him in Grange Hall.'

'So what if I have?'

'What did you talk about?'

'The economy, whether Wales will be independent and who'll be the next archbishop.'

He managed a grin.

I could think of all sorts of smart answers but I kept them to myself.

'Jimmy Walsh and Bevard go back a long time too.'

Norcross shrugged.

'Did Walsh ever talk about Bevard?'

'No, why would he?'

'Did Walsh talk about his plans for his release?'

'I can't remember.'

'No celebration party?'

Norcross shook his head.

'Do you know the café at Roath Park?'

Now I saw a faint shadow cross his eyes. The spectre of a worry.

'Place near the lake. Passed it a few times.'

'When were you in there last?'

'Can't remember.'

An evasive and vague answer wasn't going to work.

'Try. It's important.' I paused and sat back, staring him straight in the eye. He looked away.

'Last month? Last week?'

He shrugged again. He was making it an art form.

'I need you to tell me when you were in the café last.' This time I sounded serious.

He retreated into silence.

'We have your fingerprints from the café. It places you there. We have ongoing inquiries to determine how recently the prints were left but last Wednesday night Felix Bevard was killed there. We suspect that Jimmy Walsh was behind the killing, and that, Owen, makes you a prime suspect. So can you account for your movements on Wednesday evening into early Thursday morning?'

Norcross thrust out his chin, blinking at the same time. I could see the realisation dawning that two weeks in the sun was a faint hope. We finished the interview and stood by the custody sergeant's desk as he authorised Norcross's detention.

He probably hoped that once we'd checked his alibi he could be flying off to the sun.

'One final thing,' I said. 'We'll need you to surrender your passport.'

I was eating lunch when Inspector Ackroyd arrived in my office and handed me his dedicated source unit file. He hesitated before leaving.

'Are you making progress?'

I thought of Norcross sitting in the cells and the possessions removed from his home that morning.

'Early days, Malcolm. You know how it is.'

'Of course ... You ... I hope ... I mean all of my team are clean, John.'

'I understand.'

First rule of policing – defend your team until hell freezes.

'No, I really mean it. I'd trust them with my life.'

Walsh got the information from somewhere.

'Leave it with me.'

He gave me a weak smile and left. I dumped the file on a corner of my desk and finished my sandwich. By early afternoon I had an email from the search team supervisor who had emptied Norcross's house. Then I called Alvine Dix.

'There's no way I can get a team together to look at the evidence until Monday,' she said.

'And there's a vehicle that needs to be examined.'

'You can't possibly expect me—'

'I've got a suspect in custody.'

'Then release him.'

She slammed the telephone down. She was right. The initial twenty-four hours we could keep Norcross in the police cells would be up in the morning. In time for him to be released for Sunday lunch. And hopefully enough time for us to interview his girlfriend.

I called her mobile but the number rang out.

From the Incident Room I heard chairs being moved and chatter from Wyn and Jane. Lydia had arrived back after lunch as I walked through from my office. I had turned down her offer to join her at one of her favourite vegetarian restaurants in the city, preferring a bacon sandwich from the local delicatessen. I looked over at Wyn and Jane. 'So how did you get on today?'

Wyn was the first to answer. 'We've checked out all the various pubs and clubs Kendall alleges he was visiting on the night Bevard was killed. It surprised me the publicans and their staff recognised him. He only sticks in their minds because he made a point of paying with £50 notes.'

'Clever bastard.' I spat out the words realising it was another part of Jimmy Walsh's plan. The photograph of Felix Bevard stared down at me from the board. Underneath were the images of Jimmy Walsh, Martin Kendall, Bernie Walsh and Owen Norcross, a rogues' gallery, and our only realistic suspects.

'I've checked out some of the venues Bernie Walsh visited and the results are the same,' Jane added.

I stared at the image of Norcross praying there would be forensics we could use.

'Let's focus on Norcross. We need to talk to his girlfriend. Wyn and Jane, go and talk to his neighbours, the postman, the local supermarket. Examine his computer. And his mobile. I want to know everything about him.'

'Still doesn't help us establish how Walsh found out about the supergrass deal,' Lydia said.

I rubbed both hands over my face. It would be another long day and I could tell now that the inquiry meant another ten-hour shift tomorrow. I even contemplated postponing my visit to my parents' tomorrow evening but decided against it, knowing how disappointed my mother would be.

'Lydia. Let's go and talk to Norcross's girlfriend.'

Lydia punched in the postcode for an address in Grangetown into the satnav as I started the engine and pointed my Mondeo into the early afternoon traffic. We headed down through the Bay area passing the Millennium Centre on our left and the modern slate-clad Assembly building behind it. If Cardiff City football club had been playing at home the traffic around the stadium would have cast its tentacles through the narrow streets so we were lucky that the team were away playing one of the Sheffield sides. Streets of terraces fanned out ahead of us and I followed the instructions until I spotted the number of the property screwed to a fading plastic door.

I parked and scanned the various houses. It was the part of Cardiff trying its best to gentrify but then a door opened in front of us and a wave of rap music flooded out. Lydia followed me as we crossed the street and I hammered on the door. I heard footsteps after a radio had been silenced.

A woman, late thirties, give or take a few years, opened the door. She stared at our warrant cards that we pushed in her direction. 'We're looking for Olga Crumlin.'

'Sorry, she's not here.'

'Where can we get hold of her?'

'She's working. I can give you a mobile telephone number. What's this about?'

'We need to know where she works.'

Lydia jotted down in her pocketbook the details of the furniture warehouse where Olga Crumlin worked. We headed back to the car and it took me fifteen minutes to navigate from the house in Grangetown to the retail park near Cardiff City Stadium. Enough time for Olga to be called by her housemate and warned to expect us.

Laid out in front of me in the anonymous-looking warehouse were rows of three-piece suites. In a far corner were piles of various-sized rugs. Lydia pointed towards a glass-fronted office. As we approached I could see two women talking animatedly, glancing out over the shop floor. I pushed open the door. Two pairs of eyes turned to look at me. I tried to guess which one was Owen Norcross's girlfriend. It wasn't difficult: the older of the two women was touching sixty, the other had high heels and lavish make-up.

'I'm looking for Olga Crumlin.'

I guessed right; the older woman excused herself, giving Olga a conspiratorial glance as she left. We had our warrant cards at the ready but she paid them little attention.

'What do you want?'

'Do you know Owen Norcross?'

'Yes, of course.' She seemed to relax as though being questioned about Owen Norcross might be second nature.

'We want to establish his movements for Wednesday night.'

She paused, staring at me and then at Lydia. I wondered what was going through her mind.

'What's this all about? What's he done?'

There was a clear implication that she expected him to have done something. Obviously, she knew all about his background.

'Can you tell me what you were doing on Wednesday night?'

She frowned. 'We went to the cinema. We saw that film with Leonardo DiCaprio where he gets attacked by the bear.'

'Where did you watch the film?'

Lydia already had a pocketbook in hand and jotted down the details as Olga dictated the location of the cinema and the timing of the showing they'd watched.

'What time did the film finish?' I said.

'I can't remember exactly. Is it important?'

Nice try, Olga.

'Where did you go afterwards?'

She narrowed her eyes, obviously calculating what answer would best serve Norcross.

'It was late; I didn't keep track of the time.'

'Do your best.'

She paused again. She had probably been texting Norcross frantically since her housemate had warned her to expect us. I anticipated with interest the possibility that she had texted Norcross knowing such texts might make interesting reading when I got back to Queen Street. Now I decided I had to raise the stakes for Olga Crumlin.

'We are investigating Owen Norcross as part of a murder enquiry.' I watched her struggle to keep her eye contact with me as colour slowly drained from her face. It served as a warning to her that trying to be clever wasn't going to work. 'So where did you go after the film finished?'

She swallowed hard. 'We went for a Chinese.'

'Where?'

She named a restaurant in the Bay.

'When did you leave?'

She shrugged noncommittally.

'It's important, Olga.'

'I was back home by half twelve. I didn't keep track of the time.'

'Perhaps your housemate will remember?'

More colour drained from Olga's face and she slumped into the nearest office chair. She had returned to the house she shared before one o'clock which meant that Norcross had the rest of the night to rendezvous with Bevard. But I knew that *Acting* Detective Chief Inspector Hobbs wouldn't support the continued detention of Norcross unless we had more evidence. We had his passport; he wasn't going anywhere.

'We may need to see you again in due course,' I said to Olga as we left.

She gave us a brief frightened nod.

'Do you think she's telling us the truth, boss?' Lydia said as we approached the car.

Knowing Kendall and Bernie Walsh had taken time to build careful alibis it seemed odd that if Norcross was involved he had been careless with his. 'Let's check out the CCTV coverage from the cinema, ask the staff.'

I jumped into the car; we had hours' more work ahead of us.

Chapter 9

I had left Queen Street just before ten o'clock the previous evening, returning to my apartment in good time to see *Match of the Day*, which was showing the highlights of the Spurs against Swansea game. I woke at two o'clock in the morning when the television was playing a black-and-white film, my orange juice and a sandwich still on the coffee table.

Immediately I started thinking about Owen Norcross. Wyn and Jane had returned to the Incident Room last evening an hour or so after Lydia and myself reporting that Norcross's neighbours thought he was a chartered surveyor. Even the local shopkeeper thought he was a professional. Given the impending review of Norcross's detention required by the rules I had nothing to suggest he was other than tucked up in bed the Wednesday evening Bevard was killed.

The manager of the cinema complex had promised to send us the CCTV images and details of the members of staff who had worked the previous Wednesday evening. It all meant more delays and even if Norcross and Olga had been to the cinema it still gave him the rest of the night to have murdered Felix Bevard.

After getting a few more hours' sleep, the alarm woke me at eight and after a hasty shower I dressed. I chose a white shirt, a tie with blue-and-red stripe, a pair of moleskin trousers and a jacket that had recently been dry cleaned. I even gave my brown brogues a cursory polish before leaving the apartment.

Queen Street was quiet, the revellers from the night before sleeping off hangovers.

In my office I read the final report from the search team. Every piece of clothing that Norcross possessed was now in the forensics department waiting to be processed. It would all take time. A commodity we didn't have. I glanced at my watch repeatedly, counting down the time until my meeting with Dave Hobbs.

Olga's flatmate had said that she was watching television when Olga returned between midnight and one o'clock on the night Bevard was murdered. It wasn't going to be enough to justify the continued detention of Owen Norcross.

At the allotted time I trooped through to see Hobbs. I knocked on his door, but I didn't wait for a response before barging in. He furrowed his brow in a brief angry rebuke before nodding to one of the chairs.

'Bring me up to date.'

He elevated the chair, just enough to make him look down at me with a superior officer's glare.

'Owen Norcross is our prime suspect. Forensics found his prints in the café where Bevard was killed.'

Hobbs scribbled the occasional note as I gave him a summary of our interviews with Olga and her flatmate. And I handed him a printout of Norcross's convictions and explained that he was a close associate of Jimmy Walsh who had visited him regularly in prison.

Hobbs chewed his lower lip. 'It's not enough, John.'

'He cannot account for his movements in the middle of the night.' I waited. 'And he couldn't explain how his prints were found in the café.'

'As your senior officer I have considered all the available factors in determining whether we can authorise Norcross's continued detention.'

Acting senior officer I felt like correcting him.

'Do we have his passport?'

'Yes.'

'Then I cannot authorise his detention any longer. We'll have to release him on bail.'

I left the meeting knowing that Hobbs was right but thinking of any reason to disagree with him. I returned to the Incident Room, which was quiet. I sat down heavily by one of the desks and looked up at the faces on the board. Hobbs was right of course. If Norcross had killed Bevard then leaving the fingerprints was clumsy, especially when Bernie Walsh and Martin Kendall had gone to so much trouble to give themselves watertight alibis.

I read the time again and then I walked down to the custody suite.

Once Norcross had been brought out of his cell I went through all the formalities. None of it was new to him and he gave me a sullen stare when I explained that he had to return to the police station in twenty-eight days and that he shouldn't leave the country.

'And how the fuck could I do that without a passport?'

I smiled at him but said nothing. I watched as he left the police station and I wondered when I would see him back again.

Chapter 10

In Mario's I dragged a spoon though an Americano while staring out of the window gathering my thoughts. A breakthrough from forensics looked like the best chance we had to get Norcross back to Queen Street. But the prospect of him implicating Walsh was remote. I watched a mother dragging a screaming youngster past the café. My mind wandered. Bevard must have faced a tough choice – give up everything he and his family valued for a new life. Even if in that new life he might never be truly safe. He would always be suspicious of every stranger, guarded in his conversations and distrustful of any inquisitive remark.

And I still had to determine how Walsh had discovered that Bevard was going to sign a supergrass agreement in the first place. There had been a leak and it meant someone had a link to Walsh.

I paid and left Mario's, winding my way back to Queen Street. We still had to complete the picture of Bevard's life, so back in my office I found the contacts that Gloria Bevard had given us. The first thing I found was Jack Ledley's number but it went straight to voicemail. Years of ticking boxes and following protocols made me request a PNC search on him. I spent an hour on the papers from Bevard's pub before turning my attention to the files from Ackroyd's dedicated source unit. I worked my way through the papers, focusing on the names of the team members. There were financial reports on the six people involved: three police officers, including Ackroyd, and three lawyers, all of varying seniority in the Crown Prosecution Service. I frowned. Ackroyd could never have signed off on that sort of deal without senior management input. I picked up the telephone and called his mobile.

I got straight to the point. 'Who signed off on the

supergrass deal?'

'For Christ's sake, John. It's Sunday.'

'And I've just spent all weekend with a possible suspect. I need the complete picture, Malcolm. You promised cooperation, remember?'

I sensed the reluctance down the telephone. 'It was the chief super in central command.'

'And why wasn't his name in the file?'

'Don't get tetchy, John. You know how it is.'

'Did it go any higher? Was one of the assistant chief constables involved?'

My throat tightened as I realised that this could go all the way to the chief constables' office.

'I don't know, John. I guess that will be something you'll have to find out.'

Then he rang off. So there were seven names at least. Maybe even more. Enough to make the case full of holes.

It took me the rest of the day to read the reports of meetings, memoranda from lawyers who complained about the inadequate time given to evaluate the case. And then there was detailed analysis of the available evidence. Two witnesses had confirmed that Walsh was in a restaurant for a big family celebration on the evening Mr Oakley was killed. I had to get full financial searches and background checks on everyone involved in the supergrass deal. Normal protocols meant that I should have gone to *Acting* Detective *Chief* Inspector Hobbs for the authority I needed.

I imagined his artificial sneer, as he'd be asking for all the relevant and pertinent information for him to make an informed decision. Hobbs was expert at using ten words when three would do. I would keep him as far away from the case as I possibly could, so I picked up the telephone.

'Are you serious?' Cornock gave me a sullen look.

His face still looked the colour of a dirty pavement slab and his cheeks had hollowed out a fraction too. The enforced sabbatical wasn't doing him much good. I nodded back with a suitable degree of severity.

Cornock nursed a latte into which he had poured two sachets of sugar. The café was in the middle of a row of shops in Whitchurch equidistant from Queen Street and Cornock's home in Cyncoed. I couldn't remember ever having seen Cornock without either a white or powder-blue shirt with a neatly knotted sombre tie. His short-sleeved casual shirt in bold yellows and greens was entirely out of character.

'You know that you should ask Dave Hobbs for this authorisation.'

I rolled my shoulders, then my eyes in a sort of casual way, hoping to win his trust. 'He was one of the officers on the original enquiry into the death of Mr Oakley. I didn't want to compromise his integrity.'

Cornock raised his eyebrows. The expected reproach for my lame reply didn't materialise. 'From what you tell me Inspector Ackroyd has already completed potential searches into all of these officers and the three lawyers involved. I don't see what else you can hope to achieve.'

Cornock took another mouthful of his coffee.

'He might have missed something. After all, the searches are out of date and I need authority to requisition all personnel files, which Ackroyd didn't have.'

Encouragingly Cornock nodded. 'Are you getting accustomed to working with Dave Hobbs?'

'He's got a different style.' Searching for the right words strained my vocabulary. 'It will take me and the team time to become accustomed to his routine.'

He leant over the table a fraction, lowering his voice. 'You need to work with Dave Hobbs. The temporary promotion might be permanent. And he could be promoted even further. Sometimes you have to work with people you don't like. That doesn't make them incompetent police officers.'

I hesitated, uncertain if he expected me to respond. 'How are you enjoying your sabbatical?'

Cornock sighed.

'It's difficult not having the regular routine. I never thought I would say this, John, but I actually miss coming to work.'

It was the nearest Cornock had ever got to discussing his personal affairs with me. He was the first to break eye contact, staring around the place. Noise from the counter behind us interrupted his daydreaming and he glanced at a crowd of young girls, at a guess, the same age as his own daughter, giggling excitedly. He turned his attention back to the various authorities I had prepared for him to sign. With a flourish he added his name to the bottom of each and pushed them over the table towards me.

'I would ask you to keep me informed. But I ... think it would be better if you built your relationship with Acting Detective Chief Inspector Hobbs.' He gave the full rank an ominous permanence.

Back in Queen Street Lydia was deep in conversation with Jane who had an ordnance survey sheet on her desk. They broke off when they saw me.

'I've just got back, boss,' Jane said. 'I spoke to Bevard's golfing buddies who told me that he left their game early the afternoon he was killed. He was gone for over two hours.'

I frowned. 'Where did he go?'

'They had no idea. One of them thought he was seeing a woman but he had no evidence to back this up.'

Wyn cleared his throat. 'I have found something in Bevard's bank statement that might help.'

'Get on with it, Wyn, it's Sunday afternoon. I don't want to be here all day.'

Jane was busy pinning the map to the board.

'Bevard made a withdrawal of two hundred pounds from a cash machine in Cwmbran on the same afternoon that he was killed. And he made a purchase in a convenience store there.'

I walked over to the board; Wyn and Lydia joined me alongside Jane as we stood staring at the highlighted section identifying the golf club. There was no easy explanation for Bevard leaving the golf course. Was he meeting someone? And if so who? I glanced at the various faces on the board. I had to know what Bevard was up to that afternoon. I tapped on the map.

'Tomorrow we go to Pontypool and talk to the owner of the convenience store.'

Chapter 11

As I drove up the valley towards Aberdare, skirting round Mountain Ash, Tracy wasn't far from my thoughts. It had been late in the afternoon when I sent her a message that had gone unanswered. Now it occurred to me that I perhaps should have texted earlier and that maybe she was annoyed with me.

An urgent edge had crept into my father's voice when we'd spoken earlier that week. He had family business to discuss and made it clear I had to be punctual. A property in Pontypridd bequeathed by my grandfather – Nonno Marco – had a complicated legal provision that meant I was dragged into deciding the property's future. Only Uncle Gino, my father's older brother, had any interest and he had been pressurising my father into agreeing to sell. The third sibling, Uncle Franco, was an ageing hippy, still touring small venues with his rock band, who let my father and Uncle Gino make all the decisions.

I pulled into the drive at my parents' home, the final bars of 'You Were Always On My Mind' filling the cabin. My father opened the door before I pressed the bell.

'How are you, John?'

He had a mass of hair that always made him look younger than his age.

'Busy.'

'You're always busy. Come in.' He turned and I followed him into the house.

My mother was preparing a meal in the kitchen, and she reached up with one hand and cupped my left cheek, drawing her hand along the stubble. 'Not shaving now, John?'

'What are you cooking?'

'*Spezzatino di manzo.*'

'That's beef stew to you and me,' my father said behind me.

'You talk to Papa.'

Upstairs in one of the bedrooms that he used as an office he settled into his chair by the paper-strewn desk and took a long slug from a bottle of Peroni. He gave me a businesslike look. 'I need to talk to you about the property.'

I sat in an office chair.

'Nonno made a bloody complicated will with that idiot of a lawyer.'

My father had complained about the will before, many times.

'Nonno put the property in trust because he wanted everyone in the family to pull together once he'd died. It was old-fashioned but he hoped that somehow we could work together as a family.'

'He hadn't reckoned on Uncle Gino and Jez.' I almost spat out my cousin's name. He was lazy and if Nonno could see the way he had treated the family he'd be rewriting his will.

My father nodded slowly.

'While the property was producing a decent income then there wasn't a problem. But now Gino needs the cash and he's been talking to some property developer who's interested in buying it.'

'With the sitting tenant?'

'Apparently. They've bought up some of the adjoining properties and they want to demolish and rebuild the place. The local council is supporting them.'

'Uncle Gino must be salivating at the prospect of getting his money.'

My father drank some more beer and let his gaze wander around the room. 'I've got lots of memories from that place. Nonno was a good man but it's like he's trying to control events from the grave.'

'What do you want to do?'

He sighed. 'We might think about getting rid of the old place. Too many memories and if the price is right ... And we might avoid all the hassle of arguing with the tenant about the rent and negotiating a new tenancy.'

'So the new owners would take on the problems with evicting the tenant?'

'I suppose so.'

'What's happened so far?'

The smell of oregano and tomato drifting from downstairs made me feel hungry.

'Gino has sent me a pile of paperwork. We need to go through it before we meet the lawyers at their offices in Pontypridd. I'll let you know when it's been arranged.'

He passed over a thick wad of papers and took me through each one. There were documents and letters which he tried to explain in layman's terms. An hour passed quickly and Papa started tidying his papers when the front door bell rang. I heard Mamma's footsteps and then the sound of a greeting as she opened the door.

'Mrs Marco, lovely to see you.'

The voice of my ex-partner, Jackie, was unmistakable. I had seen more of Jackie in the last three months than I had in the previous three years – Dean's recent admission to hospital had seen to that. Thankfully he had survived the operation he needed on his brain after a fall, but I had spent hours in the hospital and it had thrown Jackie and me together.

Mamma had always liked Jackie and the feeling had been mutual. I silently cursed my mother for having orchestrated an invitation for her to join us for dinner. I flashed an angry glance at my father but he was staring at the computer screen reading emails so I went downstairs.

'Nice to see you, Jackie.'

She gave me a smile and held my gaze a little longer than normal. I gave her a brief kiss on the cheek. Her skin felt smooth; her perfume lingered in my nostrils.

'I didn't know you were joining us.'

For a moment, she looked puzzled. Then my mother cut in. 'Of course you did. I told you last week.'

Jackie wanted to reply but Mamma fussed over her, leading her by the arm into the kitchen, telling her the finer details of the recipe she'd been assembling. I followed them, helped myself to some sparkling water and listened to their conversation. Mamma still treated Jackie like a daughter-in-law, sharing the occasional confidence, asking her advice – both ignoring me.

'Where's Dean tonight?' It had taken a degree of her prior planning to make these arrangements.

'Dean's staying with some friends.' She paused, a serious look in her eyes. 'I've been thinking about moving back. There are some jobs going in one of the call centres in Cardiff Bay. And I don't think I can afford to keep the house once my divorce from Justin is finalised. So I'll probably sell up.'

'You'll be able to see a lot more of Dean then.' Mamma's tone was upbeat and positive.

I wondered how much of Jackie's arrangements were not being shared with me.

Papa joined us in the kitchen before we went into the adjacent dining room where a bottle of Chianti stood on the table with two bottles of water. Mamma's beef stew was up to her usual high standard and Jackie made all the right complimentary comments. It still annoyed me that Mamma was trying to interfere in my personal life, but criticism was futile. There was a careful analysis of whether Dean was fully recovered after his accident and brain operation. Then his current schooling was scrutinised before the discussion focused on the quality of schools near Jackie's mother.

After panna cotta my father made espresso and by eleven I was stifling a yawn. I mumbled my excuses about having to work the following morning and needing a good night's sleep and Jackie joined me as we left my parents' home. I didn't know exactly what to say as we stood on the driveway.

Jackie squeezed my arm. 'I wanted to tell you how much I valued your help when Dean was ill. I could never have done it without you.' Then she lingered too long with a simple kiss on my cheek before getting into her car and driving away.

Now Jackie dominated my thoughts as I drove back to Cardiff. I was uncertain of my own emotions and unclear how I would react if Jackie tried to rekindle our relationship. I had reached Taff's Well just before the M4 when my mobile rang. I fumbled with my jacket on the seat by my side and answered the call.

'Inspector Marco. You're needed at a murder scene.'

Chapter 12

I slammed the car into third gear and hammered up the slip road of the motorway where I raced into the outside lane. The traffic was light and soon the car reached a hundred miles an hour. I thrust the mobile into the cradle on the dashboard and dialled central operations. The call was answered after a single ring.

'Are the CSI team on their way?' I said.

'Yes, sir. Miss Dix and her team are en route.'

Then I rang Lydia. 'Just had the call, sir.'

'I'll meet you there.'

Mentally I calculated the journey to Llantrisant – it was two junctions on the motorway and then a few miles to the north. Twenty minutes maximum. I made it in twelve. I pulled the car onto the pavement as Lydia parked behind me. We strode over to the semi-detached property where a uniformed police officer stood outside.

'He's in the kitchen.'

I snapped on a pair of latex gloves and walked down the hallway.

Brian Yelland sat upright in a chair by a pine table still wearing his prison officer's uniform, a blank look on his face, a bullet wound in the centre of his forehead. I stared over and recalled the only time I had met him. I had caught the smell of alcohol on his breath when he showed us Walsh's cell in HMP Grange Hall. Drunks always tried to overcompensate, I knew that only too well, and his loquaciousness had become grating. I stood for a moment and scanned the scene – first the body, then the table, before slowly turning to the rest of the kitchen. The realisation gripped me that a killer had stood in this same room. I couldn't escape a feeling of foreboding that the finger was pointed at Jimmy Walsh, safely locked up in the prison where Yelland worked.

Lydia stood behind me. 'Jesus, it's just like Bevard.'

I nodded. 'Looks like another professional kill.'

'One of his neighbours found him. He called to see Yelland about some problems with the boundary fence. He looked in and saw the body.'

A slice of buttered bread sat alone on a cream-coloured plate and near it was an upended yogurt pot. Tomato ketchup smeared the plate in front of Yelland: his last meal had not been fine dining.

'We'll need to know if he had a family.'

'Looks like he lives alone.'

I turned my attention to the rest of the kitchen. It had all the usual accessories: a kettle and a toaster, crockery on a drainer – and the smell of decaying food. And amongst this domestic normality I had to hope there would be some trace of the killer.

Behind me, I heard the muted sound of vehicles arriving and then voices.

Then a white-suited Alvine Dix appeared in the doorway.

'What have we got, Marco?'

I glanced towards Yelland.

'We'll get started then.'

I retreated with Lydia out of the kitchen and into the sitting room at the front of the house. It had a cheap three-piece suite, its arms scuffed and the cushions sagging. I peered out of the window. The markings of the patrol car glistened under the street light. It still had its blue warning light flashing. Then I noticed an A-Class Mercedes parking. Paddy McVeigh jumped out and I walked through into the hallway to meet him.

'Hi, Paddy.'

'Hello, John. Where's the body?'

I pointed down the hallway. The pathologist hurried towards the kitchen and I heard Alvine complaining about being disturbed.

'Shut up, Alvine,' Paddy shouted. He knew well enough how to handle her. Not that there was any ill will towards Paddy or me from Alvine but she had to get things done and if anyone got in her way then she complained. A lot.

I was about to return to the sitting room when I heard a frantic woman's voice. 'Is it true?'

'This is a crime scene, madam.' I recognised the voice of the uniformed officer. 'You cannot go in there.'

She shouted. 'I need to see him. Is he in there?'

'Madam …'

I heard the sound of scuffling and then a small woman with auburn hair burst into the house. Lydia had emerged from the sitting room by now and we stood between the woman and the kitchen so she stopped.

'My name is Detective Inspector John Marco and this is Detective Sergeant Flint.' I kept my voice soft and low.

'Is it true?'

'Who are you?'

'Sharon … Sharon Yelland. I'm Brian's … At least …. We were separated. One of the neighbours called me.'

I raised an arm, pointing her into the sitting room and then towards the sofa where she sat. Now I could see the bags around her eyes where the tears had left their tracks.

'I'm afraid Brian has been killed.'

Her lips quivered. 'How?'

'He was shot.'

Her face crumpled and she pushed her hands to her face.

I glanced over at Lydia who took my prompt. 'Sharon, can you tell me about Brian?'

She was still crying but Lydia had managed a kindly tone and Sharon glanced over at her, swallowed and then calmed herself. 'We were separated.' She fidgeted for a tissue from her bag and blew her nose.

Lydia leant forward again. 'How often did you see him?'

'He'd come to pick up the kids and we'd meet to have coffee sometimes.'

It suggested that despite the problems in their marriage she still had feelings for Yelland.

'And he'd been having trouble at work.'

Lydia shot me an urgent glance before continuing. 'What sort of trouble?'

'The governor had started disciplinary proceedings against him.'

'Do you know the details?' I said.

'Bad time keeping and unprofessional conduct. But that was an excuse – it was really about the drinking.'

Suddenly I tuned into what she was saying. 'Did he have a problem with drink?'

She grunted. 'Problem? He'd get into work pissed. I pleaded with him to get help but he ignored me.'

Once we had all her contact details we ushered her outside where two neighbours were waiting. A comforting arm was placed over her shoulder as they walked over to one of the houses nearby. Conversation between Paddy and Alvine, from down the hallway, broke my concentration and seconds later, Paddy appeared in the doorway. 'John, I've finished.'

'It looks straightforward enough. Bullet wound to the head. Death would have been instantaneous but I'll let you have the full report after the post mortem.'

'Thanks, Paddy.'

I stood for a moment watching him drive away as I smoked a cigarette. Counting each one had become almost as much a ritual as the smoking itself. But I had promised my mother it was only a five-a-day habit. I gazed around the housing estate: the development was a mixture of some semis with small garages and then larger detached houses with bigger gardens.

Llantrisant was another dormitory town for Cardiff. In fact most of the valleys that had once housed heavy industry were now residential areas for the larger conurbations. The politicians talked about the Cardiff City region and they dreamt of greater employment but the valleys of South Wales offered scant opportunity for businesses to develop. Everything seemed focused on the big cities now.

And the residents of this road would all have to be interviewed and their details recorded and their records checked. The killer might be amongst them. Most murderers are known to their victim. But everything told me we already knew where to look for the killer.

Lydia stood with me outside 'This is connected to Jimmy Walsh, isn't it, sir?'

I nodded. Someone else was doing his dirty work. I blew out a lungful of smoke. 'Of course. All we have to do is prove it.' But the prospect felt daunting.

It had been after two o'clock in the morning when I left Queen Street and back in my apartment I slept badly. I could still feel the tiredness in my eyes as I returned to the empty Incident Room after a few hours' sleep. Lydia arrived and we spent time organising house-to-house interviews near Yelland's property, checking when the forensics would be finished and calling the mortuary who confirmed the time of the post mortem. Yelland's mobile telephone and his computer would be available later so our priority would be to establish his movements on the day he was killed. It was the mundane stuff of every inquiry and by mid-morning when I read an email from the PR department asking for a briefing, I realised I needed to get out of Queen Street and do some real policing.

The mortuary was a modern addition to one of the old hospitals in Cardiff. After years of attending post mortems in a cramped old building with ceramic tiles from the Victorian era it had been a welcome change to visit a new and clean environment. The receptionist who doubled as an administrative officer gave me a friendly smile. 'You know your way, Inspector.'

Paddy McVeigh was already preparing as I could hear classical music from beyond the double doors at the end of the corridor.

'That's the 1812 overture.' Lydia hummed along.

There was a loud crash of cymbals as I pushed open the door. Paddy waved his arms in the air as though he were standing in front of an enormous orchestra. Then he gesticulated over at us as the mortuary assistant wheeled in a blanketed gurney.

'Just in time.' Paddy raised his voice enough for us to understand.

Attending a post mortem was a task I never particularly enjoyed. The sight of blood and a human body being pulled apart hadn't been on the application form when I joined the police force. But as the senior investigating officer it was an inevitable part of every murder case. I glanced over at Lydia; her gaze settled into a frown as her jaw tensed. With the volume dimmed Paddy got to work and we watched a man contented with his lot in life. Finally he gave a satisfied sigh and then looked up at me. 'A single gunshot wound to the head. It was a small calibre handgun. At a guess it was a 19 mm, may be Walther P99.'

'Is it the same weapon that killed Felix Bevard?'

Before answering, he set his gaze to Yelland's forehead. Then he tilted his head slightly. 'The tests on the bullet will tell you, but I would say it's a similar handgun. But the nature of the killing is different somehow. This is more clinical. The killing of Felix Bevard was a frenzied, angry attack. The killer pumped six bullets into him.'

'But could it be the same killer?'

I should have expected one of Paddy's sharp one-liners to my rhetorical question. Instead, he sounded stoical. 'I can't judge, John. It is a similar gun, possibly the same one. However, the nature of the killing suggests a different perpetrator. Or a killer who really hated Bevard.'

Paddy turned up the volume as we left. At the main entrance Lydia glanced towards the mortuary entrance. 'He must be having a Tchaikovsky day. He's playing the *Nutcracker* now.'

Outside, a shower freshened the air and we scampered to the car. It hadn't given me time for a cigarette although I sensed the guilty presence of the pack in my jacket pocket.

'Do you reckon we are looking for two killers?' Lydia said once we were in the car.

Paddy's comments had been troubling me as well. 'Could be, but if there are, then they are both linked to Walsh.'

I switched on the engine and let the wipers swish back and forth before I added, 'Hopefully the forensics from Yelland's house will yield some more clues.'

I started the car and negotiated my way out of the

car park. Lydia tapped a postcode into the satnav and we headed to the north of Cardiff to speak to Sharon Yelland again. The earlier shower had turned into something more intense and the rain battered against the windscreen. It was half an hour before I found the village where she lived.

Lydia parked by the terrace of houses but before we left the car she glanced over. 'If you don't mind, I'll take the lead, boss.' She hesitated. 'She might respond better to a woman.'

After working with Boyd Pearce, who had been my sergeant for several years, the advantages of working with Lydia had taken time to bed in. The inspector who trained me would have been horrified to see a woman working alongside him.

Sharon Yelland lived in the middle of a terrace of six properties and she led us into a small kitchen at the rear where we sat by a table as she made coffee. Evidence of the tears she had shed for her late husband had disappeared and a discreet amount of make-up made her look younger than I remembered.

'This is a lovely property,' Lydia began. 'How long have you lived here?'

'It's only been a year.' She reached for three mugs from a cupboard.

'It must have been tough for the children when you separated. How old are they?'

I could see Sharon relaxing in response to Lydia's interest in her children.

'The youngest is five and the oldest eleven.'

'Have they settled into their new schools?'

The electric kettle bubbled and then frothed before switching itself off. Sharon heaped instant coffee into each mug and after establishing our preferences she added milk.

'The kids have settled fine. My mother's taken them

today. None of them are sleeping well.'

'It must be terrible for them.'

Sharon put the coffees down on the table and pulled out a chair to join us. I could sense Lydia's mood changing, engaging a serious cog. 'Why did you and Brian separate?'

She peered down at the steaming surface of her drink. 'His drinking was the big problem. And I found out he was shagging some tart from the prison.'

I wanted to interrupt and ask her all the details but I could see the concentration on Lydia's face.

'I told him ages ago he needed counselling. I warned him he'd lose his job if he wasn't careful.' Sharon held her mug with two hands and took a first mouthful. 'Governor James wanted to get rid of him.'

Lydia leant over the table towards her. 'You mentioned he was having a relationship with one of the prison staff. Can you tell me who she was?'

'Janice, I think. I never knew her full name. One of my friends who's married to one of the other prison officers saw them together in Cardiff one weekend. I expect you can find out all about her on his Facebook page. He spent huge amounts of time on Facebook. First thing he did when he got up, during every meal, and then last thing at night. I got sick of it. And I got sick of the lies about money. He was forever drinking or gambling or both. I'm better off now living on my own, than I ever was living with Brian.'

Lydia allowed a lull to develop so I cleared my throat. 'Did he owe money to any particular bookmaker?'

'There was this betting shop in Llantrisant he used regularly.'

'Do you remember the name?' I said, thinking there'd be half a dozen betting shops in the town.

'The betting shop chains had banned him over two

years ago. It was that small independent one.'

I made a mental note to get a search done once I was back in Queen Street. 'You mentioned he'd been to Alcoholics Anonymous meetings.'

She nodded briskly.

'Do you know where those meetings were? We might be able to talk to those present.'

'Pontypridd or maybe Llantrisant?'

'When did he last see the children?'

'It was last weekend. Something wasn't right. He didn't seem himself.'

'Was he worried about the disciplinary proceedings?' Lydia said.

'It wasn't that. He was elated. He said things were looking up. But I didn't know what to believe. He could be delusional. Maybe he had a good tip for a race. When we first got married Brian was full of good intentions. He wanted to get a promotion. He even talked of applying for governor grade. He was clever enough, but it would have meant moving around the country and he knew I didn't want to do that. My family is all from this area and I didn't want to move.'

'Did he have any other family – parents or siblings?'

'He was an only child and both his parents died when he was in his twenties. His only family were the kids really and he doted on them. He was a good father most of the time. He got completely addicted and then he couldn't help himself. I did love him once, you know.'

She looked surprised when we asked her if he had any enemies. Had he mentioned any prisoner or former prisoner who might have threatened him? Again more head shaking. We left Sharon and headed back for the car.

'I wonder what caused the sudden change in Yelland's behaviour?' Lydia said as she fired the engine into life.

'We'll talk to his mates at the prison tomorrow, maybe they can shed light on what was happening.' Lydia clicked her safety belt into place. It was my turn to choose the soundtrack for our journey and I thought 'Suspicious Minds' was entirely appropriate.

Wyn and Jane were sitting at their desks in the Incident Room when we got back, an air of expectation clear in the way they almost jumped up when we entered.

Wyn was the first to speak. 'We tracked down that cashpoint in Cwmbran, boss. It was outside a shop where Bevard bought food. The owner couldn't remember the transaction and looked blank at us.'

I sat on one of the desks.

'They must have hundreds of transactions each day,' Lydia said.

Jane continued. 'The owner hadn't been working that day. So he suggested we visit his other shop. He thought one of his staff might remember something.'

Jane settled comfortably into recounting their movements that morning. 'He runs two convenience stores in the town. And he thought one of the staff in the second shop might remember the transaction. The man wasn't working so we had to track him down in his flat.'

'Grotty place, too, boss,' Wyn added. 'Place stank.'

'But he *was* able to remember Bevard when we showed him his photograph. Not because of what Bevard bought but because he was wearing his golf clothes. And he had an expensive car that attracted a lot of attention.'

'Okay, anything else?'

Jane glanced at Wyn who took the prompt to speak. 'Bevard was with another man.'

Now I stood up and straightened.

Jane continued. 'The man described was quite distinctive: tattoos all over his arms and a narrow ponytail extending down his back.'

I recognised the description and for a moment struggled to make sense of my thoughts. I turned on my heels and headed back to my office. 'I've seen that man.'

I rummaged through the papers we had taken from the Lemon Grove until I found the photograph of Bevard and his football-playing friends. I stared at one face in particular before marching out to the Incident Room and pinning the image to the board.

One of the men had a ponytail and the tattoos were evident on his right arm.

'Jack Ledley,' I said. 'Gloria Bevard identified him as one of Bevard's friends.'

I looked over at Lydia. 'Get your coat. Let's see if Ledley's at home.'

This time I hammered on Ledley's front door. But the result was the same. The next door neighbour came out of his front door when he heard me shouting.

'Jack hasn't been home since you were here last.'

'Do you know where he might be? I need to speak to him.'

He stared at me as though I was deranged. 'Like I said. I don't know where he could be.'

He stood there for a few seconds before going back inside and firmly closing the door.

I jerked my head up the street. 'You take one side. I'll take the other. Somebody must know something about him.'

I could see the scepticism on Lydia's face but I headed off before she could say anything. I spoke to several people who shook their heads when I mentioned Ledley's name. After a dozen houses I crossed over and waited while Lydia finished with a portly man who kept her talking on the doorstep.

'Nothing, boss. It's as though he's invisible.'

'Damn. Let's go to the sports centre where they played football. They might know something.'

We spoke to a receptionist who knew nothing about the members of the five-a-side football teams and she looked blankly when I mentioned the name of Felix Bevard and Jack Ledley. He was quickly becoming someone that we needed to find.

Someone who had spoken to Bevard on the day he died. Someone with information about Bevard's last few hours.

Chapter 13

I was at my desk early and the message from Jackie reminding me about the arrangements for me to spend Saturday afternoon with Dean surprised me. It was longer than the messages I was accustomed to, and it sounded friendly. I texted her back and afterwards kept an eye on my telephone, half expecting a reply.

I worked my way through the preliminary reports of the house-to-house inquires in Yelland's estate but they told us little of value and then the forensics report and the post mortem results took us no further. The prison had emailed his personnel file to us and I scanned the details.

I knew there had to be a connection to Walsh. And the only concrete one we had was Norcross who had once worked for Walsh and whose fingerprints were found at the Bevard murder scene. But we still couldn't tie him directly to the murders.

So I called the forensics lab and spoke to one of the scientists there who snorted in disbelief when I inquired about progress. Frustrated, I turned to the papers on Norcross and wasted an hour until I read the result of the PNC check and read the name of HMP Newport where he had spent part of a sentence years ago. I had seen an earlier reference to the prison in the paperwork and a knot of tension developed that I had missed something obvious.

Then I recalled the details on Yelland's personnel file and clicked on my mouse until his CV opened on my screen. He had spent six months in HMP Newport too, and I turned back to the papers on Norcross. My mouth dried and a sense that I was making progress filled my mind. Some progress, at least.

I picked up the telephone handset and called Newport prison.

After a brief conversation I strode out into the Incident Room and peered at the board. 'Owen Norcross was in Newport jail at the same time that Brian Yelland was working there.'

None of the team said anything.

I stared at the image of Norcross. 'Get him in for questioning. He's on bail. Tell him we need to ask him some more questions.'

'What if he refuses, sir?' Wyn added.

I turned to him. His eyes had a troubled look. 'Then arrest him.'

'What for?'

'For? Being an associate of Jimmy Walsh – that should be more than enough.'

For a moment Wyn thought I was serious. Jane sniggered.

'And while both of you get Norcross into the cells Lydia and I will go and talk to Yelland's mates in the prison.'

I walked back to my office for my jacket and then I joined Lydia as we made our way to the car park. After the usual formalities it was late morning before we were shown through to see Governor James. She had a harassed look on her face.

'The press have rung every hour.' She waved us to the chairs by the table.

I sat in one of the visitor chairs, Lydia by my side.

'Is there any indication who might have killed Yelland?'

'It's far too early to say,' I said.

'It means a complete investigation.' She sounded crushed. 'Headquarters have these protocols.' Her gaze couldn't settle on anything. 'They're sending a team.' She made it sound very cloak and dagger. 'Yelland was subject to disciplinary proceedings. The whole thing is being handled by the HR section here in consultation with the Prison Officers Union.'

'We'll need the file.'

She nodded. It was a tired, worried nod. 'These things take time. You have no idea about the paperwork we need to go through to discipline a prison officer. And my predecessor was useless. He ignored any problem and hoped it would go away.'

'You could fill me in about his background while Sergeant Flint speaks to the POU representative.'

James reached for the telephone, tapped in a number and barked some instructions at the person at the other end. She smiled weakly at me.

'Tell me about Yelland.'

'He was a drunk. But I expect you know that. And if he worked weekends there were complaints from families in the visitor centre that he smelt of booze and that he was slurring. One Saturday he fell over and broke a chair.'

'When did he finish work on Sunday?'

'He should have finished his shift at six but he filled in for a colleague and did some overtime. He left at ten.'

There was a knock on the door and a woman drifted in with an armful of papers she deposited on James's desk. 'The POU representative will see Detective Sergeant Flint now,' she announced.

Lydia left and I turned my attention back to James.

'Had he been threatened by anyone?

'Not that I am aware, Inspector.'

'Did he have any contact with Jimmy Walsh?'

James stared over at me open-mouthed in astonishment. 'Surely you don't still think Walsh was responsible?' She shook her head slowly as though my approach was to be pitied.

'Yelland was the officer who showed us Walsh's

cell.'

'I know but, for Christ's sake. Walsh is a prisoner here, he couldn't have been responsible unless ...'

'He conspired with someone else.'

She sat back in her chair with a thud. She shifted through the papers. 'We had only gone so far with the disciplinary proceedings. We had to get risk assessments of his work and evaluate his performance.' She paused. 'And now the poor man is dead. This is awfully sad. Have you spoken to his wife? I understand they were separated.'

Eventually she extracted a thin plastic envelope and riffled through its various contents.

'I'll need to speak to HR about releasing all the papers.'

A growing sense that the reason for Yelland's death did not lie in his disciplinary file made me appear deferential. 'I will need everything in due course. Perhaps you can get back to me once you've spoken to HR. I'll need full details of where he worked, what his duties were, etc. And I need to know whether he made any enemies in the prison? Both from the prisoners and the staff.'

'His colleagues can give you a better picture. I understand years ago he was considered material for governor grade but things got on top of him. And then the booze got a hold of him. Terrible thing being an alcoholic.'

Every time a person was portrayed in this way, I thought the speaker must know about me and then my shirt tightened around my neck and the hairs on my neck stood up. So I found myself blanking out her comments.

'I understand he was having a relationship with one of the female staff.'

James gazed over the desk, astonished. 'First I've heard of it.'

'Wouldn't such a relationship be relevant in the

disciplinary proceedings?'

'You cannot seriously expect me to know everything about the private lives of all the staff here.'

'I'll need a list of all your staff in due course.'

'Of course.' James was surveying the carnage on her desk as I left. I joined Lydia in the entrance lobby and we were escorted to another administration building.

'The representative of the POU is a right fascist. He wanted to know if there was written authority for all the paperwork to be disclosed. Then he went through a list of things the prison authorities had done wrong and how they had contributed to Yelland being a drunk.'

'Yelland's dead and he wants to play the union game.'

'That's what I told him. I couldn't believe he was being so awkward. Obviously he wants to protect his own little empire.'

'Prison officers are notoriously defensive. There's a great *esprit de corps*.'

Eventually we were led into an airless room in a two-storey building in the middle of HMP Grange Hall. We hadn't been offered coffee or tea or water and my throat felt parched. After an hour listening to the jaded comments from various prison officers who knew Brian Yelland I sympathised with Governor James's dilemma. They all shared a cynicism about the effectiveness of the prison system and how shorter sentences in the relaxed regime at HMP Grange Hall made their life difficult, increased crime and generally contributed to the decline of civilisation.

The final officer was younger than the rest.

'Glyn Vaughan.' He reached out a hand, which I shook. He sat down and gave us an open smile that encouraged me to believe he might be more helpful than his colleagues.

'Were you friends with Brian Yelland?'

Vaughan nodded. 'We worked together. I got on well with him. I suppose you know he was facing disciplinary proceedings.'

I flicked through the file of papers in front of me until I found Yelland's personnel details. I looked up at Vaughan. 'You're a bit younger than Yelland?'

'I had probably more in common with him than some of the other officers. I came into the prison service after university not really knowing what I wanted to do. Most of the other officers are ex-servicemen which is a bit ironic when you consider the ex-servicemen we lock up.'

'Did you work the same shifts as Yelland?'

'For most of the time. We shared responsibility for looking after the four "F" billets and we supervised the gardening section.'

'Is that where James Walsh works?'

Vaughan's direct eye contact told me so much more than his simple nod.

'Was Brian good at his work?'

Vaughan cleared his throat as though he wanted time to compose an answer. 'He was a very experienced prison officer but I think he got too familiar with a lot of the prisoners. Although this is an open jail and we've got our fair share of dodgy accountants and crooked lawyers, there are still career hardened criminals here too.'

Lydia stopped scribbling notes and gazed over at Vaughan.

I continued wondering what else he could add. 'What do you mean by "familiar"? Any specific examples you could share?'

'Oh, you know, he would hang around the billet for longer than he needed. Then he'd get talking to the prisoners. We are not here as social workers, Inspector.'

'Was he ever over familiar with Jimmy Walsh?'

Vaughan pursed his lips. 'I warned him about Walsh. I saw him in the greenhouses and sheds where Walsh worked, talking and sharing a joke with him. As though they were mates.'

'Can you remember if you were working last Wednesday evening? It was the night Felix Bevard was murdered?'

'There were a lot of disturbances that night.'

I frowned. 'What kind of disturbances?'

'It happens occasionally when the tension boils over. Younger prisoners from the other billets had been fighting earlier in the day. Then there was an argument between two prisoners over a game of poker.'

'Was Jimmy Walsh involved? Did Brian Yelland work that evening?'

'Brian was working for sure. He'd asked for overtime. He needed the money apparently. But then he always needed money. As I recall Jimmy Walsh had been ill.'

'Was he seen by a doctor?'

Vaughan guffawed. 'If the prisoners are sick then they're sick. There's no doctor on site. Walsh might have got paracetamols from the other prisoners.'

I tidied the papers but Vaughan remained seated. 'Look, Inspector, there's one other thing. I can't prove this but I think Brian was taking money from Walsh.'

I let out a slow breath. I saw the tension in Lydia's face.

'You had better explain.' I used a measured tone.

'It's not unheard of for the wealthier prisoners to make certain their time inside is made easier by paying prison officers to make sure they get the right privileges and the best food. I noticed Brian was bringing in ready meals — far more than he would ever eat on duty. If Walsh got hungry, all he had to do was use the microwave in his billet. And Brian made sure Walsh got the quietest cell and the cosiest job in the prison.'

'Did you ever voice your concern to your superiors?'

Vaughan gave me a crooked smile. 'Brian was a colleague. What he did was stupid but nobody escaped. Nobody absconded.'

After Vaughan left I wondered what Governor James would make of all this. We left the administration block and made our way to the main gate. I could understand the indignation of the red-topped newspapers whenever a prisoner absconded but there had to be a system for trying to rehabilitate offenders. I pointed my remote at the car and it bleeped open.

'What did you make of Vaughan, boss?'

I stopped and put a hand on the roof of my car. 'I think it brings nearer that conversation I need to have with Jimmy Walsh.'

A tray with the dried-up remains of a half-eaten lasagne lay on a plastic plate on the floor of the interview room. The room smelt thick from dirty clothes and unwashed bodies. The custody sergeant had warned me that a couple of drunks had been interviewed in the room earlier that day. Lydia took the tray outside and I put the tapes and my papers on the table. Before leaving my office I had read an email from the governor of Newport jail. The paragraphs that told me about the conflict between Norcross and Yelland had made interesting reading.

Owen Norcross appeared in the doorway moments later, this time with a solicitor. Chris Humphreys was one of the regulars from one of the less fashionable firms in Cardiff and the quality of his suit and the scuffed brogues suggested he needed a better class of client.

'What is the basis of this interview? Have you arrested my client?' Humphreys pumped himself up before continuing.

'Your client is on bail and has agreed to assist us with our inquiries.' I smiled at Norcross. It had little effect. He sat down, crossed his arms, and stared at me.

Once Lydia and I were settled at the desk I turned to Norcross. 'I'm investigating the murder of Brian Yelland.'

More blank stares.

'Mr Yelland was a prison officer at HMP Grange Hall.'

'No comment.' Norcross glanced at Humphreys.

'He was killed on Sunday evening.'

Humphreys made his first contribution. 'Are you suggesting that my client had a motive to kill Mr Yelland because he was a prisoner when Yelland was an officer there?'

'Did you know Mr Yelland?'

'No comment.'

Moving some of the papers to one side, I checked the dates of Norcross's incarceration in Newport jail.

'You knew Brian Yelland from your time in Newport prison. He was one of the senior officers on the wing where you spent the last six months of your sentence.'

He moved in his chair as though he were sitting on something uncomfortable.

'Did you have an argument with Yelland?'

He shook his head back and forth.

'Is it true that there was an argument between you both about your privileges and that you threatened Yelland?'

Norcross glanced at Humphreys. He gave the slightest of nods.

'Yelland was a vindictive bastard and he was drunk all the time. I didn't kill him.'

Humphreys stopped scribbling in his notepad and announced, 'And you've got no reason to hold my client or suspect that he was involved.'

I ignored Humphreys and kept looking at Norcross. 'Where were you on Sunday night after you left the police station?'

He unfolded his arms and placed his palms on the table; there was a note of defiance in his voice. 'I went to see my mum, then I went home. I was back before midnight.'

We left Norcross and his lawyer, who protested vehemently about his client's continued detention. I went outside to smoke a cigarette while Lydia spoke to Norcross's mother. I returned to the custody suite as Lydia finished her call. 'She confirms he visited but she can't recall when he left.'

She shrugged. 'We don't have any eyewitness evidence, boss.'

An hour later we had released Norcross. My reminder that he was still on bail met with a dull stare. I watched him leave Queen Street with Humphreys. It sickened me to think that he would be on the telephone with Bernie Walsh once he got home, laughing and gloating.

Chapter 14

Lydia had chosen to play a CD of *La Traviata* on the car stereo during our journey the following morning. Our agreement to alternate musical tastes meant the theme tune to our next trip would be Elvis' greatest hits. She took the M4 west until the junction for Bridgend and then she followed the road north for Maesteg. After the decline of the coal industry the town was nothing more than a dormitory area for Port Talbot. Gloria Bevard's extended family still lived there and she had given us the address of her parents' home where she was staying. I mulled over her father's name: Walter Underwood. He had been a childhood hero of mine who had played half back for Swansea before they reached the heights of the English Premier league. Nobody remembered him much but he had played for Wales on the first occasion I had watched an international game, and he had scored the only goal.

'Did you know *La Traviata* is the most popular opera?' Lydia said, clearly aiming to embarrass me over my knowledge of Italian opera.

'It was first performed in Venice in 1853.'

'How did you know that?'

'I can be full of useless information.'

After Aberkenfig and Tondu, Lydia powered the car up the valley towards Maesteg. The town hadn't lost its end-of-the-line feel but it was the sort of isolation that gave it a strong sense of community. The satnav took us to a street of well-maintained dormer bungalows with neatly trimmed gardens and shrubs.

Lydia pulled up once the disembodied voice told us we had reached our destination. At the same time a message arrived on my mobile from my father telling me a meeting had been arranged for Saturday morning with the family lawyers in Pontypridd. It felt like a long way in the future and I hoped that despite the demands of the inquiry I'd be able to attend.

Walter Underwood stood in the door as we approached. He still had a strong head of hair and it was difficult to guess his age from his tall stature although the makings of a paunch suggested he wasn't as fit as he once was.

'Mr Underwood, Detective Inspector Marco.' I reached out a hand. His shook mine fiercely.

'I'll call Gloria. She's sleeping.'

'Thanks. It's a pleasure to meet you. I was in the Cardiff City Stadium when you played for Wales in that game against Cyprus.'

He gave a brisk acknowledgement. 'I scored that game. Shame we didn't progress in that competition. We had some good players then.'

I wanted to talk football and Welsh football in particular. Especially as the national team was in one of the more favourable groups for the next World Cup. However, Walter left us in a sitting room with mementoes from his playing career littered across various sideboards and cupboards. I cast an appreciative eye around them all including the photograph of him receiving his fiftieth cap.

I hadn't finished admiring the collection when I heard movement behind me. Gloria walked in, sank into a chair and then yawned.

'What do you want?'

'I was admiring your father's collection. I enjoyed watching him play years ago.'

'He still loves his football. He trains the local team and helps youngsters. It's a pity there wasn't the money in the game when he was playing. He'd be dead rich by now.'

'Where does he help out?'

'Local sides mostly. And Mam does the teas after the game on a Saturday.'

She tucked both legs underneath her on the chair.

Lydia butted in; talking football wouldn't find Bevard's killer. 'We need to ask you about a Martin Kendall.'

'Who?'

I switched into detective mode quickly enough when I noticed the casual lie. It was the averted glance and the slight evasive tone to her voice that sharpened my concentration.

Lydia continued. 'He worked with Jimmy Walsh.' Then she described Kendall in detail even down to the colour of his Porsche.

'I think he may have mentioned him. Yeh, he did. Felix was forever getting involved with Jimmy Walsh.'

I glanced over at Lydia. She was gathering her thoughts.

'Have you got a big family?' I said.

'Two sisters, like. We're close, *really* close I mean. We do everything together and the boys are best mates with their cousins.'

Talking about her family was obviously something she enjoyed. 'I don't know what I'd have done without Mam this last week. I was a wreck. So I've been staying here with the boys. I can see my sister too. They live nearby, see.'

Lydia got back into the swing of her questions. 'We're trying to build a picture of what Felix was doing on the afternoon he was killed. We can't account for two hours in the middle of the afternoon. Do you know if he was meeting anyone?'

She straightened in her chair. 'Are you suggesting he was playing around? My Felix would never do that.'

'I didn't say that. Do you know if he was meeting anyone?'

'No, definitely not.'

'We believe he might have been in the Cwmbran area that afternoon.'

'But that's miles from the golf course. What was he doing there?'

'We hoped you might help us. We believe he may have been with a man called Jack Ledley?'

She gave a disinterested shrug that sat uncomfortably with the earlier belligerence.

'Do you know Jack Ledley?'

She started chewing a nail before shrugging. 'Sorry, dunno.'

Discussing with her the fact that Felix was contemplating signing a supergrass deal had to be faced. These agreements meant a complete change for the entire family, a new life, a break with everything familiar. Gloria looked tired; the skin around her eyes looked parched and cracked as though she had aged since her husband's death.

'I need to ask you about one other matter.' I cleared my throat. 'Were you aware that Felix was going to give evidence against Jimmy Walsh?'

She glanced away before adjusting her hair. 'What do you mean?'

'Jimmy was implicated in the murder of a man called Robin Oakley a few years back.'

Gloria looked at me with a neutral expression.

'Felix had enough evidence to have Jimmy Walsh convicted.'

I waited for a response. Lydia filled the lull. 'Gloria, did Felix ever mention the witness protection scheme to you?'

'What do you mean?'

'Felix,' Lydia paused, 'and you and the boys would have been given new identities and a new life.'

'Don't be daft.'

'He mentioned nothing about this to you?'

She pulled her legs closer to her now.

'It would have meant a fresh start for you as a family without the risk of Jimmy Walsh ever finding you.'

She shook her head. 'My Felix wouldn't do that. Nobody knew him better than me and I'd swear on my gran's grave Felix wouldn't do that. He knows how close I am to my family. He'd never make me leave them.'

Gloria adopted an increasingly fractious response to the rest of our questions. We left soon after and headed back for Cardiff. I cursed silently when a message reached my mobile from Hobbs requesting a meeting later.

'Perhaps she was right, boss, and Felix Bevard was never going to contemplate being a supergrass.'

'I find that hard to believe when he was facing a murder charge. Remember, Robin Oakley's blood traces in one of his taxis would be enough to get him convicted.'

Lydia didn't seem convinced.

Back at Queen Street a uniformed officer was sitting by a desk in the Incident Room. 'Detective Inspector Marco?'

I nodded.

'Constable Colin Young, sir. I'm with the traffic department.'

I waved Young through to my room. 'How can I help?'

He was about my age, clean-shaven, with a lean powerful build.

'I've been on a week's holiday.' It explained the bronze tinge to his skin. 'I understand you are investigating the death of Felix Bevard.'

I cast my watch a surreptitious glance, aware I

didn't want to keep Hobbs waiting.

'I stopped Bevard that afternoon for speeding.'

It stopped me thinking about Hobbs in an instant. I pulled my chair nearer the desk, scrambled for a ballpoint and a clean sheet of paper.

'Where was that? I'll need all the details. Where have you been?'

'On a beach in Tenerife. I always go for a week this time of the year.'

'We know Bevard was in the Llanymerlin golf club on the afternoon he was killed. So what time did you stop him?'

Before Young started, I bellowed for Lydia. She took seconds to appear in my room and after hearing why we needed to speak to Young she sat down on one of the visitor chairs.

'I was doing a regular patrol along the A472. It's a known spot for speeding motorists. I was parked on one of the slip roads—'

'Where exactly is that? Wait, Lydia will get the map.'

Lydia returned moments later with an ordnance survey sheet. She spread the map out over the desk and we looked on as Young found the exact location where he had stopped Bevard. We exchanged a troubled glance. It was miles away from the golf club and the shop he'd visited the same afternoon.

I looked over at Young. 'I want you to remember everything.'

Young sat back in his chair. 'He was in Pontypool driving north in the direction of Blaenavon. There was another man in the car with him.'

'Can you describe him?'

My brusqueness startled Young who hesitated.

'I didn't see his face but ...'

I leant over the desk. 'Anything at all. I need to know who this other man was.'

'He had tattoos and I think he had a pony tail.'

I glanced at Lydia. She nodded sternly.

Young continued. 'I checked the car through the DVLA system and it belonged to Bevard. There wasn't anything wrong with the car. He was pleasant and polite. He even apologised for speeding but he was doing far too much for a warning so I issued a ticket.'

'Did you see anything in the car? Anything, it's important.'

Young puckered his brow. 'Come to think of it there were shopping bags on the back seat. Two or maybe three carrier bags. I wasn't paying much attention. I think it might have been frozen foods, ready meals.'

'Did he say where he was going?'

Young gave Lydia a puzzled look. 'We don't pass the time of day with speeding motorists.'

Then I read the time again and I quickly tapped out an email to Hobbs telling him I was delayed. I turned back to Young. 'I need your help.'

It took Young twenty minutes to give us an idea of how long it would have taken Bevard to travel from the golf club to the shop in Cwmbran and then to the spot where he was stopped for speeding. Lydia jotted down his comments about the likely road conditions. By the end I was no clearer why Bevard was driving around the eastern valleys. Young left us huddled over the map promising that if he remembered anything else he would contact us.

'What do you think, boss?' There was eager anticipation in Lydia's voice.

'Let's concentrate on what we know. He was buying food. So he must have been buying it for somebody else. Let's double-check ...'

I clicked into the computer and found the forensics report from Bevard's car that had been parked near to Roath Park. There was no sign of any shopping. It had his fingerprints on the steering wheel, and nothing to suggest any foul play.

'There wasn't anything in Bevard's car?' Lydia said.

I shook my head. I found a pencil on my desk and drew a circle around an area between the golf club, Cwmbran and Pontypool where Young had stopped Bevard. 'Somewhere here we're looking for Jack Ledley who was with Bevard. We'll need to get Wyn and Jane working on all of Bevard's known associates. Have we had the list of the prisoners released from HMP Grange Hall in the last three weeks?'

'No, sir. I think we're still waiting …'

'Well, tell them to pull their finger out.'

'Yes, boss—'

'And we'll need to talk to the drivers in his minicab business.'

I glanced again at my watch. Hobbs' patience would be running thin by now.

'I've got a meeting with Chief Inspector Hobbs.'

'I know, sir. He asked me to attend as well.'

I narrowed my eyes but Lydia couldn't possibly know why Hobbs wanted her to attend. We walked through the emptying corridors of Queen Street as the building readied itself for the night shift. I tapped on the door to Cornock's office; I still couldn't bring myself to think of it as Dave Hobbs's office. There was a brief businesslike shout for us to enter. The room was still stuffy. Dave Hobbs had a china teacup and saucer set on the desk and his best pompous air.

'Do sit down, Inspector Marco, Sergeant Flint.'

'Thank you, sir,' Lydia said.

I mumbled something under my breath. Hobbs cast me a condescending glance.

'My apologies about being late. We had an interesting development late this afternoon.' I found a comfortable position on the chair and settled my right foot over my left knee.

'So you're making progress.' Hobbs raised an eyebrow.

I galloped through a summary of the events of the week, dwelling specifically on the unresolved journey Bevard had taken on the last afternoon of his life.

'Do you have any direct evidence to implicate Walsh, yet, Inspector?'

'It's only a matter of time.'

Lydia made her first contribution. 'I think our best option is to trace Jack Ledley, the man Bevard met the afternoon he was killed.'

'That sounds very sensible, Sergeant Flint.' Hobbs looked in my direction. 'Perhaps you could let me have a written report by the morning.' Then he paused and added. 'Inspector.'

I could see what he was playing at. He was like a parent with a naughty child who wouldn't say please. Would I play his game? Would I say the magic word for him?

'Of course. I have another couple of hours of work before leaving tonight. Sir.'

Then Lydia and I left. Walking back to the Incident Room I gradually unclenched by fists and then counted to fifty and then even more slowly to one hundred.

Chapter 15

After a morning reviewing all the house-to-house inquiries around Yelland's home, and listening to Wyn and Jane recounting another wasted morning trying to track down Jack Ledley, I settled into a hope that forensics from Yelland's blood-spattered kitchen might give us something we could use. I even managed to keep an even temper when I called the forensics lab for an update on the clothing recovered from Norcross's home only to be told it would take time.

Lydia stood in the doorway of my office. 'We've had details of the staff at Grange Hall and there's nobody by the name of Janice working there.' Lydia sat down opposite me, her hair drawn into a tight ponytail. The blusher on her cheekbones gave her face a sculpted appearance.

The window behind my desk let in enough cool air to remind me it was early September although the forecasters had been predicting more mild weather. Noise levels from the shops and offices increased as the weekend approached. Our main suspect for both deaths was Walsh. All I had to do was join the dots. If I could find them.

And Martin Kendall and Bernie Walsh had cast iron alibis. My frustration was off the scale at being unable to see what linked both murders. It meant another conversation with Sharon Yelland to establish who had seen her late husband with 'Janice' and then get a detailed description. It would all take time.

'Get Wyn and Jane to speak to Sharon Yelland so we can track down this "Janice" woman.'

'Yes, boss.'

I scanned the to-do list I had printed first thing that morning. Acting Detective Chief Inspector Hobbs would have been pleased with my approach to paperwork. 'And

Wyn and Jane can talk to the bookmakers Sharon mentioned at the same time.'

After booting up my computer I scanned the dozens of emails that clogged my inbox, hoping I wouldn't miss anything too important. Then I turned my attention to the various financial reports on the lawyers and police officers involved in the Bevard supergrass deal. I read financial summaries for the three police officers involved in the case, including the chief superintendent who had signed off on the agreement although the final decision must have gone to one of the ACCs.

Inspector Ackroyd had a house in Caerphilly with a small mortgage. I read about his investments in tax-free savings products and that his wife worked as a teacher. They had two children and everything seemed glaringly normal and unremarkable. The other two officers on his team had no financial problems that merited our attention. Ackroyd's assurance that his officers were not the source of the leak seemed right. I was pleased, of course. Discovering that a police officer might have been indirectly responsible for Bevard's death would have been unpalatable.

The most senior of the Crown Prosecution lawyers had more ready cash than I earned in a year, which piqued my interest. After establishing that his bank account had the same level of liquidity for the past three years and that he had disclosed a substantial inheritance after his father died two years previously, which included a flat in a French ski resort, I stopped digging any further.

The last two CPS lawyers had addresses in the more desirable parts of Cardiff. I scanned their CVs and turned to the financial records. Roger Stockes had little in his bank account at the end of each month. I noticed regular payments to a private school and an internet search told me it charged annual fees of more than five times my monthly salary. Having a financial drain on his income would be a motive enough. I dwelt on his file in more detail and found there were irregular patterns of expenditure so I burrowed further.

Lydia appeared at my door. 'Coffee, boss?'

A niggle worked its way into my mind as I tried to ignore a feeling I had missed something important amidst the bank statements and financial summaries. I went back to Stockes' CV. I stopped when I reached the details of his university degree: astronomy. It was when I read the name of the university he had attended that my pulse flipped sideways.

I looked over at Lydia. 'Something wrong, boss?'

I knew exactly where I had read the same information. 'Roger Stockes went to the same university as Yelland. They both studied astronomy.'

Lydia sounded surprised. 'So one becomes a prison officer, the other a lawyer for the CPS.'

'And by happy coincidence one works on the Walsh supergrass deal and the other is a prison officer on Walsh's billet. Stockes would have had access to all the information about Walsh. He could have mentioned it in passing to Yelland and he sees it as a smart way of making a few extra pounds.'

'So we need a complete picture of Yelland's finances.' Lydia sank back into the visitor chair in my office, a look of resigned acceptance on her face.

'And we need a complete analysis of Stockes' finances too.'

The prospect of interviewing a Crown Prosecution lawyer was almost as daunting as interviewing police officers, and with Dave Hobbs more than a ghostly presence in the background I had to be careful how I proceeded.

'But are we saying that Stockes killed Bevard and

then Yelland?' She gave me a perplexed frown. Lydia was right: this possibility looked remote.

Lydia left and I turned my attention to the file of papers relating to the financial affairs of Roger Stockes. It always amazed me how far back the banks and financial institutions could go when we asked for information as part of a criminal inquiry. I spent the first hour getting a clear picture of his financial position. A generous salary reached the account on the twenty-fifth of each month. Other regular credits into his bank account would need an explanation so I opened a spreadsheet I named 'queries/income'.

If Stockes was in hock to Walsh, it would be fairly recent so I had decided to go back three years. Then I turned my attention to his outgoings. He had a mortgage, a car loan, regular payments to finance and credit card companies with fancy names. I punched the figures into another spreadsheet I called 'expenditure' and which I hoped I could use to establish any unusual patterns. The possibility that Stockes had been the original source of the leak about Bevard's supergrass agreement appalled me. If he had shared the information with Yelland for some extra cash flow then he deserved a stretch in a high security jail. Perhaps it had been only a casual remark at the end of a drunken evening. And for Yelland it had been a meal ticket he couldn't ignore.

I noticed that Stockes made regular payments to one of the large supermarket chains and a quarterly subscription to a wine club. I sat back hoping I could make sense of the information on my screen, but all I saw was a tangled web of figures, dates and abbreviations. This was a task better suited to an officer in the economic crime department and I thought of Boyd Pearce. He could help but I knew I couldn't risk any word of my investigation being shared around Queen Street or the other departments of Southern Division. I dialled his number.

'Good morning, sir.'

'Boyd, how's Mandy and the family?'

Boyd had transferred from my team to the economic crime department before his wife gave birth to their first child and I'd rarely seen him since.

'They're great thanks, busy of course. Not a moment of peace when I get home... Are you working on that Bevard murder enquiry?'

I sensed a wistful edge to his question, laced with regret and the possibilities that working on my team again offered an excitement and challenge he missed.

'I need help with constructing a spreadsheet to analyse income and expenditure for one of the suspects.'

'That's not difficult.' I listened as he explained how to go about creating a document in Excel, using formulas. 'You need to colour code various months and then calculate totals for each month to see if your suspect has a pattern for taking cash out of his account. That way you can identify any months with irregular payments or withdrawals. For example, everyone has to eat, so if there's a month when he's not spending money in the supermarket and he's not dead then he's buying food with cash.'

I thanked Boyd, promising to buy him lunch sometime. Our conversation had given me a renewed focus.

It was late afternoon by the time I had anything resembling a working spreadsheet. My euphoria at having succeeded with the paperwork was tempered by a complete lack of any useful information. There was nothing about Roger Stockes' financial affairs to suggest he was handling large amounts of cash.

I pushed my chair back and threw a ballpoint across the papers on my desk before stalking out into the Incident

Room where Lydia was staring at her monitor.

I sat down heavily on one of the office chairs. 'I've been through Stockes' finances for the last three years. There's nothing.'

Lydia sat back with a satisfied look on her face. 'I've been working on Yelland's financial position. It was a complete mess. He was making regular payments to various finance companies. Once he was in arrears with one company he got a loan from another at a higher interest rate to pay off the first. Then he got into a cycle of high interest loans.'

'How did he break out of that vicious circle?'

'That's where things get interesting. In the last year he paid off some of his smaller loans. He had two credit cards with two thousand pounds owed on each. They were both paid off. It helped him with his cash flow but then within two months he was paying money out to online bookmakers.'

'So once he paid off one debt he starts another.'

'It looks like that. Perhaps Wyn and Jane will have more information from the bookmakers.'

I stood up, walked over and stared at the image of Yelland pinned to the board. The Incident Room door opened and Wyn and Jane, voices loud in animated conversation, entered carrying large mugs of coffee.

'I hope you've got something positive to tell me,' I said.

Wyn blinked furiously, and Jane slipped off her fleece and threw it over one of the desks. Once their drinks had been safely deposited Wyn cleared his throat.

'We spoke to Mrs Yelland, boss,' Wyn began. 'All she could give us was the name of the woman who'd seen Yelland in Cardiff. We tracked her down after speaking with the admin section of the prison. She gave us a description but something was lost in translation – the woman had made no reference to Yelland's girlfriend working in the prison.'

'Damn, bloody hell. We still need to identify her.'

Jane took a large mouthful of her coffee before announcing in her most important voice, 'We had a very helpful conversation with the manager of the bookmakers. He knew all about Brian Yelland. He'd run up debts of about three thousand pounds in a twelve-month period.'

It surprised me a bookmaker would allow such extended credit.

Jane continued. 'A month ago the debt was paid in full. In cash and it wasn't Yelland who paid the bill. We got a detailed description of the man who called in with a wad of twenty-pound notes.' She paced over towards the board and pointed at the face of Martin Kendall. 'He described Kendall down to the hairs on his nose.'

For the first time since the case started my pulse beat a fraction faster.

Chapter 16

I reached the top of the stairs in Queen Street and felt my chest tightening. My five-a-day habit was reminding me that I should be cutting down. I pushed open the door to the Incident Room and noticed a short man in an immaculate grey suit standing with Lydia. From the unsettled look on her face and the way her eyes darted around I could tell she wasn't comfortable.

'Inspector Marco, good morning,' he said, his hand outstretched. 'I'm Roger Stockes. I'd like a word.'

I darted a glance at Lydia and then at the board, hoping that nobody had added Stockes' name to it. We shook hands and I showed him into my office. Lydia followed.

Stockes made himself comfortable in a visitor chair. 'I was in a meeting with DCI Hobbs this morning and I thought I would take the opportunity to speak to you. I'm sure you know by now that I was friends with Brian Yelland.'

A meeting with Dave Hobbs? I wondered what they talked about.

'Brian and I studied at university together.'

I couldn't make out the accent. It wasn't Cardiff or South Wales. It had a rounded crisp edge to it that professionals develop to make themselves sound important.

'We had established that you were associated with Brian Yelland.'

'We were good friends. And his death was shocking.' He paused for effect and shook his head solemnly. I could see that Stockes and Hobbs would get along just fine.

Lydia had a suspicious frown etched on her face. I stared over at Stockes wondering why he had decided to come and see me. He had seized the initiative but he could only guess how much we knew already. I found a notebook and reached for the buff folder of papers we had on Stockes from the pile on my desk.

'What was your involvement with the supergrass agreement?' I said.

'The initial case involving the discovery of the DNA in Bevard's car came onto my desk. The case was handled by one of the dedicated source units. I coordinated the paperwork with a senior prosecutor. The whole thing was signed off correctly.'

'I'm sure it was.' I looked down at the papers on my lap reminding myself of all those involved in the decision-making process. 'So can you tell me who was involved?'

Stockes reeled off the names of police officers and lawyers and I mentally ticked off each one against my list.

I spent half an hour listening to lots of legal jargon and his assessment of the evidence. Occasionally Lydia interrupted with a question, but Stockes handled the interview with ease. But I was still curious about why he had made the initial approach.

'Have you made any progress with identifying who murdered Bevard?'

I shook my head. Stockes continued. 'I suppose you consider Walsh to be the directing mind behind the murder?'

'I'm sure you appreciate that we have to entertain the possibility Walsh was aware that Bevard was contemplating giving evidence against him.'

'Of course.'

'We're talking to everyone involved.' I looked over at Stockes. He didn't avoid my eye – in fact he kept staring straight at me.

'We believe there might be a link to the death of Brian Yelland, too.'

He couldn't hide the anxiety in his face. He drew two fingers under his cheekbones as though he had a developing toothache.

Lydia cut in. 'Yelland was killed with a gun similar to the one used to kill Felix Bevard.'

'Can you tell me more about your relationship with Yelland?' I said. 'Did you see him regularly?'

'We went out occasionally for a drink. After he and Sharon were separated I saw him more often.'

'Did he ever tell you what happened between him and Sharon?'

Stockes shrugged. 'Not really. I suppose the drinking didn't help.'

'Do you know if he had been seeing anyone else?'

'He'd been using some internet dating sites and he'd been on some dates but nothing came of it.'

'He didn't mention anyone called Janice?'

He shook his head.

'When was the last time you saw Yelland?'

He thought for a moment before answering. 'We went out one night two weeks ago.'

'What was his mood like?'

He shrugged but avoided eye contact. 'He was in good form. He even mentioned going on holiday which surprised me when he always complained about money.'

'Did he ever talk about work?'

'The usual small talk. There was a lot of bad feeling at work. He was facing disciplinary proceedings and he was worried.'

'Did he ever mention any prisoners by name?'

Stockes gave me a puzzled look. 'No, why would he?'

'Small talk I suppose.'

He narrowed his eyes, hardened his gaze.

'When he was working in Newport jail a man made a complaint against him. Did he ever talk about that?'

'He mentioned it but prisoners often make unfounded claims against prison officers. A lot of them know how to milk the system.'

'Did he ever mention a man called Owen Norcross?'

Stocked puckered his lips and shook his head. 'Not that I recall.'

A typical evasive lawyer-like reply only made me feel more suspicious.

'Norcross was the prisoner who made the complaint about Yelland. Did Yelland ever mention James Walsh to you?'

Mention of Walsh bridled him. He made an odd sort of coughing sound and shook his head.

'I'm sure you must realise that we have to look at every possible thread in this case. Otherwise you wouldn't have come here to see me. We believe that Walsh found out about the supergrass deal. He must have realised that it meant he was going to face a life sentence.'

'I don't suppose it has occurred to you that Bevard might simply have told someone. These people are toe-rags, Inspector, and they all swim round in a big pool of their own shit.'

I stared at him for a couple of seconds. Any initiative he had when he arrived had gone by now and it only made me more suspicious of Stockes. When he left he handed me a business card with his direct line number and an assurance that if he could help in any way I should not hesitate to call.

After he left Lydia turned to me. 'Do you think he told Yelland about Bevard?'

Contemplating that a Crown Prosecution lawyer had lied to me meant there was something much bigger at stake.

'I don't like coincidences especially when they're linked to someone like Walsh.'

'Maybe he thought we wouldn't dig into his private life if he came to us first.'

'Then he's mistaken.'

Stockes' appearance that morning wouldn't stop me turning over every part of his life.

I sat in my car, Lydia by my side, nursing a double-shot Americano in one of those plastic beakers with a clever lid that was supposed to make drinking from it easier. I had worked ten days straight and part of me knew that I needed a day off although I wasn't certain that my meeting in the morning with Uncle Gino and Jez at the solicitors counted.

Across the road from my car the ACE minicab firm occupied an old garage on a side street: convenient for the motorway and near enough to make it a short drive into the middle of town. Lydia and I looked over at the various cars parked untidily on the forecourt. A big sign over the entrance boasted it was a 24-hour guaranteed service – special rates to the airports of Cardiff and Bristol.

We left the car and headed over towards the entrance. Behind a counter, a woman with leathery skin and a sun-bed tan peered over at us.

'Where to, love? Only it's our busy time now. There might be a bit of a wait. There's a coffee machine by there.'

I held up my warrant card and she squinted over. 'You after that dirty bitch who stole Robbie's money last week? Only he's not here.'

'What's your name?' Lydia said.

'Sonia.'

'We're investigating the death of Mr Bevard.'

Suddenly her mood changed. She straightened and approached the counter. 'You had better come through.' She nodded at the door in reception.

A large whiteboard dominated one wall with the names of all drivers and vehicle registration numbers. It looked an unintelligible jumble. The smell of oil and grease and dirty food hung around the place.

'How many drivers have you got working here?' Lydia asked as she looked at the board closely.

'There are twenty different drivers. Some of them work part time, some own their own cars.'

I stared at the tangle of names. 'Do you know a man called Jack Ledley? Big, lots of tattoos and a ponytail?'

She frowned. 'Sorry, love.'

'Do any of the drivers live up in Cwmbran or Pontypool?'

'Don't think so. So you haven't found who killed Felix?'

Lydia persevered. 'We'll need a list of the drivers. Are any of them here now?'

'There are five of them on their break. Is it true he was killed with a machine gun, like one of them Steven Seagal films? I like them.'

I stepped over towards Sonia and lowered my voice. 'It's all a bit confidential. A need-to-know basis.'

Her mouth fell open, her eyes wide with astonishment.

'Now ... How about that list?'

She sat down at her desk and started rummaging through paperwork. Lydia sat next to her.

'Do you know if Felix Bevard had any enemies?' Lydia said.

'What, like someone who'd want to kill him?' she murmured.

'Someone who might have threatened him. Business rivals or disgruntled employees.'

She curled her lips into a frown. 'Don't think so.'

It surprised me how quickly Sonia was able put her hands on the necessary records in the midst of such chaos. Then she walked over to a photocopier, piled sheets of paper into the top of the machine and waited until it had pinged out all the copies. She handed us the various sheets and we left through a side door before heading towards the restroom at the back of the garage.

Five men sat around a table drinking from large dirty mugs. One of them was picking at fish and chips from a plastic container, another flicking through a men's magazine. They all scanned Lydia from head to toe when she followed me in.

I flashed my card at them, and Lydia did the same. 'DI Marco. We're looking for someone who knew Felix Bevard. We believe his name was Jack Ledley. He had long hair and tattoos on his arms.' There were blank stares mostly; two of the men shook their heads and as Lydia ticked off their names from Sonia's list I had the impression they were telling us the truth. But there were fifteen more names on the list. Somebody must have known Ledley.

A car drew up in the main body of the garage and the atmosphere inside the restroom changed. They craned to look outside, some frowning. 'That's Gloria,' one of them said under his breath. I followed Lydia outside. She reached Gloria Bevard before me.

She peered over at us. 'What the hell are you doing here?'

'We need to trace Jack Ledley,' Lydia said, using her most diplomatic tone.

'Don't come back here unless you notify me in advance. I mean ... I want to know what's going on. I want to know who killed Felix.'

It was difficult to make her out. I paused and stared at her. Was this the natural reaction of the grieving widow?

Gloria seemed out of place amongst the old cars, the oil and the grime. Lydia repeated the description of Ledley, but Gloria ignored her. She looked over my shoulders to the back of the garage and then over to the office.

Adopting a casual tone, I said, 'What will you do with this place now?'

She scowled at me as though the answer was obvious.

'I'll keep it of course. It's my business now and my livelihood. Felix loved this place. He built it up from scratch with just one car, you know. I'd never sell it if that's what you mean.'

Habit made me reach for my pocket to give Mrs Bevard one of my cards. 'Please contact us if you think of anything else or you see Jack Ledley.' She read it with a perplexed look and we turned to walk away.

'I don't like that Gloria Bevard.'

As police officers we weren't paid to like people but Lydia was right in thinking that there was something odd about her behaviour. I flashed my headlights at a van that pulled out in front of me. The traffic into town was building up.

'She seems to have gotten over her grief quickly enough,' I said.

'She's distrustful of us which is worse. I guess that's what I don't like.'

I mumbled my agreement. Lydia continued. 'And I

cannot imagine her leaving her family and her way of life in South Wales.'

'I wonder how Felix was going to tell her that she had no choice and that it was either a bungalow in Adelaide and a cleaning job in the local pizza restaurant or a bullet through the brains.'

I reached Queen Street and pulled into the car park.

'Are we working tomorrow, boss?'

As always with Lydia it was what she implied in a question that was important. She probably felt as jaded as I did. I shook my head before reaching for the handle. 'Recharge the batteries.'

She smiled her agreement.

In the Incident Room Wyn and Jane looked up from their monitors and I nodded an acknowledgement. I sat down and stared at the board, hoping for a miracle. There was something amidst all the images on the board that connected them. Some thread and all I had to do was find it and tug at it until I had enough evidence. Enough evidence to charge Jimmy Walsh. That afternoon I needed to review and revisit everything so that by Monday morning I'd have a fresh mind.

'What do we do about the Kendall connection to Yelland?' Wyn said.

Glyn Vaughan's comments came to mind about his suspicions that Walsh was paying Yelland for favourable treatment in jail. The explanation for paying Yelland's betting office bill was probably that simple. 'It means we keep Kendall as a person of interest. Wyn and Jane go over the house-to-house statements again and then go through his mobile telephone records and his computer. There must be something, for Christ's sake. And we need to find Ledley.' I said it out loud, not expecting anyone to answer.

'I've spoken to the detectives covering the

Pontypool area and nobody recognises the name,' Jane said.

I stood up and walked to the board. 'There's two hours in the middle of Felix Bevard's day that we cannot account for. Maybe he made arrangements to meet up with Ledley later that night and that's when Ledley killed him.'

'But we don't know what the motive might be, boss?' Wyn said.

He was right of course. I was speculating. 'We'll need to chase the forensic lab for the results from Norcross's clothes.'

I stared at the photograph of Jimmy Walsh and although his face was expressionless, I knew he was gloating. Walsh had been in other prisons, shared cells with various convicts. There must have been somebody with a connection to Walsh.

'Have we had a list of Walsh's cell mates, yet?'

'In your inbox, sir,' Wyn said.

'Back to the start.' I tapped Walsh's image. 'We need to establish how he knew about Bevard and the supergrass deal.'

I could sense the futility behind me from the sighs and unspoken criticisms.

'We have no idea who Bevard might have told about the deal,' Lydia said.

'He might even have spoken to Ledley about it,' Jane added.

All I knew was that somehow Walsh had the details of the supergrass deal and that he had been instrumental in having Bevard killed. The only suspects we had, Norcross and Ledley, stared down at me. And behind them directing everything was Jimmy Walsh.

I headed back to my office where I spent a restless two hours watching the coverage from the CCTV cameras on the night Bevard was killed from around the centre of Cardiff. I followed Martin Kendall as he traipsed from bar to bar and it was like looking at him auditioning for a part in some cheap real-life game show. It sickened me by the end because it was so obvious he was constructing an alibi. The same was true of Bernie Walsh although she kept the ham acting to a minimum.

Then I turned my attention to the list of men Walsh had shared a cell with during his time inside. Checking them all would take days. It was a mind-crunching task Wyn would enjoy. I read through the names of all those that had been released from Grange Hall in the last month and then cross-referenced them to the names of the prisoners who had been on the same billet as Walsh. It surprised me there were only six and I quickly dismissed five of them who had given addresses in various parts of England. I requisitioned a PNC check against the remaining name.

By mid-afternoon my boredom levels were getting dangerously high so I trooped out of my office. Lydia followed me out of Queen Street and we headed for Mario's where we ordered coffee.

'I've been checking the house-to-house inquiries for Roath Park for the night Bevard was killed. But there's nothing of any significance,' Lydia said. 'And all the staff from the café have been interviewed. Nobody remembers Norcross being there but they have hundreds of customers each day.'

It curdled my thoughts that soon Hobbs would ask me some awkward questions. A waitress brought my Americano and a tall milky concoction for Lydia. I picked up my spoon, giving the black liquid a therapeutic stir.

'I feel uncomfortable with this supergrass stuff,' Lydia said.

I didn't reply. The truth was I hated these

supergrass deals too. It was like shaking hands with the devil and watching him laugh at you. Bad men got away scot-free in order to put equally bad men in prison. Maybe that was what the authorities thought was a good deal. For me it always meant bad policing which explained why they had little publicity.

Chapter 17

The sound of accents from the Rhondda Valley as I walked down the main street of Pontypridd took me straight back to my childhood. I smiled to myself as I remembered Saturday mornings going from one shop to another, flirting with girls who had travelled on the same bus from Aberdare. And then feeling important sitting in the Marco café with a milky coffee and some buttered toast. I stopped by the travel agents and looked up at the first floor window that had the name of the lawyers' office stencilled in sombre black lettering.

Walters and Sons had written Nonno Marco's will, which contributed to the conflict within the extended Marco family. The original Mr Walters had long since passed away and it was one of his sons we were seeing, although I recalled gossip from years ago that the other son had been caught in one of the public toilets with another man, an event that had scandalised the community. Soon after, he had left to live in Australia.

There was a gentle climb along a tarmac path to the imposing black glossed door to the lawyers' offices. I took the stairs to the first floor. Reception was empty, piles of paperwork littered the desks, monitors blank, computers silent. I followed the muffled sounds of conversation from a room at the end of a corridor until I pushed open the door to a large well-lit room at the front of the building overlooking the main street. It had a large conference table in the middle and Gareth Walters jumped to his feet as he saw me. Whippet-thin with strands of greying hair taken from the base of his head to form a comb-over made him look ridiculous. He shook my hand warmly enough and pointed me to a chair next to my father who gave me a cursory nod.

Uncle Gino stared over the table at me. Thick clumps of silver hair protruded from his ears; his shirt opened to two buttons exposing a mass of cobweb-like hair over his chest. His eyes were still the two small dark balls I remembered. He got up clumsily and reached over. 'Hello John. Good to see you.'

Jeremy Marco sat alongside his father. 'Hi, Jez,' I said, using the nickname he loathed.

He opened his mouth, bared some teeth like a snarling dog and settled into a sneer. 'Hello, John.'

'Let's get started then,' Gareth said. 'We have lots to discuss.'

The lawyer circulated a detailed memorandum to everyone around the table. Uncle Gino rolled his head back and forth as he read it and I scanned Jeremy's face, intense and serious, before I read the document myself. I skipped over a lot of the legal jargon until I read the details of the money being offered for the café building. A single-page letter from a local valuer stated they thought the sum was 'reasonable' but it had a hurried feel and a paragraph of disclaimers did not fill me with confidence. Gareth let us read on for a few minutes and then cleared his throat noisily. 'Let's get on shall we? The trust provision in Mr Marco Senior's will provides that all the beneficiaries need to agree to any proposal for the sale of the café building.'

'We've been hanging on to the property for far too long,' Jeremy announced. 'It makes little sense keeping it any longer.'

Gareth butted in. 'I think John needs to hear all the details.' He gave me a brief conciliatory smile before slowly dragging three fingers over his meagre hair. 'There is a rent review due imminently but a recent proposal has emerged for the sale of the property to a development company.'

Uncle Gino had been fiddling with the sheets of

paper in front of him – patience wasn't one of his greatest virtues. 'Let's get on with this Gareth.'

'There's a redevelopment proposal that includes the old café. The council is supporting the plans.'

'Is it likely the council might buy the property?' I said.

'Don't be stupid,' Jeremy said. 'Councils haven't got the money to do property development. Look, this offer is the best we could achieve. Let's get rid of the old place and we can all move on.'

'I don't know anything about the offer.'

Jeremy sounded tired when he replied. 'Goldstar Properties have got lots of development sites. They specialise in this sort of thing, developing two or three properties together with commercial and social housing. Look it's a good deal. We've had a valuation confirm it's a good price. What's your problem, John?'

'Don't get in a flap, Jez.'

'I'm not in a fucking flap.'

Gareth attempted a conciliatory tone. 'Let's not get diverted from the main issue. In principle does the family wish to retain the property?'

'Goldstar Properties,' I said. 'Have I heard of them before?'

The name sounded familiar and I listened to Uncle Gino's monologue about the unfairness of Nonno Marco's will. My father sat back, folded his arms, and gave his brother an angry look.

'Papa, shut up for now,' Jeremy said sharply.

'Don't talk to me like that,' Uncle Gino added equally sharply. 'Everyone knows Nonno Marco should have changed his will. The property should have been left to me.' In temper he raised the papers in front of him and threw them onto the table. They scattered over the floor by my father's feet and he reached down to pick them up and then threw them back at Gino.

Jeremy raised his voice at us. 'Do you want to sell or don't you? It's simple: if we don't sell now then we could be landed with the property for years. And who will pay for all the maintenance? The redevelopment might go ahead without the property so it could be worthless in a few years' time. We might not be able to get a new tenant.'

My father unfolded his arms and leant on the table. 'Don't raise your voice at me. I'll decide when I'm good and ready. And let's get one thing clear, Nonno Marco's will was perfectly fair. He knew what you were like.' He spat out the last sentence at his brother.

I turned to the lawyer who appeared stunned into silence. 'What do you think, Gareth?'

He threaded the fingers of both hands together and placed them on the table in front of him. 'Well, if you retain the property there will be future expenses but you have to remember the possibility of the value going up.' Jeremy snorted. Gareth ignored him and continued. 'So you have to measure that against the present offer. You might be advised to get more valuations.'

'For Christ's sake,' Jeremy almost shouted. 'We all know the present valuation is fair.'

A gut feeling from years of working as a police officer sounded an alarm bell. 'Have we had a written offer from Goldstar Properties?'

'Don't you accept my word they've made a proper offer?'

I had never trusted Jez. I paused and looked over at him wondering if there was something underhand going on, some backroom deal. His attitude put my back up.

'It's only you and Uncle Gino that have spoken with Goldstar Properties,' I added. 'At least you can tell us about who is involved.'

He sighed impatiently. Then he shook his head back and forth. 'I don't believe this.'

Gareth joined the conversation. 'I think it might be helpful if we had a more complete picture.'

Jez feigned annoyance. 'I have met Mr Kendall and David Shaw a couple of times. They've even taken me around one of their developments in Bridgend. And—'

When he said the name Kendall, it was like a brief electrical shock to my brain. Momentarily I was stunned. 'What was the name?'

'The man who runs the business is David Shaw. But a Martin Kendall was with him.'

'Martin Kendall.' As I raised my voice I sensed four pairs of eyes staring at me.

'What's wrong?' Jez said. 'Do you know him?'

The saliva in my mouth felt like a paste.

I stared at the papers in front of me. Jez continued. 'They run a very successful property business and the council officials I've spoken to mentioned the work they've done with other developments.'

I threaded the fingers of both hands together and clasped them tightly. Telling Jez that Kendall was implicated in the murder of Felix Bevard meant breaking every protocol. I looked at Jez and then Uncle Gino: I had to say something.

'You have no idea.' I slowed my speech right down.

'This is all bullshit,' Jez replied. 'What's your problem, John?'

'No fucking idea.'

'You've said that before. We need to move on with our lives and get the property sold. They've made a good offer.'

I stood up abruptly and kicked back my chair.

'They're gangsters and we should have nothing to do with them.'

I turned to the lawyer. 'This meeting's over.'

I gathered up the papers and left with Papa. The investigation had just become personal. Jimmy Walsh had seen to that. Now my family were involved in one of his schemes. Then I thought about the Oakley family and what they had been through. The file of that investigation was in my office unopened. There had been no need to reopen the case, but now I wanted to know everything about the inquiry and how Jimmy Walsh had reacted and what he had said. I reached the main street and stopped. I heard Papa's voice but his words didn't register.

'Are you all right, John?'

I spotted a café and Papa followed me in. We found a table out of the way and ordered. I lowered my voice. 'Kendall is involved with a man called Jimmy Walsh who was implicated in the murder of a business man several years ago. That man owned a property in the middle of Bridgend.'

'But Jez mentioned—'

'Yes, it's probably the same property. Walsh was investigated for murder after the family refused to sell the property to him. He was found floating in a boat in Roath Park lake.'

'Jesus, I remember that.'

I leant over the table and whispered. 'Be careful, Papa.'

Tracy sat by my side in the kitchen of my flat, a half-eaten lunchtime sandwich on a plate on the table. She must have realised I was distracted after my meeting that morning. I had resolved after Dean's accident, when he had spent a week in an induced coma, that my feeble attempts at fatherhood had to be replaced by something more meaningful. Jackie was staying with her mother and messages to my mobile had confirmed the arrangements for me to collect Dean. Until Jackie had told me of her plans to move back to South Wales from Basingstoke I had accepted that seeing Dean would mean travelling regularly. Now she was thinking of relocating it unsettled me. There was a comfort in knowing Jackie and Dean lived a distance away from me. Now she was likely to be nearby I wanted to avoid slipping back into casually ignoring my son.

'Are you all right, John?' Tracy peered at me.

'Yes, of course.' I didn't sound convincing.

'You seem distracted.'

'Cousin Jez was a complete knobhead this morning.'

I imagined Jez being impressed by Martin Kendall, with his flash clothes and expensive car. The thought of Kendall being involved with my family business filled my stomach with cold bile. Then I saw the smiling face of Martin Kendall as he toured the pubs and clubs of Cardiff constructing a watertight alibi for the murder of Bevard. The whole thing seemed staged. Jimmy Walsh had been expecting us to speak to his wife and Kendall. Had he expected me to be appointed to the case, when he knew one of his construction companies wanted to purchase the old Marco café? My paranoia took me to another dark place as I contemplated the possibility a senior officer had made certain I was the SIO. Then I imagined the small piggy eyes of Dave Hobbs looking at me over Superintendent Cornock's desk and the possibility he was involved flashed into my mind. Maybe it was Cornock? Or one of the other senior officers pulling the strings.

'When are we collecting Dean?'

I stared out of the window not listening to Tracy. She tugged my arm. 'Planet Earth calling Inspector Marco.'

'What?'

'Dean,' she said impatiently.

'What about him?'

'We're taking him to Castell Coch this afternoon.'

'Of course, of course.'

It was early afternoon before we headed out to collect Dean. Jackie gave me a warm smile but no peck on the cheek although I sensed her scanning the car making certain Tracy was with me. It was a short drive to the Victorian castle outside Cardiff. Spending time with my son gradually unwound my tension. Tracy seemed more relaxed too and she settled into a steady rhythm of asking Dean about his schooling, his friends and how he was feeling after his accident. It was football that preoccupied most of his thoughts and he had an encyclopaedic knowledge of Queen's Park Rangers football team and their various players. It brought a smile to my face because I remember being exactly the same about Cardiff City as a boy. Maybe I could wean him off this Queens Park Rangers business after he moved.

Dean was more amenable than I thought to wearing an audiovisual guide and we wandered around the old castle learning it was built in the Gothic revival style to indulge the desires of the Marquess of Bute for a grand home for occasional summer use. Its name as the red castle came from the sandstone used in its construction and we roamed around the grand old buildings and ornate bedrooms.

We finished the afternoon at a tenpin bowling alley and then at a McDonalds where Dean demolished an enormous burger. The sound of a Scottish accent startled me and took me back to my first meeting with Martin Kendall and the smell of fish and chips that had clung to my clothes.

By the end of the meal, Dean was busy scrolling through his smartphone. I glanced over. 'Who are you texting?'

'Facebook, Dad,' he said, adding disbelief to his voice.

Despite having relaxed for most of the afternoon my mind switched immediately to the comments made by Sharon Yelland. I had ignored her comment about Brian's use of Facebook. So I turned to look at my son.

'Do you mind showing me how Facebook works?' I had little interest in pictures of other people's kids so I had made a concerted effort to ignore the social media site.

'Yeah, suppose.'

I watched intently as Dean explained all about storing photographs on Facebook, finding people, liking them, and generally helping me join the twenty-first century. By the end, I knew exactly what Wyn and Jane would be doing Monday morning.

Chapter 18

The following morning I woke early from a vivid dream where I watched Jeremy talking to Jimmy Walsh and Martin Kendall in a bar. A bottle of champagne stood in an ice bucket on the table before them and I joined them as they raised their glasses in a toast. They all smiled at me. The dream turned my stomach so I got up without waking Tracy and traipsed through to the kitchen where I made instant coffee and sat watching early morning television.

It was supposed to be a rest day. A chance to relax. Spend some time away from Queen Street. I had even declined an invitation to watch the televised Cardiff against Burnley game with Robbie, my regular footballing companion, in order to spend time with Tracy.

But Martin Kendall and Jimmy Walsh dominated my thoughts.

The Oakley inquiry had been in the background. The murder of Robin Oakley had been fully investigated. I dragged the barest details to the forefront of my mind. Walsh had wanted Oakley's property and had done everything possible to force Oakley into selling until he had only one option left. I shuddered at the prospect that Walsh was trying the same thing with my family.

I had to read the Oakley papers. My family were involved now and, ignoring the bad feeling between us, we were still family. Perhaps there was a statement or some piece of evidence that might help me in the Bevard case. After all, Oakley's blood had been found in one of Bevard's taxis.

I glanced at my watch. If I was lucky I'd be finished by lunchtime and I could still spend the rest of the day with Tracy. So I walked through into the kitchen and made her tea. I put the mug down by the bedside light and sat on the side of the bed. I ruffled her shoulder and she looked up at me through bleary eyes.

'Look, I'm really sorry. Something has come up at work. I should be finished by lunchtime.'

'I thought ...'

'I know, but there's something I have to do.'

'We were going to do something together today ...' She drew the duvet over her head.

I showered quickly, dressed and was in my car twenty minutes later heading into town, my mind resolved that Jimmy Walsh wasn't going to get near my family. He'd made it personal and now I felt the same.

I started with the statements from Mrs Oakley. It sickened me to read how Walsh and Martin Kendall had flattered them about all the money they'd make from the sale of the property. Kendall and Walsh had entertained Robin Oakley and his wife lavishly but when they changed their minds things got nasty.

Noting down the Oakleys' contact details I turned my attention to the list of witnesses. I read down the names and I stopped at one that looked familiar. I flicked through to the statement from Philip Bryant, the landlord of the Dog and Whistle public house and friend of Jimmy Walsh. His evidence was one part of the alibi Walsh had for the night of Oakley's death.

His name was familiar because he had been a regular visitor to see Jimmy Walsh at HMP Grange Hall.

I rang Lydia. 'There's a development. We need to interview—'

'I thought we were—'

'It's important.'

She said nothing for a while. 'Give me half an hour.'

'Thanks.'

It gave me time for breakfast so I left the station

and walked over to Mario's where I ordered a bacon sandwich and a double-shot Americano. The café was quiet and I read a newspaper while I waited. The latest immigration figures and the chorus of disapproval from various politicians dominated the headlines. Nothing changes. By the time I got back to Queen Street Lydia was waiting in the Incident Room.

'Good morning, boss. What's the urgency?'

'This bastard Kendall is involved with my family.'

I turned and watched a worried veil fall over Lydia's face. 'What do you mean?'

She listened as I explained about the property in Pontypridd, occasionally nodding her head. Finally she said, 'What has this got to do with the Bevard inquiry?'

'Background,' I said, too quickly.

She gave me a dubious look. I continued. 'Bevard was implicated in the Oakley death. The initial impetus for the supergrass deal came from that murder case. We should have been looking at the background sooner.'

I ignored her raised eyebrow.

Half an hour later we drew up outside the Dog and Whistle. It was a large old building at the end of a row of shops north of Cathays Park. A crowd of young men on gleaming bicycles congregated outside one of the takeaway restaurants nearby. Before leaving Queen Street I showed Lydia the statement from Bryant that provided Walsh with the alibi he needed in the Oakley investigation.

'Let's hope Phil Bryant is working.' Lydia was already out of the car as she finished what sounded like a reproach.

We sauntered towards the pub. It was tired, like the pubs I would visit at the end of a drinking session, untroubled by the decor, surroundings, or quality of the beer. I had wasted too many hours propping up the bar in places like this, forcing the last dregs of cheap beer down my throat. Somebody once asked me if it was difficult sitting in a pub and not drinking. Not drinking wasn't the hardest part, it had been waking up and not being able to remember how I got home or where I had been. Even so, I didn't make visiting pubs a regular part of my new social calendar and when I reached the door I hesitated.

The smell was the same as any other pub, warm and almost welcoming as though the place wanted to wrap itself around you, push a pint of beer into your hand and tell you that drinking it was the most natural thing to do. A large man with a thick beard paced around the bar area that filled the centre of the pub; behind him the optics glistened under the artificial light.

Luckily the place was quiet, readying itself for a busy Sunday lunchtime. I walked up to the bar and flashed my warrant card.

'Detective Inspector Marco and this is Detective Sergeant Flint. I need to speak to Philip Bryant.'

He stared at our warrant cards before nodding towards the end of the bar.

We passed through into the rear section under a sign that said 'restaurant', which was a grand term for a room that had half a dozen bench-like tables. Bryant adopted a wide-legged stance.

'What's this about? I don't have any trouble here.'

'I'm investigating the death of Felix Bevard.'

'Who?' His face told me he knew all about Bevard, so it annoyed me he wanted to play games with me.

'He was a business associate of James Walsh.'

'What has that got to do with me?'

'You've been to see Jimmy in Grange Hall.'

Bryant cast a gaze over my shoulder at the sound of voices from the bar. 'What if I have? I've known him a long time. Look, we'll be busy soon.'

'A few years ago you were interviewed as part of the inquiry into the murder of Robin Oakley. Jimmy Walsh was the main suspect. Do you remember what you told the police at the time?'

'Christ almighty, that was years ago. Are you like those cold case cops on the TV? It must be fucking boring.'

I slowed my voice. 'I asked you a question, Mr Bryant.'

Lydia reached for a file of papers.

'For fuck's sake. I am trying to run a business here.'

'And we are investigating a murder.' Lydia's voice sounded deeper than normal but just as professional. She thrust a photograph in front of Bryant. He scanned it, pulled a face and turned away. 'He was shot at point-blank range.'

Bryant showed no emotion and my annoyance grew at his casual indifference.

Lydia clutched a closely typed statement. 'This is a copy of the statement you signed a few days after Robin Oakley was murdered in Roath Park. Quite a coincidence, but Felix Bevard was killed there too.'

The noise from the bar increased. Bryant cast agitated glances over my shoulder more frequently now. He feigned irritation, not very successfully.

'Look, it was a long time ago. I was at this party with Jimmy. There were lots of people there. I can't remember how many. What I do remember is Jimmy was there the whole night with his missus.'

'When did you arrive?'

'Early, about seven. It was in that fancy Italian place on Albany Road. The place was buzzing, full of people. Ask anybody and they'll remember Jimmy was there all night.'

'So why did you visit Jimmy Walsh in jail?'

'I don't need a reason.' Now he folded his arms and stared. Gone was the urgency to help out in the bar.

'How long have you known him? Did you visit him when he was at any of the other jails?'

The concentration on Bryant's face slipped.

'Only Grange Hall then.' I stepped towards him. 'I think Jimmy Walsh had Bevard killed. And because you are one of the kind, charitable friends who visited him in jail I'd like to know what you talked about.'

Bryant narrowed his eyes. 'Go fuck yourself.'

Lydia opened the plastic bag she had bought from the convenience store near the Dog and Whistle and handed me a soft drink can. It fizzed as I snapped it open.

'That went well,' I said.

'We're wasting our time, boss.'

I hated it when Lydia sounded like a teacher telling me what I should do to get better results in a school exam. 'We should concentrate on the Bevard murder. Don't you think we might tread on someone's toes if we're seen to be reopening the Oakley inquiry?'

I took a mouthful of the sugary drink. My determination stiffened; we had to discover what linked Bevard to the murder of Oakley and Jimmy Walsh. After talking to Bryant I realised I was being led by Walsh like a poodle on a chain. Even from prison, he was directing things but, for now, I would play along.

'I don't want anyone to say we didn't give the whole case our complete attention.'

Lydia cleared her throat. 'There's nothing to justify us spending time on looking at the old case. There is no way we can reopen the case against Walsh for the Oakley murder.'

I held up my hand. 'I want Walsh to know we're working on the original case because that way he'll believe we're wasting our time because he knows there's nothing we can do. That fat slob in there ...' I looked over at the Dog and Whistle. '... will have been on the telephone to Bernie Walsh the minute we left. And then when she visits dear Jimmy this weekend she'll give him all the details.'

'Okay, but I'm still not convinced.'

'Can we record the conversations between Jimmy and his wife in the visitors centre in Grange Hall?'

Lydia gave me a disdainful glare and didn't bother to reply.

We finished our drinks as I explained to Lydia that Jimmy Walsh's empire extended to various allegedly legitimate businesses. An acquisition in the year before his incarceration had been a second-hand car showroom and the name of one of the employees appeared on the witness list in the Oakley case. On a weekday the journey would have taken half an hour through the Cardiff traffic but that morning we pulled up outside the garage in half that time. I strode over the tiled floor towards a beaming woman standing behind a spotless counter. She had a smart jacket and enough hair spray to give a climate change activist a stroke. I flashed my warrant card, Lydia did the same.

'I need to see your boss.'

The smile disappeared and she turned sharply and walked towards a door behind her. I heard her say my name and Lydia's before she glanced back at me. A moment later she was back forcing a smile. 'Mrs Parks will see you now.'

A nameplate on the door informed us the occupant was the general manager.

Joanna Parks was a short stout woman in her fifties who almost lost her balance reaching over the paper-strewn desk to shake my hand. 'Excuse the mess. The accountants are in next week so I need to get my paperwork organised.'

I pulled up a chair and we sat down.

'What's this all about?'

Lydia opened the file on her lap. 'We're investigating the death of Felix Bevard.'

The second less-than-surprised look of the day confirmed the Walsh family had been hard at work.

Lydia continued. 'He was a known associate of Jimmy Walsh.' She paused and Joanna Parks gave a weak smile now. *Of course, I know all about it. Bernie called me last night.*

'I understand you made a statement when Mr Walsh was being investigated in relation to the murder of a Mr Oakley. You were at a party with him in the La Scala restaurant.'

Parks nodded. 'I remember. Jimmy and his family were there all night. We had the run of the first floor. There was a disco and an amazing buffet. The Italians certainly know a thing or two about entertaining.'

At least I could agree with that sentiment.

I scanned her statement that Lydia had given me. 'Tell me what you remember about the evening.'

Parks launched into a detailed recollection, repeating almost word for word the statement on my lap. Expecting her to have rehearsed her recollection of events didn't lessen my rising anger. Abruptly I cut across her. 'Thanks for your time, Mrs Parks. We may need to see you again.'

I stood up and led Lydia back to the car.

'You were right, boss. We're being set up.' Lydia sat in the passenger seat. 'She'd been rehearsing her statement.'

'You think?' I said it too sharply and it earned me a reproachful turn of her head. 'Sorry. I didn't mean ...' I slammed my hand against the steering wheel. 'Jimmy bloody Walsh thinks we're all muppets. What the hell is that bastard playing at?'

Lydia crunched on an apple she found in her bag. Even that put my nerves on edge. I wanted to smoke, badly, but instead I found an old packet of chewing gum in a storage compartment and chewed on a dried-up segment. 'Let's go and talk to the other witnesses from that night.'

Lydia gave me a world-weary look as I suggested the sort of questions to ask two other witnesses who had confirmed Jimmy's alibi. After an hour and a half her scepticism had been proved right. We had spoken to a man who ran a coffee shop and delicatessen who feigned surprise at our visit with the flamboyance of an actor accepting an Oscar the whole world knew he would win. A woman married to an estate agent did her best to sound vague but there was enough clarity in her comments to make it clear she had read and reread her original statement in advance.

Outside her home, I put a cigarette to my lips, sparked my Zippo and drew the smoke deep into my lungs. Lydia walked back to the car and when I caught up with her she wafted the smoke away with her hands before giving me a serious motherly scowl. We reached the car and I leant on the door.

Lydia stood waiting for me to finish. 'That was a waste of time.'

'Now we know Jimmy Walsh has primed several of the original witnesses who gave him an alibi. That means he was covering his back. And that makes him as guilty as hell.'

'But we can prove nothing. The case is closed.'

'Even so, he's guilty. We need to find the evidence.'

I ground the butt into the pavement and we headed off to see the final witness.

Chapter 19

Ristorante La Scala was located down a side street off Albany Road. Large white sheets shrouded the pavement outside as two painters dabbed finishing touches to the woodwork of the windows. The building looked prosperous and I peered at the menu displayed in the window. It had all the usual classic Italian dishes with an English summary underneath in smaller letters. It surprised me that my mother hadn't heard about this place and I made a mental note to tell her.

'Have you ever been to La Scala?' I said to Lydia standing by my side.

'I've never heard of this restaurant before.'

'I meant the opera house. In Milan.' Lydia's love of opera had taken her to Glyndebourne and the Welsh National Opera's performances at the Millennium Centre.

'No, but … It is on my to-do list.' She sounded hopeful.

I pushed open the door. A voice bellowed from the rear. 'Sorry, we're closed.'

'Police. I need to talk to the owner.'

I heard the sound of glasses clinking together. Moments later a tall thin man emerged from behind the bar area and walked towards me. He gave my warrant card a cursory look. 'He's upstairs. They're very busy.'

At the top of a broad staircase covered with a deep red carpet was a room full of men in casual clothes rearranging tables and chairs. I scanned, hoping I could make out the owner, but a name like Williams didn't suggest he was an Italian. A man, mid-fifties, receding hairline and heavy paunch, walked towards us.

'I'm sorry but the restaurant is closed. Didn't you see the sign downstairs?'

I held up my warrant card. 'Are you David Williams?'

'Yes. What's this about?'

'Detective Inspector John Marco and this is Detective Sergeant Flint.'

'What do you want?' There was an intense, worried look on his face.

It was the reaction I had expected from Bryant and Parks. A visit from two police officers isn't a daily occurrence and I could sense the anxiety in Williams' voice.

'We're looking again at the murder of Mr Oakley several years ago when a Jimmy Walsh was a possible suspect. His alibi was that he had been here all evening at a family party.'

'I remember. It was a big party. They were using this room for a disco and the buffet.' He jerked his head over his shoulder. Behind him, two members of staff were hanging prints of Italian beach scenes.

'What can you remember?'

'You're joking right?' He drew a hand over his head. 'The place was rammed. We were rushed off our feet trying to organise everything, all the food and the booze. And I seem to recall we were short-staffed.'

'At the time you made a statement confirming Jimmy Walsh and his wife Bernie Walsh had been here that evening.'

'That's right.'

'Can you remember anything about when they arrived and when they left?'

The incredulity on Williams' face was obvious. 'I can't remember what I said all those years ago. I remember seeing Walsh with his wife but ...'

'Could Walsh have left during the evening?'

There was a shout from one corner as one of the prints fell onto a table, glass smashing over the tablecloth.

Williams turned and shouted. 'For Christ's sake. That's coming out of your wages.' Both men stood transfixed, staring at the ruined print. 'Get it cleared up and then take it downstairs. We'll get it re-framed.'

He stared back at me. 'How the hell would I know about Jimmy Walsh? I haven't seen him for years. Why don't you talk to Mickey and Frank over there?' Then he strode over to the men struggling to hang the prints, shouting at them to be careful.

I glanced at Lydia. She frowned slightly. From the file of papers under her arm she found the original list of witnesses. I couldn't recall anyone called 'Frank' on the list.

'There's a Michael Prentice, two girls, but nobody by the name of Frank, boss.'

I approached both men. 'Which one of you two is Mickey?'

'I'm Mickey Prentice,' the taller one said. The man standing by his side had a ruddy complexion and flabby cheeks. There was innocence about his face.

'You must be Frank?'

The man nodded.

'I want to ask you both about a party a few years ago. The police were investigating a man called Jimmy Walsh in relation to the murder of a Robin Oakley.' Frank blinked rapidly.

'Do you both remember that evening?'

Mickey was the first to reply. 'I made a statement years ago.'

Lydia had found what I assumed was his original statement from the file. 'I want to clarify if you can remember what happened?'

After five minutes it was clear Mickey hadn't been primed to expect us. He scanned through the original statement Lydia gave him, shrugged and then thrust it back at her.

I kept my questions neat and simple. Both remembered seeing Jimmy Walsh, neither could tell me exactly when he arrived or when he left and my question about whether he could have left during the evening met with raised eyebrows and incredulity. I turned to Frank. 'Do you recall what happened that evening?'

'It's a long time ago.' He swallowed self-consciously.

'You were both working together?' I kept my gaze firmly on Frank.

'The place was super busy.'

There wasn't the vagueness I had expected from his replies. The evening had been fixed deep in his memory. My anticipation grew at the prospect of a new witness. In the background David Williams kept shouting instructions.

'Do you remember a Mrs Parks?'

Both men shook their heads.

'And what about Philip Bryant?'

Mickey snorted. He glanced at his colleague. 'You tell him, Frank.'

'Tell me what?'

'That slob Bryant had been shagging his girlfriend.'

Frank folded his arms. 'It was all a long time ago. She was working in the Dog and Whistle. He couldn't keep his hands off her.'

'So was Bryant at the party?'

Mickey replied first. 'He was here all right. He got wrecked.'

'What time did he arrive?'

'He was pissed when he arrived.' Frank added slowly, 'It was late – half ten or eleven. I remember he complained like hell about there being no food. And more than anything I can remember her perfume on his clothes.'

Sitting in the car I fumbled for the satnav.

'Philip Bryant lied to us.'

I must have sounded desperate but Frank's evidence weakened Walsh's alibi.

'Boss, how is this helping with the Bevard inquiry?' Lydia said.

Bryant arriving late at the party meant Walsh's alibi could be challenged. We would have to put him in Roath Park for him to murder Oakley. 'I want to work out how long it would have taken Jimmy Walsh to drive to Roath Park.'

'We *know* Walsh had to time to leave the party, sir.'

I couldn't ignore Lydia for too long nor could I ignore her comments about how the investigation into Oakley's murder would help us with the Bevard case. But for now her concerns could wait. I answered my own question.

'Ten minutes, maybe more.' I tossed the satnav towards her. 'To hell with this bloody machine. I know the way.'

I started the car. Then I looked over at Lydia. 'Get your phone out and time us.'

Now it was her time to fumble in her bag before she produced a mobile and found the time setting. 'It's not going to be *real* evidence.'

'I want to *know* how long the journey would have taken. Start it *now*.'

I glanced in the mirror, accelerated towards the junction with Albany Road and then indicated left. I pulled into the traffic; luckily it was light and I headed west. I'd almost reached the junction of Wellfield Road but instinct made me decide not to turn right. Walsh would have taken the shortest route with the least traffic and he might have been delayed on Wellfield Road leading towards the junction with Ninian Road. So I drove further along towards one of the residential streets and headed right down Alfred Street. It was quiet, and I increased my speed as much as I dared. Three minutes later we were at the junction with Ninian Road. Roath recreation ground opened out in front of me. The pleasure grounds and Roath Park stretched out northwards. The quickest way towards the park itself was along Ninian Road towards the roundabout and then up Eastern Avenue. Would Walsh have taken this route?

I sped along Ninian Road. It had to be the quickest route.

I slowed at the end of the road, my irritation rising as we got snarled up behind half a dozen cars waiting to cross the roundabout. Lydia announced that five minutes had passed. I tapped my fingers on the steering wheel. Eventually I negotiated the tight roundabout and then drove under the flyover feeling a sense of relief as I saw the railings for Roath Park to my right. I drove sedately up Lake Road West until I reached the entrance and saw the Captain Scott Memorial lighthouse perched at the bottom of the Roath Park lake. I braked, too hard and too suddenly for the driver behind who blasted his horn.

'Seven and a half minutes, boss.'

I let my breathing return to normal.

'So it would have been a fifteen-minute round trip.'

'Assuming the traffic was the same.'

I turned towards Lydia. 'And, he would have needed time to kill Oakley.'

Chapter 20

First thing Monday morning I strode into the Incident Room and headed straight for the board displaying the images of the victims and Jimmy Walsh. The way Martin Kendall and Bernie Walsh had orchestrated their alibis reinforced my determination that Walsh was guilty. But gut feeling and intuition could always be an excuse for a lack of evidence. And if I was wrong then I'd be issuing speeding tickets on the motorway soon enough.

Lydia caught me in the middle of rearranging the photographs and she gave me a startled look. I had Bernie and Martin Kendall directly underneath Jimmy Walsh and underneath both of them Phil Bryant and alongside him Owen Norcross.

Lydia dumped her bag on the desk and shrugged off her coat. 'I've been thinking, boss.' She measured her words, which I knew meant I had to take her seriously. 'We still need to establish where Bevard was on the afternoon he was killed and we need to find Ledley.' She paused; I could see where this was going. 'I can't help think that spending time on the old Oakley case is a dead end.'

I folded my arms and Papa's worried frown came to mind when I told him about Martin Kendall and Jimmy Walsh.

'It's personal.'

'That's what worries me, sir.'

'Jesus, Lydia, yesterday we established that Walsh's alibi for the Oakley case wasn't as watertight as everyone believed.' I paced back to the board and pointed at Bryant. 'And we know that he has been to visit Walsh in jail.' I stared at his face. 'I wonder where he was the night Bevard was killed?'

Listening to myself I knew we had to focus on

Bevard but the Oakley case still niggled. 'You're right we focus on Bevard. But first we speak to Mrs Oakley.'

Lydia scowled but I used a tone that suggested my decision wasn't a matter for debate. In order to make progress with Bevard I had to speak to Mrs Oakley, be satisfied in my own mind that the investigation into her husband's death had been completed properly. And I needed to hear from her what Jimmy Walsh had done to them. At least then I could tell Uncle Gino and Jez what sort of people they were dealing with, although I doubted that either would listen to me.

Behind her, the main door opened and Wyn entered. The weekend had resulted in a haircut, a neat short back and sides, and there was purposefulness in his stride. Seconds later Jane walked in already yawning and dragging her feet.

I acknowledged their greetings and quickly gave them a summary of the position with Martin Kendall and Jimmy Walsh. Wyn tugged at his nose while Jane frowned, gazing over at the board.

'What we haven't looked at are the social media accounts for both Bevard and Yelland. And Roger Stockes told us that Yelland was using some internet dating sites.'

After half an hour I had allocated various tasks.

'And I need a complete trawl through every available CCTV camera within ten miles of where Bevard was stopped for speeding.'

I sensed Wyn's early morning enthusiasm already waning.

Once we were off the motorway temporary traffic lights delayed us and I drummed my fingers over the top of the steering wheel. Lydia continued to hum along to the recording of Rigoletto she'd chosen for the journey.

'Do you think Mrs Oakley might have anything new to tell us, boss?'

It was Lydia's way of saying – *I hope this isn't another waste of time.*

I mumbled a reply, recalling Mrs Oakley's disinterest when I called first thing that morning to arrange our visit. The lights ahead of me turned green and I pulled away as the satnav gave more instructions. The disembodied voice led us through various suburbs of Bridgend. I indicated left and pulled into a cul-de-sac of a dozen bungalows, some with dormers and others with converted garages. Mrs Oakley's property was at the end and I parked the car in the drive behind a red Alfa Romeo Brera sports car. The rims of the alloys were scuffed, the paintwork scratched and as we walked to the front door I noticed the car's tired leather upholstery.

A man in his twenties, heavily built with a polo shirt a size too small that accentuated the pumped-up muscles of his arms, gave us an intense stare. 'I'm Howard Oakley. You'd better come in.'

Mrs Oakley stood at the end of the hallway staring at us. She was thin, flat-chested and her clothes made her look shapeless. Her lips were colourless. 'What do you want?'

I held out a hand and shook hers. It was bony, the skin flaccid. 'I'm investigating the death of Felix Bevard.'

'He was involved with Jimmy Walsh wasn't he?'

'Is there somewhere we can sit down?'

Mrs Oakley darted her head towards the door into the living room. A television was on mute but before sitting down she pressed the remote to switch it off.

'You know Jimmy Walsh killed my Robin don't you? There was nothing you lot could do about it. Perfect alibi –

that's what I was told.'

The old springs of the sofa groaned as Lydia and I sat down.

Mrs Oakley looked up at her son who had followed us into the room with an upright wooden dining chair. He sat, legs apart, hands propped onto solid knees. 'Howie can tell you. He knows all about that scumbag.'

I looked over at Howard. The deadpan look on his face remained unchanged.

'I want to go over some of the details you told the police at the time of your husband's murder.'

Lydia passed me a copy of the statement Mrs Oakley had provided.

Before I continued Howard piped up, his voice surprisingly reedy. 'That bastard Walsh is a fucking murderer. Detective Webster in charge of the enquiry was a useless piece of shit. He had no interest in Mam or me.'

'I appreciate your strong feelings on the matter.' I wanted to say – *you're right and I'm going to nail the bastard*, but years of policing kicked in. 'At the time Jimmy Walsh had an alibi we couldn't challenge. It was considered carefully by the prosecution lawyers.'

'Then Jimmy must have paid somebody off.' Howie folded his arms, defying me to challenge him. I turned to look at Mrs Oakley but Howie continued. 'And Felix Bevard was up to his neck in the same shit as Walsh. So if you ask me he's had what's coming to him. Good riddance to a bad load of shit.'

As I turned to look over at Howie I shared a worried glance with Lydia.

'I need to talk to your mother,' I said, lowering my voice.

He pouted. I turned back to Mrs Oakley, giving her the barest of smiles. 'Can we review what you told the investigating officers at the time?'

I went over everything again in detail: the time when Oakley had left the house on the morning of his death, the meetings he had had with Walsh and Bevard and the various telephone calls and late-night visits heavy with veiled threats and ultimatums. Howie couldn't resist interrupting but when I pointed a finger at him with my hardest glare he sank back into his chair.

'At first Walsh and his scumbag son-in-law were as nice as pie. They wanted to make us rich so we could retire. They took as to the races near Llanelli. Robin drank a skinful of champagne and puked in the car on the way back.'

'Tell them what happened then, Mam,' Howie said.

Mrs Oakley started chewing a nail; as though it was the first thing she had eaten all day. 'We got second thoughts. The property had been owned by the family for donkeys' years and with so many memories we couldn't bring ourselves to sell it. And other shopkeepers and stallholders in the nearby market didn't want us to sell.'

Howie stood up and paced around the room. 'Dad told them right enough. He wasn't going to sell.'

'It was the worst thing ...' Mrs Oakley brushed away a tear. 'He had his greyhounds. Loved them like they were little kiddies. One morning we found them dead and then Felix Bevard came round, pretending to be all nice. Telling us selling up was really for the best.'

An unsettling fear clung to my mind as I dreaded what Uncle Gino and Jez were concocting with Martin Kendall.

'I hate them. All of them, for what they done to me ...'

'Tell them, Mam. Tell them everything.' Howard stopped pacing, put his hands on his hips and stared down at Lydia and I.

'I'm not well.'

Howard took a step towards us. 'After Dad was killed by those mad fuckers the business went under within a year and they picked up the property dirt cheap. So until now it's cost them nothing.'

I narrowed my eyes as I looked over at Howie. 'What you mean "until now"?'

'Well he's fucking dead isn't he? You need to ask Mam what it's like for her. Walsh will come out of jail healthy and fit. He's had three meals a day, best gym for miles and satellite TV all paid for by the taxpayer.'

Mrs Oakley had finished chewing the nail of her left hand but had started another on her right before mumbling. 'I'm sick.'

I paused. Lydia adjusted her position on the sofa by my side. 'Mrs Oakley, can you tell us what's wrong?'

'I've got cancer.'

'And it was all as a result of those two lizards Bevard and Walsh.' Howie tempered his voice this time.

'I'm very sorry.'

The dining chair sagged under Howie's weight as he dropped his body onto it. 'The cancer won't go away. Mam is going to start chemotherapy next week.'

I could see how tangling with Jimmy Walsh and Bevard had led to this. They blamed both men for Mrs Oakley's illness. And I could see they had been innocents caught in a web drawn by Jimmy Walsh.

'He's coming out of jail soon,' Howie said, rocking back and forth slowly. 'Two years. That's nothing for being a mainline drug dealer and killer. Where is the justice in that? It makes my fucking blood boil.'

I felt helpless. I wanted to tell them I knew Walsh could have left the restaurant, gone to Roath Park and killed Robin Oakley. For the sake of my career, I decided a gentle reassurance would have to suffice. 'I can appreciate why you are angry. Cases are reopened, sometimes.' I could sense Lydia getting uncomfortable by my side. 'I'm not reopening the inquiry into your husband's death; all I'm doing is identifying if there's anything that might link the case to the death of Felix Bevard.'

Mrs Oakley managed a harsh cough that rattled her ribs. 'You should talk to Maggie.' There was more coughing until she crumpled back into a chair.

'Maggie?'

'It was the best thing that came out of the whole business. Maggie Evans came to see me with Ben. She was ignored by you people too. Nobody believed a word she told 'em even though Ben was in the park the night Robin was killed. She wanted to tell me how sad she was about Robin and everything. Then we got to be friends.'

I turned to Lydia; she was already flicking through the sheets of paper in the file. She handed me the list of witnesses from the original case. I scanned down until I found the name Margaret Evans with an address in Roath. I searched but I couldn't find a reference to any other witness called Ben.

The possibility that the investigating team had overlooked a witness raised my optimism. I measured every word. 'Who was Ben?'

'Ben Evans? Her son of course. He was a nice lad but there is something not right with him. One of them *syndromes* – it was probably why the cops ignored him. They moved away afterwards. I don't think she wanted to stay around near Roath Park.'

'Do you have an address for her?'

Mrs Oakley took a deep breath and her whole body shook violently.

'Mam has had enough now. It's time for you to go.'

'Do you have a phone number for Margaret Evans?'

Mrs Oakley walked slowly to a sideboard and returned with an address book. Lydia jotted down a telephone number and address. I promised to keep Mrs Oakley informed of developments, although in truth the only development she would care about would be Walsh in jail for her husband's murder. I didn't blame her for one minute.

Howie pushed the door firmly closed behind us.

'I thought you might be here.'

Lydia sidled into the bench seat opposite me. She drew a finger along the table top and grimaced. Ramones was the best greasy spoon in Cardiff and as a regular all I had to was smile at the nearest waitress and a full breakfast would be on its way. I folded away that morning's *Western Mail* having read the sports pages in their entirety.

Lydia looked over at the menu board. 'Does everything involve fried bacon?'

'They don't do vegetarian here.'

A waitress arrived at our table before Lydia could reply. 'What do you want?'

Lydia ordered tea and two rounds of toast. 'What did you make of Mrs Oakley, boss?'

'I think we should run Howard Oakley's name through the PNC. He looks mad enough to have killed Bevard himself.'

Lydia nodded slowly.

I tapped the file of papers sitting on the table. 'I've checked the list of witnesses from the Oakley inquiry and there's no mention of a Ben Evans being interviewed.'

Lydia curled up her lips. 'That means—'

'We need to speak to him.'

'But that really does mean reopening the Oakley case.'

I knew exactly what was on her mind. 'We can't simply ignore this.'

Her tea arrived and she gave the chipped mug a suspicious glance. 'But it's not really part of the Bevard case.'

Walsh and Kendall had involved my family and I wasn't going to leave any loose ends – not on the Bevard inquiry, nor now with the Oakley investigation which looked more and more flawed. Next stop was an interview with the man himself.

Chapter 21

I placed two chairs opposite each other, either side of an old metal table. I dropped a buff-coloured folder onto the surface and sat down. I scanned the room wondering if there was a microphone. But this was HMP Grange Hall and not some set from a television drama.

To my right was a large Perspex window. Prison officers could still see into the room, which was reassuring. Governor James had sounded puzzled by my request to interview Jimmy Walsh, but I had brushed aside her concerns about his imminent release. I glanced at my watch: Walsh was late.

I wanted to invade his personal space. Tell him I was in charge. Make it clear if he ever bullied my family then …

Jimmy Walsh passed the window, a prison officer opened the door and Walsh entered. He was shorter than I imagined, but broader and thicker around the neck. The prison reports had mentioned his regular attendances in the gym that contributed to the bulk.

He dragged a chair from underneath the table and sat down.

The door pulled closed behind the prison officer and I sat looking at Walsh.

He wore standard prison clothes: blue striped shirt and denims with a grey sweatshirt. Hair trimmed closer to his skull than in the images in his file.

Frustration tightened around my chest as I stared at Walsh. I would prove his guilt for Bevard's death, and he'd be going down for life. I noticed the prison officer staring in at us and I glanced over at him. He nodded back. Walsh stared at me.

I pushed my warrant card over the table towards him. Walsh leant forward, peered down casually, and then made eye contact with me again.

'Detective Inspector Marco. I'm investigating the death of Felix Bevard.'

'So I hear.'

'He was a business associate of yours.'

'Why am I here, Inspector?'

'Answer the question.'

'This isn't an interview under caution is it?'

'I'm sure you want to cooperate with the inquiry. You might know something of relevance.'

I stared into the whites of his eyes: there was a trace of yellow there too.

'I'm in prison, Inspector.'

'Did Felix Bevard ever contact you?'

'I'm sure you've checked the visitor log.'

I opened the papers on my desk.

'You and Felix go back a long way.'

He stared straight at me, through me.

'Did you visit him on your last weekend release?' I checked the dates with a flourish. 'When was that exactly?' I recited the dates.

He adjusted his position. 'Somebody told me you're from the Aberdare Marco family.'

My lips dried as he drawled. 'It's the Marco ice cream family isn't it?' He paused. 'I always liked their ice cream as a boy.'

I closed the file of papers and pushed it to one side.

'Is it the same family that owns the Marco café in Pontypridd?' Walsh managed a narrow smile without opening his lips but there was no emotion in his eyes. 'Somebody told me there are big redevelopment plans pending.'

My body tensed. I grasped both hands together. I wanted to reach over the table and calmly throttle Walsh until he agreed never to contact my family again. Somehow, I managed to keep my voice calm. 'Tell me about Felix Bevard?'

Walsh knew our interview wasn't being taped and that gave him confidence and composure. 'Felix was an old friend of mine.' That smile was back again but now his eyes sparkled like sunshine reflecting off finely sharpened steel. 'We went back a long time.'

'And you had him killed.'

He feigned disbelief and outrage with a shake of his head.

I placed my chin on steepled arms. 'You must have known about Felix Bevard, about his plans to grass you up?'

He stared over at me, blinked once, then tried his mean smile again. He knew, of course he knew.

'I thought you and I should have this chat. Off the record. You found out Bevard would give evidence that you killed Robin Oakley. You were going down for murder. And for you, that would mean life.'

He narrowed his eyes.

'You do remember Mr Oakley? His widow certainly remembers you.'

Even sitting quite still Walsh exuded a menacing quality.

'Tell me about Yelland?'

'He was one of the prison officers here. It was very sad, his death.'

I curled my left hand into a fist.

'He was making your life easy wasn't he? You have the cosiest job in the jail, best food, he brought in bottles of whisky and brandy for you. So what do you know about his death?'

He raised his hands, scanned the room. 'I'm in jail, Inspector.'

'We know that you arranged to pay off his gambling debts.'

There was something different in his eyes now, surprise perhaps, and I felt pleased that I had the advantage. 'How much did you pay him to make your life easy?'

He paused. 'So I slipped him a few quid. I wasn't the first and I won't be the last to have done that.'

'So did Yelland get greedy?'

He shook his head. 'I don't know what you're talking about.'

'I've spoken to Martin Kendall. And I've seen your wife. But I'm sure you know that too.'

I sat back in the chair as one of the prison officers walked to the window, raising an eyebrow and tapping on his watch. I nodded briefly; Walsh had to be back in his cell for the afternoon roll call.

'We are reopening the Oakley murder case ...'

He frowned, then rolled his eyes. 'Somebody told me you've been rummaging around my cell. Did you find anything?'

I should have expected that. Nothing was secret in prison.

'Somebody told me you might even be a good detective.'

I leant over the table. I was staring at the man who had conspired to kill Felix Bevard. He might not have pulled the trigger but it was only a matter of time before I proved who did. And his involvement with Uncle Gino and Jez and Papa had to stop.

'Tell Kendall to steer clear of my family. You may be released soon but this place is your real home. So don't get too comfortable. You'll be back inside, dead quick.'

He smirked, a long, fixed snide-like grin. I stood up,

kicked back the chair, and made for the door.

Outside I smoked a cigarette walking to my car and then another as I sat contemplating my conversation with Jimmy Walsh. Paying off Yelland's gambling debts was more than 'slipping him a few quid'. It was the only time that Walsh had engaged with me and I wondered if he was distracting me.

I had hoped for more clarity but how exactly I would achieve that eluded me as I sat with the window open, flicking ash onto the tarmac of the car park. My frustration was draining me. I reached for my mobile, thinking I should call Papa. Professional necessity cut in and I threw the mobile onto the passenger seat. I had to find the person who pulled the trigger. I had to hope Walsh's release would be short lived. I drove away leaving my despondency behind.

Chapter 22

The following morning I was back in Queen Street, refreshed after a decent night's sleep. I stood in front of the Incident Room board staring at the collection of images. Lydia's admonishment that we had already spent two days on the Oakley case came to mind but I knew that the case had been handled badly. Detective Chief Inspector Webster, the SIO on the case, had recently died and his sergeant at the time was now sitting in Cornock's office throwing his weight around as my superior. I had to be careful. If I could finish that inquiry, close the file knowing that I had been as thorough as possible, I'd have been more thorough than the original team.

The silence was broken when Lydia arrived with Jane and Wyn. Once jackets and coats were removed and pleasantries exchanged Lydia joined me by the board.

'How did you get on with Jimmy Walsh, boss?'

I stared at his face on the board. 'He's a scumbag.' I paused. 'How much did Martin Kendall pay to that bookmaker?'

I sensed Wyn and Jane moving uncomfortably in their chairs.

Wyn answered. 'It was three thousand pounds.'

'Walsh said it was a few quid.'

'Probably was for Walsh,' Lydia added.

'I want every aspect of Yelland's finances examined. We need to know exactly how much he owed and to who and when. When I told Jimmy Walsh about the supergrass deal he didn't even bother to try and hide the fact that he knew all about it.'

'I did a check on Howard Oakley and he has a string of convictions for violence. And there's mention he has a link to an organised crime group in Swansea. At the time of the investigation into his father's death he made threats against Bevard that were taken seriously enough for him to be given a formal warning.'

Wyn piped up. 'I've still got contacts in one of the serious crime teams in Swansea.'

'Good, make contact.'

Now we had Howard Oakley added to the name of Owen Norcross as more than just a person of interest in our inquiry.

'So Howard has a motive to kill Bevard,' Lydia said. 'But Yelland ...?'

Oakley's possible involvement didn't fit with my conviction that Walsh was responsible for both deaths.

Lydia continued. 'Maybe there were two killers?'

'Let's assume they are connected. Someone wanted them dead.' I didn't say *and that someone is Jimmy Walsh* no matter how much I wanted to. I turned to face the team. I nodded at Wyn and Jane in a joint instruction. 'Do some more digging into Oakley.'

I scanned the team. 'And is there any sign of Bevard on the CCTV from Pontypool?'

Three heads shook in unison. 'Damn. Send it all to my computer. I'll check it out myself.'

I headed for my office and from a bottom drawer I found a large piece of paper and started drawing a mind map. In the middle I wrote the name *Jimmy Walsh* in large capital letters. Then I drew a circle around his name. On the right I printed the name of Owen Norcross. His connection to Walsh was enough to make him a prime suspect and because he tangled with Yelland in Newport jail he had motive enough. We still needed the results of the forensic analysis of his possessions and an email to the lab only resulted in a swift, terse reply telling me they were still working on them.

On the left-hand side I printed the name 'Ledley' and pondered where he was and how he fitted into Bevard's world. All we knew about him was his name and that he played five-a-side football with Bevard. And that he had a ponytail and tattoos. It wasn't taking us very far.

I added the name 'Phil Bryant' to the right-hand side, deciding that his dishonest alibi earned him a place underneath Norcross. And underneath Bryant I added the name 'Howard Oakley'. I drew a wavy red line around his name as a reminder that we had no obvious motive for him killing Yelland. Finally I scribbled the name 'Felix Bevard' and 'Yelland' in smaller circles at the bottom and left of the page underneath Walsh. It was only a matter of time before I could find a thread to pull them all together.

I pondered my mind map, blanking out the sounds from the Incident Room.

Then I started at the CCTV coverage from around Cardiff on the night Bevard was killed. I clicked through hours of coverage from the various pubs and clubs that Kendall had visited, strutting around like some fancy peacock. Kendall had even chosen pubs with CCTV systems to make certain his face was recorded. By the end of the evening he even glanced up, searching for the cameras. I froze the images several times, peering at him. It reinforced for me that he must have known what was happening that evening in Roath Park café. And that meant that Walsh was implicated.

Sickened by all the obvious bravado I turned my attention to the CCTV coverage from the route that Bevard drove on the afternoon he was killed. He had left the golf course that afternoon and then travelled to Cwmbran where he bought food in a shop, took money out from a cash machine and then was stopped in Cwmbran. Where was he going? The CCTV coverage was patchy; I picked up his car as he left Cwmbran but it was impossible to tell if he had a passenger. The car later appeared again on some coverage from Pontypool but he soon disappeared from the recording only to be seen again on his way back to the golf course later. Alone.

All the inquiries into Jack Ledley had proved dead ends. He owned the house in Birchgrove, had modest amounts in his bank accounts and had no criminal record. By lunchtime the images from my computer monitor were swimming around my mind so I left Queen Street, strode down to St Mary Street, and stood looking at one of the pubs that Kendall had visited the night he was building his alibi. I walked to the next pub on his itinerary but, uninspired, I headed to the St David's shopping arcade and one of the big coffee chains for a watery coffee and a greasy sandwich. I started thinking about Gloria Bevard, whose movements we couldn't trace on CCTV. I decided I needed to unpick all the details of her alibi.

Wyn was on his feet when I got back to Queen Street. 'We've identified three women who have been on dates with Brian Yelland.'

Jane was nodding energetically at her desk. I sat down and Wyn explained the intricacies of the dating website that Yelland had used. It promised the latest psychological profiling to find 'your perfect partner'. The website offered a money-back guarantee although Wyn gave me a puzzled look when I asked what that meant.

'He emailed the women. It was all fairly innocuous stuff – arranging to meet in a pub for a drink, that sort of thing. We're going to see the first later today.'

'Good,' I said, turning to Lydia. 'Let's go and talk to some of Gloria's friends.'

It took me half an hour to find someone who was available to speak to us that afternoon. Lydia shrugged on her coat as we left Queen Street and we walked around to the offices of one of the large insurance companies that had made its home in Cardiff. The receptionist sounded disinterested as we asked for Ann O'Brien. We sat down in the reception and classical music swirled around us. There was little activity and I wondered what it was like to work in such calm.

I heard the tip-tap of high heels on the marble floor before I noticed Ann emerging from around a corner near the lifts. She was smartly dressed and heavily made up. She reached out a hand and a waft of perfume collided with my nostrils. We shook hands. She gave Lydia a more careful scan than I had warranted.

'How can I help?'

'Is there anywhere we can talk?'

She gave an irritated grimace. 'I suppose we could use one of the conference rooms. It means signing you in.'

I smiled an encouragement.

We had forms to complete with our personal details and were then given a lanyard with the word 'visitor' printed in large letters. We followed Ann into an air-conditioned conference room. She waved us towards steel mesh chairs with faux leather seats and we sat down.

'We are investigating the death of Felix Bevard,' I said. 'How well did you know him?'

'I am friends with Gloria.' Ann sat across the table from me.

'Have you ever met Felix?'

'Of course, lots of times. Look, is this going to take long? I'm very busy.'

'You were out with Gloria on the night he was killed?'

'I already confirmed that when another officer telephoned me.'

'I know but there are some details we need to clarify.'

And being uncooperative isn't going to help.

I took Ann O'Brien through the entire evening very slowly. Occasionally Lydia butted in to clarify an answer or ask a supplementary question. As the time ran on I could see that Ann was getting anxious.

'What was Gloria like that night?'

'She did seem on edge. She kept picking up her telephone as though she was waiting for a call. And she did text a lot.'

'Did she say who she was texting?'

She shook her head.

'Did she mention whether she was expecting a call?'

'No, sorry.'

I looked over at Ann and decided that I'd venture a different sort of question.

'Had things between Felix and Gloria improved?' I made it sound casual.

'Not really. She had been complaining about him all night but she'd been doing that a lot. They'd probably had an argument before she came out. And she was hammering the gin. I told her to cool it but she must have had a dozen by the end of the night.'

I thanked Ann and we headed back for Queen Street.

'How did you know things were bad between Felix and Gloria, boss?'

'I didn't. But Ann confirmed it. So I wonder what Gloria's hiding?'

'Lots of couples argue, boss. It's not suspicious.'

Ann's uncooperative attitude had riled me. What had been really going on between Felix and Gloria Bevard?

Chapter 23

The following morning Lydia and I headed for Bristol hoping to beat the early morning traffic jams on the M4 heading east. But we found ourselves crawling along as the motorway slowed to two lanes at the Bryn Glas tunnels.

'I'll be retired before the politicians make a final decision about the relief road to ease all this congestion,' I said.

Lydia had found the address for Maggie Evans, and the fact she was leaving for a fortnight's holiday had given me the perfect excuse to postpone my meeting with Acting Detective Chief Inspector Hobbs that morning, despite his email, with the word 'urgent' written in capital letters. I hoped Mrs Evans might contribute another missing piece of the Oakley jigsaw I could use to reopen the initial inquiry. Anything that might make Dave Hobbs's life uncomfortable was worth pursuing.

Lydia tapped the postcode into the satnav and I followed the instructions off the motorway towards Bristol and then down to Clifton. We threaded our way through the suburbs until the satnav announced at the end of a long terrace that we had reached our destination. I looked up at the tall, imposing properties.

'She lives in the ground floor flat,' Lydia said, nodding towards a large green door.

I pressed the intercom for the right apartment and a crackly voice emerged from the loudspeaker. 'Who is that?'

'Detective Inspector Marco for Maggie Evans.'

The lock on the door beside me buzzed and I pushed it open. Maggie Evans was standing in the hallway. I had my warrant card ready. 'John Marco,' I said. 'And this is Detective Sergeant Flint.'

Maggie pulled open the door and led us into a

dowdy, old-fashioned sitting room at the front of the building. Net curtains hung from a rail clipped around the window casements. The place felt stuffy, as though none of the windows had been opened for months nor a vacuum dragged over the carpets.

'You were interviewed at the time Mr Oakley was murdered. And one of our suspects had been a man called Jimmy Walsh. I'm investigating the death of a man called Felix Bevard who was linked to Walsh.'

Margaret Evans was a short woman with an apparent doughnut habit. She had nervous eyes.

'Of course. I went to see Mrs Oakley after the whole sad business. I don't know what I could have done. I suppose I wanted to offer my help.'

Last night I had read her statement and the notes from the officers who interviewed her. She sounded like a typical busybody. At the time she'd lived near Roath Park and it surprised me that her son had not been interviewed. Was it no more than a simple oversight?

'I was wondering if you could tell me about your son?'

'He's autistic. He goes to a special needs school, that's one of the reasons why we moved to Bristol.'

'Why didn't he make a statement to the police at the time?'

She gave me a kindly smile. 'I did tell the officers he had been in Roath Park. I expect they were busy.'

Her simple announcement hastened my excitement. I smiled at her, hoping Ben had that nugget of evidence we needed.

'I don't think he saw anything or at least he didn't tell me.'

'Is your son still at school?'

I imagined killing time waiting for a schoolboy to

return home and every hour was taking Jimmy Walsh nearer his release date.

'Oh, no, he'll be home soon. Would you like some tea?'

The waiting was interminable. The tea was brown and strong. Lydia left most of hers but I finished my mug having spooned two teaspoons of sugar into it. We tried small talk; Lydia was more successful than I was. Surreptitiously I kept an eye on the clock, realising we had already been there for almost an hour. Mrs Evans cleared away our mugs and a plate of biscuits.

I felt a physical sense of relief when I heard a key scratching the lock in the door.

'There are two people from Cardiff to see you,' Mrs Evans said, loudly enough for Lydia and me to hear.

A teenager slouched into the sitting room and gave us a lopsided look. His slack-waisted jeans complemented the drizzle of stubble over his chin. I smiled, wanting to put him at ease.

'My name is John and this is Lydia. We're police officers. It's Ben, isn't it?'

He gave me a reluctant pout as an acknowledgement and collapsed into one of the old sofas.

'We're investigating what happened in Roath Park a few years ago.'

Mrs Evans joined her son on the sofa and he tried to sit up straighter. 'Tell them why you were there.'

'They were filming.'

I knew from the reports that a television crew had been filming earlier in the evening Oakley was killed. But it had been raining and the filming had been abandoned before seven.

'Come on, Ben, tell them everything.' Maggie didn't give her son a chance. 'He's a *Doctor Who* fan. He's got all the DVDs. His bedroom is plastered with posters and pictures of all the actors who have taken part in every series. He could probably go on *Mastermind* with everything he knows about *Doctor Who.* Would you like that, Ben?'

'Were you near the film crew?' I said.

Ben opened his eyes wide. 'It was really cool. I kept really still. Nobody saw me. I was able to sneak through the undergrowth. I sat waiting for them to do the filming. I was there for hours.'

'By the time he came home he was soaked to the skin. I was afraid he might get pneumonia.'

'I'd like to hear what else Ben can remember.' I tried to get my reproach sounding as polite as possible. 'Did you see anybody else walking around Roath Park?' I held my breath.

'I had my camera ready to take photographs.'

My fingertips tingled; impatience built to a point where I was afraid I would raise my voice and shout. 'Did you get any photographs?'

'Only the film crew. And the Doctor himself walked right up to where I was. I could almost touch him. I wanted to take photographs but I knew if I did somebody would see me and I'd be reported to the police and may be sent to jail.'

I let out a long slow breath. 'What time did you leave?'

'It was late.'

Maggie Evans tutted.

'Mam was really angry when I got home.'

'I'd like you to remember what time it was?'

Maggie Evans butted in again. I almost snapped at her, telling her not to interrupt. 'He had a bath straight after he got home and then he watched his favourite television programme, after *Doctor Who* of course.'

'The time?'

'*Big Bang Theory* started at ten-thirty and he's watched all the repeats.'

'So how long would it have taken you to walk home?'

'Eleven minutes.'

'But when did the filming stop?'

'Stop?' Ben said. 'They were still filming when I left.'

I gaped in disbelief. It contradicted the evidence we already had that filming had stopped due to bad weather. I wanted to rush out of the house, jump into the car and scream over to the offices of the film company in Cardiff Bay. Instead I thanked Mrs Evans and Ben, warning them before we left the flat that I might need another statement. I almost tripped over in my haste to reach the car.

Lydia had her mobile phone at the ready as I started the engine.

'Whoever was in charge of that Oakley investigation needs to be taken out and fucking shot.' I realised what I had said but it was too late.

'I think we need to prioritise, boss.'

I was tempted to break the speed limits on my journey back to Cardiff, but the knowledge that Jane was already on her way to the production company's offices in the Bay eased my apprehension.

Chapter 24

I pulled up behind the pool car outside the address Jane had emailed to my mobile on the journey from Bristol. Lydia followed me as we headed for the entrance. Inside, Jane stopped talking to a member of staff once she spotted me. 'There's nobody here, boss.'

'What do you mean?' I could hear activity behind her, the occasional one-sided telephone conversation.

'All of the production staff are out on site.'

'Is there nobody in charge?'

'One of the admin staff will talk to us.'

The receptionist was a woman in her twenties with long auburn hair and enormous black-rimmed spectacles. 'I'll call Jamie.' She picked up the handset. 'There are three police officers in reception for you.'

She mumbled an acknowledgement as Jamie gave her instructions. She got up and led us through a corridor before pushing open the door of a conference room. 'Would you guys like coffee?'

'How long will Jamie be?'

She gave a noncommittal shrug. 'Do help yourself to some sparkling water.' She pointed towards the blue and crimson bottles of Ty Nant water on a sideboard. 'I'll tell Jamie you guys are waiting.'

We sat down and Jane opened a folder of papers on the table. 'I brought the file as you asked, boss.'

I flicked through the statements looking for confirmation of the names of the witnesses. Quickly I realised the file was vague and incomplete. The original investigating team must have ignored digging deeper into who exactly was filming where, and when. My annoyance turned to anger. They should have known better. I heard a fizz behind me, as Lydia opened one of the bottles. She filled three glasses and pushed them over the table.

'The only statement is from a production manager. And I bet he wasn't even there.' I read it again.

'Maybe Ben Evans was wrong all along,' Lydia said. 'Maybe they did finish filming earlier than he recalls.'

A man, late twenties, with designer stubble and wearing a shirt that clung to his thin frame and overflowed over his fashionably faded denims, breezed into the room. 'Hi guys. Jamie James.'

'Detective Inspector Marco.' I held out a hand. 'And this is Detective Sergeant Flint and Detective Constable Thorne. We're investigating the death of Felix Bevard who was killed in the Roath Park café. He was linked to the murder of Robin Oakley.'

'None of the production staff are here. I'm not certain what I can do to help you guys.'

'This statement ...' I waved it in the air at James. '... is from a production manager. I want to speak to someone who was *actually* filming on the night of Oakley's death.'

'You'll need to talk to the original production team. And—'

'I want to know who exactly was on that team.'

'It might take some time. I don't know who was in charge. All I can do is take your details—'

'This is a murder inquiry, Jamie. I need the details now. Yesterday.' The tone of my voice was intended to frighten him.

He jotted down the date of Oakley's murder, a list of everything we needed to know and thankfully he stopped calling us 'you guys' every sentence.

'Why did you do it?'

Dave Hobbs clenched his teeth together and drew

in a large breath as I explained my meeting with Jimmy Walsh. 'I think it was most ill-advised.'

'Jimmy Walsh somehow knew about the supergrass deal. I don't know, yet, how he got hold of that information.'

'You're not suggesting it leaked from the dedicated source unit? Is that why you interviewed Roger Stockes?'

'For Christ's sake, he came to see me. He was waiting for me. He must have known that we'd want to talk to him.'

'We've had a complaint from the CPS about your conduct. They are demanding that if you ever need to talk to Stockes again it be done through the proper channels.'

'Proper channels.' I snorted.

'Yes, John.'

'My discussion with Stockes was perfectly ...' I struggled for the right word. 'Cordial. He volunteered information about Yelland. They were trying to interfere with my investigation.'

'It's not that.'

'Then what is it, Dave?'

Like an exasperated parent he shook his head.

'Walsh got hold of the information from somewhere.' I paused and waited but Hobbs said nothing.

'With Bevard dead Jimmy Walsh is in the clear. There is no risk he could be facing prosecution for the Robin Oakley murder.'

'I don't want you speaking to Jimmy Walsh again unless it's under caution and you've got evidence that justifies an arrest.'

Hobbs stared.

'I understand. Dave.' I stood up and left, enjoying the discomfort on his face, but as no other officers were present there was no chance I was going to call him *sir*.

Back in the Incident Room I listened to Wyn explaining that he had spoken to one of the girls that Yelland had dated. She had left the date after an hour once Yelland had poured two pints down his neck in quick succession.

'And the other girls he dated?'

'Working on it, boss.'

Wyn launched into a detailed analysis about Yelland's Facebook page, announcing that he hoped to cross-reference some of Yelland's friends to the internet dating site. I stood up, and wandered over to the window, peering down over the rear of properties along Queen Street. Jimmy Walsh's release next week meant he'd be celebrating in one of the swanky restaurants in the middle of town. 'I wonder what he'll do once he's released?'

Nobody replied immediately.

'You mean Jimmy Walsh?' Lydia said. 'He should keep out of trouble.'

A seagull flew past my window, hovered above the barbed wire lashed to the sill and flew away, taking the sensible course. 'I don't think Jimmy Walsh knows what that means.'

As I sat down my mobile rang. My father's name appeared on the screen.

'Hi, John. Where are you?'

His anxious tone unnerved me.

Chapter 25

Papa was pacing around the sitting room when I arrived. A half-drunk bottle of Peroni stood on the coffee table. Mamma was on the sofa chewing her lip.

'I'm sure I've been followed, John.'

'What do you mean?' I stared at Papa. He wasn't one to exaggerate things but my instinctive reaction was to think he was being melodramatic.

'I went to Swansea with some deliveries on Monday. I kept noticing this black Ford transit. It seemed to follow me around.'

'Did it visit the same places as you?'

'I can't remember. It was the afternoon when I saw it again. The same van was parked outside the factory.'

'Does it belong to one of the other units nearby?'

'I rang two of the companies. They knew nothing about it. And then on Tuesday when I was driving down to work it passed me. I could swear it was the same van. And then it turned round and followed me. I spotted it in the rear-view mirror but he turned off after a few minutes.'

'Maybe it belongs to a local delivery company.'

'A black transit? The windows all blacked out. Come off it, John.'

'When did you see the van next?' I sounded too much like a police officer and not enough like a concerned son. I had never seen Papa so rattled.

He shook his head. 'This morning.'

I suppressed my growing anxiety. 'Tell me what happened.'

My father sat down on the edge of his chair and took a long slug of beer.

'It was behind me after I left the house. It got too close so I parked in the supermarket. I bought a newspaper and then drove down to the factory.'

He put the bottle back on the table.

'I left the factory before lunch. I had a meeting with a supplier but instead of going straight there I took a roundabout route. I went up to Tonypandy, then did a detour round one of the back streets and then back down the valley to Pontypridd. They weren't behind me when I went up the valley. I was checking all the time. But then once I was back and onto the A470 the van appeared behind me.'

An invisible hand grasped my throat and squeezed. I knew there was only one explanation: Jimmy Walsh.

'I'm worried, John.'

'Did you get the number plate?'

'I memorised it this morning,' Papa reached for his mobile and recited the details.

'I'll do what I can ...'

Papa nodded. I didn't need to explain the intricacies of police protocol.

Mamma made her first contribution. She kept her voice low. 'Has this got anything to do with those people who want to buy the café?'

'Has anything happened since we met with Uncle Gino and Jez?'

'Gino complained like hell about you standing in the way of progress and not understanding what family is all about. I spoke to him on Sunday and Jez had told him Goldstar Properties would get another valuation. They told him unless we signed up within two weeks we could forget the deal. And they'd make certain we'd never sell to anyone else.'

My palms felt sweaty. I could hear Martin Kendall's Scottish accent grinding out a threat.

'I'll have to talk to Uncle Gino.'

For a few seconds we stared at each other in silence. Papa finished his beer, returning with a telephone handset which he threw over to me. I fumbled with it until I found the loudspeaker function. The dialling sound echoed around the room and after four rings I heard Uncle Gino's voice.

'It's John. I'm with Papa.'

'You're causing problems. Why can't you see sense and agree to sell the old place?' I glanced at Papa who rolled his eyes. 'It means nothing to you.'

'Papa was telling me about your conversation with the man from Goldstar Properties.'

Uncle Gino coughed. 'He's a gangster, fucking gangster. But he's got money and he is prepared to pay a good price. He thinks he can give us shit but he's got no idea.'

I looked up at Papa then glanced over at Mamma who scowled. 'This is really important. Did he threaten you at all?'

'Of course he did but that won't frighten me. Who does he think he's dealing with? He should go and live in Sicily, try his luck there, see how long he lasts.'

'What did he say? Can you remember?'

'Why all these questions? He's a businessman. He wants to do a deal and he's giving me a hard time. So what is it going to take to get you to change your mind?'

'Papa thinks he's being followed. And he's worried.'

Gino went quiet.

'A black van has been stalking him.'

'For Christ's sake, this is not Palermo or some fucking crime thriller on the TV,' Gino spluttered. 'Grow up, John. Let's get the place sold.'

He finished the call and I reached over for my mobile. I punched in the number for operational support. I barked an order for a vehicle registration check. I hoped I could hide the tension galloping through my mind. Mamma left to make some food, announcing I was staying for dinner. Minutes later my mobile rang.

I'd already guessed. I looked over at Papa. 'It's a false number plate.'

It was after midnight when I got home. I sat in front of the television, channel-hopping for half an hour, thinking about my parents, hoping they'd sleep. The bottle of Chianti they'd drunk with the spaghetti bolognese would help. I showered and fell into bed exhausted.

It felt as though I had slept for only two hours when the sound of my mobile woke me. I reached a hand over and then knocked the clock off the bedside cabinet. It hit the wall and the batteries ran over the floor. I fumbled for the handset.

'Detective Inspector Marco? This is area control; we have a report of a burglary and arson allocated to you.'

I propped myself up on one elbow. 'I'm in the middle of—'

'I was to tell you it's at the offices of Goldstar Properties.'

I shot my legs out from under the duvet and sat on the edge of the bed. 'What did you say?'

'Two nearby residents have reported unusual activity. The alarm went off when the windows were smashed. And then the place was set on fire. We have a CSI team on the way but—'

'I'll be there in ten minutes.'

I yanked on a pair of jeans, fumbled for a shirt and sweatshirt and then, grabbing a fleece, raced downstairs to my car. I raced through the empty streets. Minutes later I reached the fish and chip restaurant, braked hard and parked behind one of the two patrol cars. I jumped out, slammed the car door, and ran.

A fire tender was parked at the entrance, a hose reaching down to the rear of the property. Halfway down the driveway I slowed to a walk and watched as the fire crew dampened down the last of the flames. An acrid smell of burning plastic hung in the air and drifted through the blue-and-white lights of the tender.

I marched up to two uniformed officers. Disembodied voices crackled on radios on their lapels. Despite my haste I had remembered my warrant card which I flashed at the older of the two. 'DI Marco.'

'You got here quickly, sir.'

'Have the owners been notified?'

'We've struggled to find the key holder. A second name we have wasn't replying to his telephone.'

I turned to look at the building that I had recently visited.

'Apparently the fire crew got here just in time. Whoever it was splashed petrol over the door and window. He must have hoped that the fire would take hold but the property has a sprinkler system.'

I knew that the entire economic crime unit of the Wales Police Service would sacrifice valuable parts of their bodies for the opportunity to examine the contents of the files inside. Somebody had wanted to hurt Jimmy Walsh very badly and that person must have had a death wish too.

I heard a Scottish accent swearing expertly behind me. I zipped my jacket nearer my chin. Martin Kendall bundled his way past one of the fire crew and marched right up to me.

'What are you doing here?'

'I'm investigating a suspected attempted burglary

and arson attack. Is this your property, Mr Kendall?'

'Don't get smart with me.'

'I thought it was owned by Mrs Walsh?'

'I am a keyholder. You must know that.'

'There's been a burglary. I was going to check that the building was secure. This is a crime scene. I'm the senior investigating officer.'

'And I'm the keyholder. And you and everyone else can fuck off.'

I gave him a kindly ah-well-this-is-your-business-really smile before turning to leave.

Chapter 26

By the time I was back at my apartment it was daylight and the city had woken. I showered, made a double espresso and watched the early morning television news before heading out for breakfast at Gorge with George. Contractors filled the café, piling on the calories before a morning's work on the building sites around the Bay. I ordered a full breakfast and a double strength coffee before finding a stool by a bar area at the back. The rear pages of the *Western Mail* carried depressing news about the latest injury setback for the Cardiff City team. My holidays had meant I had missed the first three fixtures of the new season. The results had been mixed, one win, a loss and a nil-nil draw. The headlines focused on the need to strengthen the attacking line-up.

I folded the paper, placing it to one side so I could read the interview with the team manager, and ate my breakfast at the same time. I swished the last piece of my floury bread roll around the brown sauce, finished the coffee and headed for my car after paying.

A few minutes later, I pulled into the car park at Queen Street, still able to taste the fat of the bacon. Lydia had arrived in the Incident Room. 'I hear you had a busy time last night?'

'Someone tried to torch the place. A window and door dowsed in petrol. So it was someone quite mad or with a death wish.'

Lydia snorted. 'Any eyewitnesses?'

'We'll need to interview the neighbours.'

'What did Bernie Walsh have to say?'

'Nobody could find her but Martin Kendall arrived and went ape shit.'

'So he doesn't want to pursue a complaint?'

'He didn't actually say those words last night.'

Lydia raised an eyebrow. 'So is this a live inquiry?'

'Of course it is. A crime has been committed.'

Lydia tapped the image of Howard Oakley on the board. We knew Oakley had a grudge against Walsh and was probably stupid enough to be an arsonist.

'Let's go and talk to the neighbours,' I said.

Lydia fell in behind me as we trotted down the stairs to the car park. It really felt like lunchtime now and tiredness scorched my eyes. Lydia opened one of the pool cars with the remote control. We took the scenic route down the western link road, skirting past the Millennium Centre and the flashy bars and restaurants of the Bay before heading for Grangetown. She slowed and I surreptitiously glanced down the driveway at the side of the fish and chip restaurant. It was quiet and I wondered when the CSI team would arrive. Thankfully there was no sign of Martin Kendall's Porsche.

Lydia drew to a halt by the kerb, away from the restaurant. I checked my paperwork and then looked over at the small block of flats where the first witness lived. We found the buzzer for Mr Riddle's flat and he opened after I had to shout down the intercom. The door of his flat was ajar when we reached the first floor. A man in his seventies with wispy thin white hair opened the door.

'I am Detective Inspector John Marco and this is Detective Sergeant Flint.' We held up our cards. 'We're investigating last night's burglary and arson.'

'You had better come in.' Inside it was suffocatingly hot and airless. Even so, Riddle wore a sleeveless sweater over a shirt with prominent stripes and a grey tie.

'You made a call about a suspected break-in last night.'

'Nothing suspicious about it. I was in the kitchen at

the time, making my wife a hot drink. She doesn't sleep too well.'

'What time was that?'

'It was just before the shipping forecast.'

Lydia tapped on her mobile telephone. She looked up. 'Shipping forecast is at 5.20 am.'

'I heard the glass smashing. It made a hell of a racket. I looked out of the window but I couldn't see anything. I didn't know what it was at first and then I heard more glass shattering. I looked out and saw the flames taking hold. So I rang the fire brigade straight away.'

It tallied with the information we had on his initial call.

'I went outside hoping I might see something. I've been to them neighbourhood watch meetings where we are told to be vigilant.'

'Did you see anybody?'

'I saw a red sports car driving away.'

Immediately I thought of Howard Oakley. 'Could you remember the make of the car?'

'I can do better than that. It was one of those Italian jobs – an Alfa Romeo. I had a small 147 until a few years ago. I loved the car but the chassis rusted away. Typical Italian cars.'

Now we had a positive link to Howard Oakley and were making progress.

We thanked Mr Riddle, Lydia asking politely about his wife as we left.

A message from Wyn reached my mobile – *Attn DI Marco Important development. Please come back to QS. DC Wyn Nuttall*. Only Wyn could make a text sound formal. The two other witnesses on our list could wait; we sped back into the city.

Wyn was pacing in front of the Incident Room board. He had a serious, determined look on his face that suggested the world was about to end.

He walked over towards us. 'I've been digging around into Howard Oakley's past. I found the name of an intelligence source that was interviewed about the organised crime groups in Swansea. He's in one of the interview rooms. I thought you should hear what he has to say first-hand.'

The rivalry between Cardiff and Swansea wasn't limited to the football field and if the organised crime groups of Swansea felt that their Cardiff rivals were encroaching on their turf then things could get messy. And I wondered if what happened last night had been just that.

Wyn led the way to the interview room.

I pushed open the door. A man, mid-twenties with a baseball hat perched the wrong way round on his head, had his feet propped on the table. 'This is Brendan,' Wyn said.

I stared at the soles of Brendan's trainers. He got the message and hauled them off the table before straightening his position on the plastic chair. His designer polo shirt was dusty pink; a gold chain hung limply around his neck.

'Brendan came across Howard Oakley recently.'

'Sure thing. He's a fucking nutter.'

'Tell the inspector what you know.'

'He was asking around for a gun.'

That certainly got my attention. I stared at him. 'What the hell do you mean?'

'Exactly that. He's been asking around; wanted to know where he could buy a pistol. He kept boasting that he'd been to a shooting club. He got himself involved with some thugs from Swansea so he wanted a gun for protection.'

I glanced over at Wyn and Lydia who were both staring at Brendan. I turned my gaze back at him, suddenly realising Howard Oakley needed far more of my time.

Chapter 27

After finishing with Brendan I headed straight for the Incident Room board where I underlined Howard Oakley's name with a yellow highlighter. He had a motive for the murder of Bevard and for the first time I seriously contemplated that Yelland's killer had been different from Bevard's. It was an uncomfortable thought that Walsh might not be involved in the murder of Bevard. My gaze drifted to the face of Martin Kendall. The smell of his stale aftershave pinched my nostrils as I thought about him almost frothing at the mouth, standing outside the property in the early hours.

I looked over at Lydia. 'We need to arrest Howard Oakley.'

Lydia nodded. 'I'll organise a CSI team.'

I turned to Wyn and Jane. 'Organise for uniformed officers to park outside his house.'

I strode back to my office, and barked instructions to Alvine over the telephone. After finding my car keys I hurried down to the car park, with Lydia, Wyn and Jane following behind us.

Once we were on the motorway heading west Wyn called. 'The uniformed lads have confirmed the red Alfa is still in the drive. But there's no sign of movement.'

I thanked him, finished the call and hurried on.

If Howard Oakley had acquired a gun that had killed Bevard then my theory about Walsh being involved was nothing more than self-delusion. An edge of apprehension crept into my thoughts as we raced along the M4 towards Bridgend. Walsh was a sociopath who wouldn't have hesitated in emptying all the bullets of a small handgun into Bevard. There had been other unsolved murders in South Wales where the motive pointed to Walsh but we simply didn't have enough evidence to convict. The sort of evidence that was now driving us to arrest Howard Oakley.

I slowed as I approached the exit slip on the motorway and then sped towards Bridgend and although the satnav bleeped instructions I remembered the route anyway. Once I had seen the marked police car parked by the kerb I pulled up behind it. A few minutes later Wyn and Jane slowed to a halt behind us but there was no sign of the scientific support vehicle. I didn't have time to wait so I gave the order and we pulled into the estate. I accelerated towards the Oakley house, braked, left the car and then waved at Wyn and Jane to cover the back door. I skirted round the Alfa Romeo still parked on the drive and hammered on the front door. A woman's voice screamed, followed by the sound of heavy footsteps descending a staircase. From the crashing of the door I guessed that Howard Oakley was making for the rear; I shouted at Wyn and Jane. 'He's making a run for it. Watch out.'

The front door creaked open and Mrs Oakley stood there in a thin dressing gown. I ran into the kitchen and then out of the back door where Wyn was prostrate on the ground clutching a hand to his nose, blood all over his face and shirt. In the distance, I could see Howard lumbering over the fields, Jane in pursuit. I ran to the bottom of the garden, kicked to one side a wooden gate and set off after them. Soon, my breathing became laboured, a wheezing grasped my chest. For a big man Howard Oakley seemed remarkably nimble. He reached a metal farm gate and vaulted over it in one smooth movement. Jane fumbled to climb over it and I reached her as she fell on the opposite side.

'Tell the uniformed lads what happened,' I said, setting off again.

Howard ran towards a farm building in the distance,

lengthening his stride. Over the uneven and broken surface of the field my brogues chafed and tore at the skin of my toes. Howard negotiated another gate near a barn and set off along the tarmac lane. This time I managed the gate quickly and sensed I was gaining on him. Something made him turn into another field; probably realising we'd have officers at the end of the lane by now. He ran down the field with an odd rhythm and a looping gait. I pressed on, past caring about the pain in my feet.

He was lengthening his stride, the distance between us increasing. Moments later I saw him disappear around the side of a barn. I dipped my head, trying to find that extra ounce of energy. I reached the concrete surface outside the barn and watched in dismay as Howard drove away in a 4x4, its owner lying on the floor.

I called in the details of the vehicle and then spoke to Lydia. Luckily the farmer was unhurt and laughed away my suggestion that I call an ambulance. The marked patrol car pulled into the farmyard a few minutes later and we returned to the Oakley house.

Mrs Oakley sat by the kitchen table staring at me defiantly.

'Where would Howard go?'

She shrugged.

'We need to speak to him urgently.'

'You're just going to set him up. I'm not going to help you.'

Floorboards creaked upstairs; something heavy was dropped onto the floor as Wyn and Jane searched Howard's possessions. Lydia, sitting by my side, leant over towards Mrs Oakley.

'Howard's in a lot of trouble, and we need to find him. Does he have a girlfriend, or can you tell us who his friends are?'

She snorted and pulled her folded arms tightly against her chest.

Lydia sat back. 'If Howard has done nothing wrong, then he's got nothing to hide.'

It had little impact on Mrs Oakley, who simply pouted. Footsteps descended the staircase and Wyn gestured over towards me. I followed him into the sitting room at the front of the house.

'We found his mobile, boss.'

'Good. Anything else?'

'A load of old clothes, a lot of sports gear and a massive amount of steroids.'

I raised an eyebrow. 'We need to find him.'

Through the window I watched Alvine and her team organising for a low loader to collect Howard's ancient red sports car. I returned to the kitchen. Realising there was nothing we could do to prevent Mrs Oakley contacting Howard once we had left I turned to her. 'You're coming with us.'

I grabbed her arm but she shook me off, screaming at the same time. 'This is police brutality. You can't arrest me. I've done nothing wrong.'

Eventually we bundled her into the back seat of the marked police car, which headed off for the local station in Bridgend.

Back in my car, my mobile rang. It was operational control. 'We have reports of the missing 4x4 breaking the speed limit along the M4 and then taking junction 45 towards Swansea. A patrol car is in pursuit.'

A few brief minutes later we reached the M4 and I flattened the accelerator, flashing my headlights and sounding the horn repeatedly as I manoeuvred through the traffic. As I drew to a halt near the roundabout underneath the motorway another message arrived on my mobile. Lydia read it out. 'The 4x4 has been abandoned in the Liberty Stadium car park.'

I knew exactly where it was from my visits to the stadium when Cardiff played Swansea city. It was another few minutes before we drew in alongside two marked police cars. Three officers in high visibility vests stood around the 4x4. We left my car, and peered in at seats covered in dirt and grime. Dog hairs covered the rear seat and a blanket was crumpled at one end. I surveyed the car park, wondering if Howard Oakley was nearby, looking on.

'Did any of you see him?' I said to the motorway patrol officers.

'He'd left by the time we arrived.'

'Where could he go from here?'

One of the officers pointed towards the houses on the other side the dual carriageway. 'It's only a short walk into Manselton from here.'

Another officer cut in. 'He could have walked over to the Morfa Shopping Park and taken a bus into the centre of Swansea.'

I gathered my thoughts. I dialled Wyn's number. 'I need you to contact Brendan – get him to tell you everything that Howard mentioned about his connections with the organised crime groups in Swansea. I want names, addresses.'

I finished the call and turned to Lydia. 'Let's go to Swansea Central police station.'

Chapter 28

The conference room on the top floor of Swansea Central police station had a large, highly polished table. We sat around it with Inspector Anderton and Sergeant Thomas as I explained in detail why I needed to speak to Howard Oakley. A third officer joined us as I finished.

'This is Harry Ogden. He's in charge of the organised crime unit.'

I reached over to shake his hand. I knew Ogden from years ago. He had aged badly – his skin was pallid, his jowls extensive. He was an old-fashioned type of detective who cracked heads together and worried about the consequences later: ideally suited to policing the organised crime groups.

'Do you have any idea if Howard has any contacts in the Swansea area?' Anderton said.

I cast a glance at Ogden. 'We know that he was trying to source a firearm.'

'Any names?' Ogden said.

I shook my head. 'I should have some details later.'

'I'll make some calls. But we'll need more information.'

'Of course. In due course I'll need a team of officers available.'

Thomas had been quiet until now. 'I can take half a dozen officers away from other duties this afternoon until early this evening. After that you'll need to talk to the superintendent for authority.'

It was exactly what I expected. The bean counters at the finance department cast a ghostly presence over everything we did.

'Is there an office we can use?'

Anderton glanced at Thomas and mentioned an

office number he thought was vacant. We left the conference room, following him through the building to a small room with two desks and a telephone. Lydia went in search of the canteen while I telephoned Wyn.

'I need a full list of all the gyms that Howard visits. Go through his mobile telephone and ring me back.'

I finished the call without waiting for Wyn to acknowledge his instructions. I booted up the computer on one of the desks and as Lydia returned with coffee and sandwiches I began an internet search for the gyms in the Bridgend and Swansea areas. An hour later I had a list of fifteen. When Wyn rang me back I cross-referenced each against numbers on Howard Oakley's mobile telephone. There were three, one in Bridgend, two in Swansea.

Ogden made an appearance as I grabbed my jacket. 'We've got the name of two gyms that Howard Oakley might have used. I want to talk to some of his mates.'

'I'll get my jacket and I'll see you in the car park.'

On my way out, I called Wyn and dictated instructions for him and Jane to visit the gym in Bridgend. Outside we caught up with Harry Ogden standing by his car, finishing a cigarette, which he ground into the tarmac. There was something reassuring about another detective smoking. We followed him to the first address in Townhill.

Perspiration and the smell of second-hand clothes assaulted our nostrils once we entered. Faces turned towards us, thin vests strained at pumped-up shoulders. We found the manager and I pushed a photograph of Howard Oakley in front of his nose. He gave it a genuine stare and as far as I could tell an equally authentic shrug of the shoulders when he told us he didn't recognise him.

Not one of the dozen or so customers recognised Howard Oakley either. I wondered why his mobile telephone had the details of this gym. As we headed back for our cars, Wyn telephoned. 'The Bridgend gym manager hasn't seen Howard for a week. But he's given us the details of some of his mates. We're going over there now, boss.'

The second gym was in Sketty. We pushed open the double doors into the first floor premises. A radio played one of those annoying Coldplay songs in the background. Another dozen men were bench pressing with an equal number working on machines.

Two men in matching polo shirts with the name of the gym embroidered on the material came over. 'Can we help?'

We flashed cards and then presented once again the image of Howard Oakley. They nodded slowly.

'We need to track down some of his friends.'

Ten minutes later we had two names and addresses. We jogged out of the building before racing back to the cars. Ogden was on the telephone screeching at Thomas to organise a team to meet us at an address in Fforestfach. Again Ogden led the way; this time he wasn't bothering about watching the speed limit.

We parked a hundred metres from the property and waited for Thomas's team to arrive.

Our mobiles crackled into life. It was Ogden. 'Everyone is in place. Let's go.'

We raced over to the property, joining Ogden as he kicked open a small wooden gate. He pounded on the door, calling out that it was official police business. When the door opened he pushed his way in, pinning the occupant against the wall. I streamed through into the sitting room and then into the kitchen, both of which were empty. Upstairs the bedrooms were a mess. A man in his thirties clambered out of a double bed complaining that he was working nights and that he'd never get back to sleep.

We left the occupants, ignoring their protests and

their threats of legal action.

Lack of success didn't deter Ogden in the least. 'Fucking toe-rags.' He slammed the gate before marching towards his car. 'Let's hope he's at the second address.'

We had more of an opportunity to coordinate with Thomas's team before we reached the address in Landore near the Liberty Stadium. I drew up a few metres behind Ogden, who called me on my mobile.

'It's the house with the white painted wooden windows and the gloss black door.'

I leant forward and stared through the windscreen. 'Got it.'

'The rest of the team are in the passage round the back. Take your time. He might be expecting us.'

Lydia and I walked over with Ogden as nonchalantly as we could. We knocked on the door. No reply. We exchanged urgent glances.

Ogden hammered on the door. I peered in through the net curtains; there was no movement or sound. Ogden's mobile rang. He barged past me after answering the call. 'Someone has just climbed out of the back window.'

He turned to Lydia. 'You stay here.' I followed Ogden towards the end of the terrace. At the rear a plainclothes officer was gesticulating towards the back of a house and shouting for someone to stop.

Ogden and I ran down the passageway, meeting Thomas on the pavement of the adjacent street. 'It was Oakley all right,' Thomas said.

'Which direction did he go in?'

Thomas nodded towards a property on the other side of the road. 'There was the sound of a door being broken. He probably went into the back door and out via the front.'

Ogden and Thomas ran over to the house. On

impulse I took a right and found myself in another terrace. In the distance I caught sight of a man running in the direction of the Liberty Stadium.

I gave chase, hoping that it was Howard Oakley and that somehow in the chaos he had been able to make his escape. By the end of the road I was breathless and sweaty. I caught sight of him running towards the main road.

He turned right and, after stopping briefly to call Ogden, I set off in pursuit. He must have been several hundred yards in front of me along Neath Road – I could see him glancing over at the Liberty Stadium. He must have been thinking that the stolen 4x4 would still be there. Then I realised that it probably still was. And Howard Oakley had a set of keys. I increased my pace as did the stitch in my side.

He reached the roundabout for the Liberty Stadium and I stared in disbelief as he raced across it, dodging between the traffic heading into and out of Swansea. He even managed to bang into a car and gesticulated wildly at the driver. I followed him, waving my hands in the air, shouting 'police' at the top of my voice, hoping the traffic would slow down. I weaved in-between various cars until I was able to follow Oakley down into the entrance of the Liberty Stadium but he had gained valuable seconds on me.

I imagined him passing me in the 4x4, grinning inanely.

I ignored the stabbing pains in my chest. Oakley was already sitting in the 4x4, trying frantically to start the engine. Behind me I heard a patrol car siren. I reached the vehicle as Oakley fired the engine into life. He started a three-point turn; the siren grew louder. I tugged at the driver's door, but he opened it and pushed me away. I fell into some shrubbery as the patrol car mounted the pavement and came to a halt immediately in front of Oakley.

He slammed the vehicle into reverse but another patrol car joined the second to block his exit. I got to my feet and ran over to the 4x4. I yanked open the door, pulled Oakley out and he fell onto the tarmac. Then I puked all over my shoes.

Chapter 29

I dragged a hand over my wrist and read the time. I was early. Saloon cars varying in age filled the car park. Most had occupants that cast urgent glances over at the gatehouse at HMP Grange Hall. I had parked at the far end hoping nobody would notice my presence. There was no real purpose for me being there either.

I was there to watch Jimmy Walsh walk free.

For now.

I had to witness Walsh walking into the arms of Bernie and no doubt a friendly embrace from Martin Kendall. Bernie Walsh's 4x4 swept into the car park and reversed into a parking slot. I made out Kendall sitting by her side and I was far enough away for them not to notice me. More cars arrived as the time for Walsh's release neared.

Most of the visitors who had congregated outside the entrance were women, a reminder that our jails are full of men. Casual conversation developed, judging from the arm gestures and nodding heads, and I wondered if they were regulars, meeting husbands and boyfriends who accepted imprisonment as an occupational hazard.

Our search of the list of prisoners released in the weeks before Bevard's death had proved fruitless. Someone had pulled the trigger that had killed Bevard and Yelland, and until our arrest of Howard Oakley I had been convinced it had been someone directed by Walsh. If Howard Oakley made a full and complete admission to both murders then I was going to look foolish.

In this case innuendo and circumstantial evidence giving Walsh a motive for Bevard's death would never be enough. I imagined the howls of laughter and derision if I suggested all the details of Bevard's supergrass deal be made public as part of a prosecution against Walsh.

The first prisoners emerged. A woman rushed over and threw her arms around a loved one. Bags in hand they headed for their cars. There were fifteen releases that morning and Jimmy Walsh was the last; the delay must have annoyed him.

He stood for a moment on the threshold and pitched his head skyward as though the air was different somehow for a free man. His denims looked crumpled, the shirt and jacket untidy after years in storage. Bernie raced over to him. He smiled, drew her close to him and kissed her deeply; even I could see the hunger in his body.

My chest tightened and I squinted over at them. I reached a hand to the door handle. I would tell him to stop his harassment of my family. But I could imagine the criticism in Hobbs' voice – *What possessed you to approach him? And why were you outside the prison?*

Martin Kendall dawdled behind Bernie. Walsh and his wife finished their embrace and then he hugged Kendall. They were smiling. Once they had finished, Kendall picked up Walsh's bag and they turned back for their car.

Without a further thought about the consequences I yanked open the car door. My family were more important than any protocols. I left the car and headed towards them. I buttoned my jacket, lengthened my stride, and kept them firmly in my gaze.

Walsh reached the 4x4 and drew a hand along the passenger-side wing as though he were admiring the car for the first time.

Bernie was already in the driver's seat and Kendall was closing the rear after dumping Walsh's bag inside. They hadn't noticed me. Kendall made for the rear driver's side passenger door.

I increased my pace and Walsh looked over in my

direction. He smirked.

I stopped a few feet away from him. He stepped towards me and we stood in front of the vehicle. I could sense Bernie Walsh staring at me through the windscreen.

'What do you want?'

'I know what you've been doing about the property in Pontypridd.'

'This is harassment.'

'Stay away from my family, Walsh.' I moved towards him clenching my fist. 'If you do anything to threaten my parents then I'll make certain you'll be back in here so fast your head will spin.'

He smirked at me again.

We stood there staring at each other, until eventually he climbed into the passenger seat and they drove away.

I returned to my car and opened the window. I smoked a cigarette in the cool September morning. Once I'd finished I adjusted the rear-view mirror and noticed the grey skin under my eyes. Tackling Walsh had been stupid. But he had given me no choice. I wasn't going to stand to one side and say nothing, do nothing.

A night in the cells at Queen Street had done nothing to improve Howard Oakley's mood. He sat opposite me in the interview room, staring. The flimsy white one-piece paper suit made a rustling sound every time he moved in the plastic chair. His cheeks looked puffy and I knew from reading the custody log that he had refused all food. A beaker of water sat on the table in front of him. His solicitor wore flame-red lipstick and a diamond stud in each ear lobe. I hadn't dealt with her before but the custody sergeant had warned me she could be aggressive.

Before the interview I had read with growing excitement the report from the CSIs. A Walther P99 wrapped in cling film had been found at the back of a shed in the bottom of the garden in Howard Oakley's property. Preliminary fingerprint analysis proved Oakley had handled it but it might take days for forensic confirmation that it had been the gun that killed Bevard and Yelland.

'Why did you run?' I said once the tape started recording.

'You were going to stitch me up.'

'There was a burglary at a restaurant in Grangetown early Thursday morning. And the place was torched.'

Howard Oakley folded his arms, pulling them into his chest.

Oakley's solicitor butted in again. 'Who are the owners of the property?'

'The premises are owned by Goldstar Properties. That's Mr James Walsh and Mrs Bernie Walsh.' The names hung in the air, as contagious as a cough.

I looked over at Oakley. 'Where were you between four and five-thirty that morning?'

Oakley scratched his neck. I could sense he wanted to reply. Very few people make no comment interviews: that only ever happens on television crime dramas.

'Several of the windows in the property were smashed before petrol was poured over the outside. Luckily the premises had a sprinkler system installed and the fire service arrived quickly.'

'What is the evidence to implicate my client?'

I ignored her. 'Are you the owner of an Alfa Romeo Brera sports car?' I looked up at Oakley and then for good measure reminded him of the registration number and its colour. He squinted slightly, then glanced over at the lawyer.

'DVLA records have you as the owner.' I pushed over a photocopy of the record; his reluctance to even confirm obvious details rankled.

He mumbled.

I tilted my head slightly towards him. 'For the purpose of the tape recording of this interview can you please confirm your reply?'

He shook his head.

'Can you tell me how you know Jimmy Walsh?'

Oakley slowly unfolded his arms and fisted both hands, which he placed on the table in front of him.

'He killed my father,' Oakley said slowly.

The lawyer rolled her eyes in frustration.

'And do you know Felix Bevard?'

'My client replies no comment.'

Oakley paused and then nodded.

'Do you blame Felix Bevard for the death of your father?'

Oakley's face flushed.

'Your father refused to sell his property to Jimmy Walsh and Felix Bevard.'

'Is that a question, Inspector? Because this interview is becoming a fishing expedition.'

'Walsh and Bevard wanted to buy the property your parents owned. It's a matter of record because your mother made a statement at the time of your father's death. The Wales Police Service investigated his death but Jimmy Walsh had an alibi.'

'Like fuck he did.'

I sat back and shared a brief smile with both Oakley and the lawyer.

'Is that why you went to the property the night before last?'

Oakley had relaxed his arms now, a hand grasping

each knee.

'Would it be fair to say you had a grudge against Felix Bevard?'

No reply.

I reached down and lifted the pistol from a bag by my feet. I placed it carefully on the table. The blood drained from Howard's face and the lawyer gave him a troubled look.

'This pistol was found at the back of the shed in your garden. Can you confirm that it is yours?'

He stared at me but made no reply.

'And your hatred of Bevard was enough to make you buy a pistol and kill him in the storeroom at the Roath Park café.'

Oakley sat there looking terrified. I savoured the open-mouthed astonishment from the lawyer. Her attitude changed soon afterwards. She became even more unhelpful and aggressive.

'Did you know a Brian Yelland?'

I watched his face closely. I couldn't read the reaction. Was it surprise or trepidation?

'Mr Yelland was a prison officer who was killed last Sunday.' I reeled off the date and watched as Howard's solicitor scribbled down the details. Howard's mouth fell open but his lawyer, a regular who got under the skin of every officer at Queen Street with an attitude that she knew better than anyone else, whispered in his ear. Howard shook his head.

'Do you have any evidence to link my client with the death of Mr Yelland, Inspector?'

I ignored her and continued. 'Can you tell me where you were on the night Yelland was killed?'

He shook his head slowly and I waited, giving him an opportunity to reply before moving on.

'He was probably killed with the same pistol that shot Felix Bevard. It was a small pistol, like a Walther P99, like the one we found at your property. It's only a matter of time before the forensics report is available but if they can link this pistol to both killings then now would be a good time to offer an explanation.'

He opened his lips a fraction. I could see his yellowing teeth. He looked at me blankly.

'Now is your opportunity to say something and it might go against you if you haven't mentioned something—'

His lawyer piped up. 'That's enough Inspector, you've explained the warning already and my client understands the position. Move on.'

I looked over at her; she obviously wanted to return to her warm air-conditioned office. But I had enough to keep Oakley in custody until I could review the evidence with a Crown Prosecution lawyer, Acting Detective Chief Inspector Hobbs and anybody else from the senior management team who wanted to contribute. The lawyer made all sorts of threats about the way I had conducted the interview, none of which I took seriously. I had a killer to find. Howard Oakley had the right motive, and had been after a gun so all I had to do was prove his opportunity.

An email from Hobbs summoned me to a meeting late that afternoon and I dragged myself to Cornock's office. I rapped two fingers on the door after listening briefly to the sound of intelligent conversation inside. There was a muffled shout for me to enter and Dave Hobbs waved me to the conference table.

Desmond Joplin was sitting at the far end. I knew the Crown Prosecutor as having a fearsome reputation and for not suffering fools gladly. I suspected it was for these qualities Hobbs had asked him to review the evidence against Oakley. Desmond had a pallid complexion, little hair, save for a monk-like ring around the base of his head. We shook hands. I sat down, Dave Hobbs at the other end of the table. It made me feel like a minnow between two piranhas.

'You have got no evidence.' Desmond had an accent polished by years of appearing in the magistrates' courts. I opened my mouth to reply but he ignored me. 'I appreciate why you were justified in making the arrest. Especially given the motive. But there's no evidence linking Oakley to the murders although I grant you that if the gun was used to kill Bevard and Yelland that changes things. And from what Detective Chief Inspector Hobbs has told me you're linking both deaths together.'

So the *acting* part of Hobbs' title disappeared. That annoyed me too.

'You must release him. You can't possibly justify further detention. He'll be released this evening.'

'What about the attempted burglary and arson? There's more than enough to justify a prosecution.'

Desmond dipped his head towards Dave Hobbs. I had a sensation things had been taken completely out of my hands. Hobbs held up a piece of paper lying on the table in front of him. 'We've had a letter from Bernie Walsh's solicitors – Tront and Tront.'

Simply mentioning the name of the solicitors summoned up the image of its senior partner Glanville Tront tearing into a badly prepared prosecution case and witnessing hours of work destroyed.

'The letter makes it perfectly clear that Mr and Mrs Walsh do not wish to make a complaint. And furthermore if we prosecute they would challenge the entire legitimacy of any evidence the investigators recovered from the property.'

My tie felt inextricably tightened upon my neck. There was finality to the way Dave Hobbs had read out the contents of the letter. 'But ...' I couldn't think of anything to say.

'Nothing I can do,' Hobbs said.

I stood up and made for the door. Joviality filtered into the conversation between Desmond and Hobbs as I left. I pulled the door closed behind me feeling like the poor relation.

Chapter 30

I joined the rest of the team in a café near the housing estate where Yelland had lived ready for a morning of house-to-house inquiries. From their truculent looks they clearly thought repeating what had already been done once was a waste of time.

I sat down next to Lydia. A dried-up Danish pastry lay on a plate in front of Wyn. Jane slurped on a milky coffee.

'I want everyone spoken to again on the estate. Somebody must have seen something.' I sounded fraught. I felt it too. Howard Oakley had been released and Walsh was a free man. My interest in the murder of Robin Oakley had been pushed to one side once we knew of Howard's involvement with the gangs in Swansea and his urgent need to find a gun. Before leaving Queen Street last night I had emailed the production company about the video of the *Dr Who* programme in Roath Park, threatening them with a formal warrant unless they cooperated. First thing that morning I had a reply confirming arrangements for me to view the recording at their offices in London next week. If I couldn't prove that Walsh had killed Bevard and Yelland then at least there was the possibility of reopening the case involving Robin Oakley.

I dictated instructions about who should go where and I watched the reluctant nodding of heads. 'Let's meet up later this morning.'

They followed me out of the café before we made the short journey to the housing estate.

Lydia and I walked up to the gate of the first house on our list. She hesitated but I sensed she had something to say. 'All the team are behind you, boss.'

There was a *but* coming.

'Only, sometimes you might explain things in—'

'Explain?' I stopped in my tracks. 'For Christ's sake, Lydia this is a murder inquiry.' I paused. 'I'll speak to them again: but it's my case.'

'Yes, boss.'

I pushed open the gate and marched up to the door wondering exactly what Wyn and Jane had been bitching about. Maybe it was working a Saturday they found unpalatable. I reached the door and forced a smile when the householder appeared.

We spent twenty minutes ticking off the various sections of the original notes that the uniformed officers had recorded and, satisfied that she could add no more, we left. The same thing had repeated itself by mid-morning with three other households. An elderly spinster opened the door before we had even rung the bell. 'I saw you coming. Jean from number three rang and told me you might call.'

She glanced at Lydia and me and opened the door, offering to make us coffee as she led us into her kitchen. She made decent enough coffee but we quickly realised that she too had nothing more to add. We made excuses and left carrying the various chocolate bars she insisted on giving us.

'Probably the only company she'll have all weekend,' Lydia said as we stood outside the gate. I scanned the list of names and house numbers noticing that the original officers had marked the next-door property as empty. The drive looked neat and tidy, the gutters clean. It didn't look unlived in so I ventured up to the front door and rang the bell. There was no response. I rang a second time before noticing a recycling bin placed near a gate to the rear. Not many empty houses put their rubbish out so I tried the gate, which was unlocked. At the bottom of the garden was a man pruning some rose bushes, earphones dangling freely around his neck.

I shouted over.

He ignored me so I walked down to him. He started when he saw me and fiddled with the smartphone, killing the music. 'Bloody hell, you gave me a fright.'

I showed him my card.

'Alan Taylor.' He proffered a hand. 'How can I help?'

'We're conducting house-to-house inquiries about the death of Brian Yelland.'

'Who?'

I told him Yelland lived in one of the adjacent properties, a near neighbour. 'I didn't know him. I only got back last night from a trip to Germany. What happened to him?'

'He was shot.'

'Bloody hell. You had better come in.'

The kitchen was functional and clear of any clutter or a woman's touch. We sat around the table.

'I live alone and I work a lot in Berlin so I don't really know any of my neighbours.'

'Brian Yelland worked in Grange Hall prison and moved into the property in the last year after his marriage broke up.'

'Sorry. I wouldn't recognise him. When did this happen?'

I gave Taylor the dates. 'That was the night before my flight.' He puckered his brow.

'When was your flight?

'It was half past seven from Cardiff International. I had to be awake before four and I left about half past.'

'Did you see any movement around the estate? Any unusual cars parked? Anybody walking the street?'

Taylor sat more upright in his chair. 'Now that you

ask I did see someone earlier that morning. I never sleep well before an early flight. I remember being up in the middle of the night. And I did see someone in the street.'

'Can you describe him or her?' I held out little prospect of any meaningful information.

'It was a man, definitely. I noticed because he stood under the streetlight outside Yelland's property. And there was a full moon that night – that was one of the reasons I peered out. He was using one of those fancy cigarette lighters. He was tall with a shaved head and he had a prominent nose.'

My heart almost missed a beat. The image of Martin Kendall's crooked nose came swimming to mind.

'Show me exactly where you saw him standing.'

'Of course.'

Taylor led us into the lounge at the front of the property where he pointed to Yelland's home and then at the streetlight. My concern as to how he could describe someone in the dark of night diminished as I realised how close the properties were. 'We'll need you to make a full statement and cooperate with an artist to make up a photofit image.'

'Of course. I'm only too happy to help.'

I dialled headquarters and arranged for Taylor to be seen by one of the force's artists later that afternoon. Then we left Taylor and I headed back for my car.

'Do you think it's Kendall?' Lydia said.

I ran a hand over my mouth. 'If it is him then he needs to explain what he was doing there.'

I looked over at Yelland's property. If he had seen Kendall the night he was killed it meant another strong link to Walsh. Maybe my gut instinct wasn't wrong after all.

It was early afternoon when I joined Tracy for the quality time I had promised her. We drove over to Barry Island. I drove sedately along Harbour Road taking in the view over the Bristol Channel. Once I'd parked we walked past beach shops and small cafés down to the wide expanse of beach. We headed over to the eastern promenade and admired the brightly painted beach huts that lined a small section. They looked pristine but the imminent winter's storms would put paid to the owners' efforts over the summer.

Back on the beach I took Tracy's hand but she slipped it loose to kneel and gather a piece of sea-worn glass with smooth edges. She placed the blue fragment in her palm and wet the top of her finger to clean off the sand. A deeper, richer colour emerged. Then she slipped it into a pocket. By the end of the month the temperatures would have fallen, the wind would be brisker and the visitor numbers fewer.

We strolled over the long beach towards the western side talking about nothing in particular. Tracy had recently been on a course and she told me how Alvine Dix had made a point of getting her to 'cascade her newly found knowledge' to the rest of the team at Queen Street. Later we sauntered around the gifts and trinket shops until we reached Marco's Café.

'Any relation?' Tracy asked.

'It's the owner's Christian name.'

A large sign hung by the door with tall images of the main actors from *Gavin and Stacey*, the television comedy that had given Marco's Café and Barry Island a new notoriety. We sat down by one of the round tables and beckoned a waitress. She took our orders for coffee, Tracy opting for a chocolate brownie as well..

'How are things going with the Bevard inquiry?'

'Slowly.'

It was indicative of the way our relationship had developed that I found small talk about work difficult. After my last case when I had briefly suspected Tracy had been sharing secrets with her brother it had become less easy to share confidences with her.

Thankfully, she sensed my reluctance and turned her conversation to her father and his medical problems. The house in Bournemouth was still on the market; the agents had suggested a price reduction in the hope they could find a buyer before Christmas. Our coffees arrived and Tracy tucked into the chocolate brownie, making approving comments.

A small minibus of tourists arrived and the café staff quickly arranged several tables together. The commotion soon died down, replaced by loud conversations and laughter at different attempts at the catchphrase used by the characters in the TV show. We paid and then retraced our steps to the car before driving back to Cardiff via Penarth.

That evening we strolled down to the Bay and mingled with the young couples, families out with teenagers and older groups enjoying the last of the September sunshine. We ate in an Italian restaurant, Tracy having relaxed – or perhaps we both had after our afternoon walk by the sea.

Back at my apartment we showered together. I drew a sponge over her back, ran my fingers around the fall of her breasts. She scrubbed my back and then my chest and squeezed me. Once she was clean of soapsuds she slid open the shower door and left me disappointed. Later we made love but Tracy's embrace and her kisses lacked the tenderness and urgency we had shared at the beginning.

The following morning she made breakfast and things seemed normal. I fetched a Sunday newspaper and we spent an hour exchanging comments about various articles. Cardiff City had one of those odd lunchtime kick-offs that suited the satellite broadcasters so by late morning we were walking through Grangetown to the football stadium. She held my hand more tightly. I bought some coffees before kick-off and at half-time we shared a compulsory pie. The packaging said chicken but I had my doubts.

Cardiff won, thankfully. We jostled through the crowds to the bar and met two of my regular footballing friends. We analysed the game, dissected the strength of the opposition and anticipated that Cardiff would at least make the play-offs for a Premiership slot this season. Tracy smiled, and shared a joke; her coolness from yesterday seemed to have faded.

Most of the post-match crowds had gone when we left. Tracy drew the collar of her jacket to her face against the chill in the air as we walked back to the Bay. Outside my apartment, she dawdled, reached up, touched my cheek, kissing me briefly. 'Thanks for a lovely weekend. I'm not going to stay tonight John. I need to get up early tomorrow morning.'

She reached into her bag for her car keys.

She smiled at me again before jumping into her car. I stood and watched her driving away, feeling hesitant about our future.

Chapter 31

I drove to Queen Street humming along to Elvis Presley crooning his way through 'Have I Told You Lately That I Love You?', wondering what things had been left unsaid between Tracy and me. I was the first to arrive in the Incident Room that morning and once I'd booted up my computer I opened the email with the attached photofit image of the man Taylor had seen. An adrenaline rush pumped through my body at the real prospect I had more evidence against Kendall. Even with the evidence that Yelland's gambling debts had been paid by Kendall I was still unconvinced there was enough to justify Kendall's arrest for his murder.

It meant another meeting with Hobbs. I rehearsed my arguments and I imagined his voice asking me – motive? And then he'd tilt his head and look down his nose before dismissing me.

We had to have a legitimate reason to organise an identity parade where we could hope that Taylor might identify Kendall. I didn't have time to think about it any further as a message reached my mobile from Papa – *van is back. Lurking around first thing this morning.*

I ran down to my car. The gearbox made a crunching sound as I found first gear and floored the accelerator. The engine whined; I cursed silently that I wasn't driving one of the pool cars that had warning lights. I resorted to flashing my headlights and blasting my horn. I hammered round Boulevard de Nantes and then right at the junction with North Road. Traffic scattered as I hugged the outside lane of the dual carriageway out of the city. I drove like a maniac, racing past the junction with Eastern Avenue and then on towards the main roundabout where the M4 reached the A470.

Once I was clear of the traffic lights I hurried

towards Pontypridd. My heart pounded as I thought about Jimmy Walsh and his cronies. There was a tailback on the exit slip so I had to stop. Using the next junction might be better. The tarmac wagon ahead of me gradually pulled away and I committed to driving down the slip road. Luckily the lorry peeled away and I took a junction towards the industrial estate.

I slowed the car but my pulse still raced as I scoured the parking slots and site streets for the black van. I approached my father's industrial unit and drove past hoping for a sight of the vehicle. But there was no sign so I retraced my steps and parked away from public gaze near a rear entrance to the factory.

The walk to the offices was one I had taken many times but never with such apprehension. Papa looked ashen faced as he stood in the office, next to one of the admin girls. He ran his hands over his arms as though he were cold. The telephone rang but when the girl answered it, she held the handset in her hand and looked up at Papa.

'We've had dozens of these crank calls today.'

'Have you tried identifying the caller?'

'It's always a withheld number.'

'The telephone company could trace them.'

I followed Papa to his office. Inside there was a small bottle of whisky open on his desk and a glass by its side. 'That's not going help,' I said.

'I never thought I'd hear you say that.'

He sat down behind his desk and gazed at the chaotic mass of paperwork. Managing his business was obviously the last thing on his mind.

I sat down in one of the office chairs. 'Tell me what has been happening.'

'We've had half a dozen calls yesterday morning and we were expecting a delivery by lunchtime. It never arrived and I called the supplier who told me he'd received a telephone call cancelling the order.'

'So whoever it is must know where you get your deliveries.'

'The girls are upset about the whole thing. Yesterday when I drove home from work the black van dropped in behind me on that last but one roundabout before the junction for the A470. To be certain it was the same one I took a random route home. But he followed me all the way.'

He reached a hand towards the glass but at the last second pulled back.

'I was later than normal leaving the house this morning. But within a few of minutes of leaving I spotted the van in my rear-view mirror. He got really close. I couldn't see the driver. And I made a note of the number plate.' Papa scrambled amongst the papers on his desk and handed me a small sheet.

'I can guess the result of this.' I dictated the details down the telephone.

Papa leant on his papers. 'Who are these people, John?'

He ran a hand up his left arm again. 'Are you all right?' I nodded at his arm.

'Yes, it's nothing. Just a bit of pins and needles. Your mother fusses too much.'

He sat back in his chair after topping up the whisky glass and taking a healthy mouthful.

My mobile rang. It was a short one-way conversation. I looked up at Papa nodding what he already knew. 'False plates again.'

'I'm going to cruise around for a while, see if I can spot them. I'll try and get some photographs but until they break the law there's not much I can do.'

'This is down to your uncle fucking Gino and Jez getting involved with those gangsters.'

I chewed my lip, racked my brains, wondering what I could do legally. I had no way of proving it was Walsh but there was no other explanation. It was his way of challenging me – telling me that he was in charge. I could see why the senior management of the Wales Police Service desperately wanted him behind bars. 'I need to get back.'

'Of course.'

'If you see them again today get the lads to take photographs.'

I stood up and left but the worry still clung to the pit of my stomach. I drove around for twenty minutes but there was no black van. I drove down towards the A470 and indicated south as my mobile rang.

'What is it, Wyn?' I snapped, recognising his name.

'Ah... We've just heard from Bevard's bank that on the evening he was killed he bought a takeaway meal in Pontypool. We've got the address of the restaurant. Apparently there was some problem with the bank's computer.' Wyn's voice shook.

I reached the sign for the motorway and on impulse headed east. 'Email me the details, I'm on my way there now.' I needed to calm down before returning to Queen Street so I floored the accelerator.

My mobile lit up as the address I needed reached the screen. I followed the instructions from the satnav and half an hour later I parked outside the Golden Sumac takeaway restaurant. It boasted the best Indian cuisine in Pontypool. I snatched my mobile from the cradle and my fleece from the passenger seat and jogged over the road.

Light reflected from the extensive optic display behind the bar of the Golden Sumac. A man with a thin moustache smiled at me as I entered, reaching for a menu at the same time. 'We don't open for lunch for another hour.'

'Is the owner here?' I flashed my warrant card.

The smile disappeared and he hurried to the back. An older, more confident-looking man strolled through the main part of the restaurant. 'I am the owner – how can I help?'

'I'm Detective Inspector John Marco.' I dictated the date and time of the purchase by Felix Bevard of what would probably have been his last meal. 'I need you to tell me if you can remember anything at all about that purchase.'

He gave me a helpless look, walked behind the bar and flicked through his records. I found an image of Felix Bevard and showed it to him. 'Do you recognise him? He was wearing golfing clothes. He bought a meal here. Do you remember him?'

The owner peered at the photograph. Then he checked his records again, and returned his gaze to the image on my mobile. He gave a brief nod. 'I served him that day. Now that you mention golfing clothes I remember him. He looked quite funny, alongside the other man.'

'Other man?' Instinctively I looked up and around for CCTV cameras. It had become second nature for every police officer by now.

'The other man had lots of tattoos over his arms. And a ponytail.'

It had to be Jack Ledley.

'Did you overhear any of their conversation?'

He shook his head.

'Have you seen the man with tattoos before or since?'

'No, that was the only time.'

'And I'll need you to give me a detailed statement

with a description.'

'I've already said all this to the other police officers who came.'

For a moment, I paused, fearing that I hadn't heard correctly. My lips dried. 'You've spoken to somebody else?'

Frantically I calculated who would risk being a police imposter. Who would take such a gamble?

'I'll need a detailed description of that other person too.' I leant over the bar a fraction. 'The person you spoke to wasn't a police officer. If anybody else comes asking about either of these men, call me immediately.' I pushed my business card towards him.

I ran back to my car, bellowing instructions into my mobile.

Chapter 32

Two hours later I stood in front of half a dozen uniformed officers in a conference room in Pontypool police station. I hadn't bothered learning their names although I'd picked up that there was a Ken and a Steve involved. A large-scale map of Cwmbran and Pontypool had been pinned in the middle of the board behind me. A circle, with the shop Bevard visited at its centre, dominated the map. Another overlapping circle spun out from the Golden Sumac. The final circle covered a radius from the point where Bevard was stopped for speeding. A thick red line connected all three of the known locations to form a triangle.

'We are looking for Jack Ledley.' I pointed to his photograph pinned to one side of the board. 'He has a long ponytail and heavily tattooed arms. On the day he was seen in the shop listed on your briefing memorandum and at an Indian takeaway, he was in the company of Felix Bevard who was killed later that evening. Someone posing as a police officer is looking for him. We need to find him before they do.'

I tapped on the various segments of the map. 'We've divided the town up into sections and we've allocated various teams to take a specific area. I want you to speak to all the shops, pubs, takeaways, and any business where there might be contact with the public.'

The officers nodded between concentrated stares.

'Ledley must have gone out to buy milk, or cigarettes or the newspaper. And remember, Felix Bevard was wearing golfing clothes, so his description should be memorable.'

After answering more questions the Incident Room emptied. Lydia was already organising her coat when I returned from my office shrugging on my jacket. 'Let's go.'

We headed for the shop where Bevard had used his card. The shopkeeper gave us an anxious look when he saw us walking up to the counter. Reluctantly he led us to a small room at the back of the building after he'd organised replacement staff on the till.

'Look, I've told you everything I know.'

'I want you to go through it again.' He sighed and then did as he was told. I listened intently for any variation, any subtle change. Nothing. It only compounded my frustration.

Next we called at the Golden Sumac restaurant. The owner offered coffee, we declined. We sat at one of the tables and listened as he repeated what he told us before. I asked if he had seen Ledley afterwards. *No, only that once*. We spoke to the other members of staff, who spoke passable English so we took far longer to establish that none of them had seen him around the town.

We fared no better with a newsagent nearby. He curled his lips and shook his head as we showed him photographs of Ledley and Felix Bevard. Three women in a launderette launched into a detailed analysis of the various single men who came in to wash bags of clothes once a week. Even Lydia's persuasive questioning and her warm smile did nothing to deflect their gossiping. I handed over business cards, accompanied by fierce encouragement for them to call me if they saw anyone matching Ledley's appearance.

The final stop on our list should have been a pizza takeaway restaurant but the main door was boarded and, peering inside through filthy glass, I noticed the floor covered with discarded newspapers and circulars. Net curtains hung in the window of the adjacent property. At the end of the row was an ironmongers with a window display of faded bleach bottles, foldable stepladders and mops and buckets. The door triggered a bell that rang somewhere in the building. It was like stepping back in time; a counter ran along the three sides of the shop with shelving units stacked to the ceiling.

'What do you want?'

I heard the voice but didn't see the face until an old woman emerged from between boxes of washing-up powder. From the wrinkles and her stiff white hair I guessed she must have been well over eighty. I showed her my warrant card and then the image of Ledley and Felix Bevard. She squinted at them both.

'Have you seen either of these men?'

'Sorry, love. We don't get many strangers in here.'

I was fast running out of business cards but gave her one of the last I had. She tucked it into one of the drawers by the till and I returned to the car.

'Any luck, boss?'

'No. That last place was like a time warp.'

A morning doing regular policing only reinforced my determination to find Jack Ledley. Driving always helped me focus, and sitting in the passenger seat helped me focus on why Jimmy Walsh had an interest in our missing man. And how did Bevard fit into all this? Then it struck me: I had ignored the obvious. I slammed an open palm against the dashboard.

'Get back to Queen Street.'

I had to wait a fractious hour, following an ill-tempered conversation with Inspector Malcolm Ackroyd of the dedicated source unit, before he arrived. Lydia pushed the door closed behind him and I waved him to a chair.

'We've been looking for Jack Ledley.' I stared over at Ackroyd but I didn't give him a chance to reply. 'He met

Felix Bevard on the afternoon he was killed.'

Ackroyd's gaze darted around.

'Bevard bought some food from a local shop. Then he bought a takeaway meal in an Indian restaurant before going back to the golf club.'

I sensed Lydia staring at Ackroyd.

'And today it emerged others are looking for him too. This morning uniformed officers are crawling over Pontypool trying to find him. And I thought to myself, why was Ledley connected to Bevard? And then I remembered that Bevard is connected to you, Malcolm.'

I pulled my chair nearer the desk. 'Have you got any idea what I'm talking about?'

Ackroyd opened his mouth to say something but I ignored him. 'My guess is you know exactly who Ledley is. He was part of your supergrass deal, wasn't he?' My voice was rising in step with my anger.

Ackroyd coughed. 'It's complicated.'

'Don't give me that bullshit. I'm investigating a double murder inquiry. And trying to unravel a murder from years ago involving Walsh and Bevard. I want to know the truth.' I slammed a hand on the desk.

Ackroyd, momentarily startled, blinked rapidly before continuing. 'Felix Bevard told us there was another man involved in the murder of Robin Oakley. Jack Ledley has been on the edge of Walsh's activities for years.'

'And you didn't think to tell us. You fucking idiot.' It was the first time I'd cursed at another inspector in the presence of a junior officer.

Ackroyd seemed to have visibly aged in front of me.

'So what was this Jack Ledley going to tell you?'

He groaned. 'That was the problem. We didn't interview him, didn't get a chance. All the information about Ledley came second hand from Bevard. We got the impression Ledley was getting cold feet.'

'Cold everything else, if Jimmy Walsh gets hold of him.'

If we couldn't find Jack Ledley I had to hope Jimmy Walsh couldn't either. But the prospect of another witness against him in the Oakley murder would eat him alive.

'Malcolm, is there anything else you haven't told us?'

Lydia peered at Malcolm Ackroyd's discomfort.

He shook his head. 'No, Bevard said that together he and Ledley could nail Jimmy Walsh. Look John, make no mistake, everybody wants to see this bastard in jail for the rest of his natural days.'

'So let's work together.' I gave Ackroyd a dismissive flick of my wrist. 'Now fuck off back to your dedicated source unit and don't ever conceal information from me again.'

There was a long silence between Lydia and I after Ackroyd left.

'I've never seen anything like it,' I said eventually.

Chapter 33

I strode into the Incident Room as Wyn finished what smelt like a sausage roll. I hated it when one of the team ate breakfast at work. Jane was noisily drinking a coffee.

'You've got an hour, maximum. After that I'm leaving for Pontypool.'

Lydia had been there from first thing that morning coordinating the search teams. Wyn nodded his understanding.

'I've spoken to the second of the three women Yelland dated and she says they went out once but she never heard from him again. And she didn't know any of his friends.'

'What about the third woman?'

'I'm still trying to find her full details. She uses a Canadian email service provider so it's taking me longer than I expected to find her.'

'Tell the Mounties to go get her on horseback.'

Wyn looked momentarily stunned before he recognised my feeble attempt at humour.

I read the time as Jane cleared her throat. She spent fifteen minutes explaining that she had spoken to four rental agencies covering the towns of Cwmbran and Pontypool. None of them had any knowledge of Jack Ledley. She got up and pointed to the map on the board. 'One of the agencies has organised a let recently in Griffithstown to a man with a ponytail. An officer is going to call this morning.'

It could be progress.

'The other agencies weren't any help at all.'

'Broaden the search,' I said. 'There may be letting agents in Newport that cover that area.'

She got back to work and I walked back to my office

intent on checking my emails. I saw the report on the pistol we found in Howard Oakley's place and I read through to the final page. The conclusion that it was not the same gun that had killed Bevard and Yelland shouldn't have been a surprise but still I felt deflated. Unless Howard had another pistol, it meant he was no longer a suspect in the murder of Felix Bevard. I was halfway through the rest of my emails when my mobile rang. It was my mother. 'It's Papa, he's collapsed.'

I stood up. My chest tightened and my heart sank to my shoes. I tried to sound calm. 'Have you called an ambulance?'

'Of course.'

'I'm on my way.'

I kept talking to her, reassuring her as I walked down to the car.

The journey passed in a blur. An ambulance was parked in the drive when I drew up on the pavement outside the house. I rushed in and found Papa unconscious on the floor, Mamma standing over him. I went over to her and held her close as she sobbed. Paramedics surrounded him talking in technical jargon as they connected various pieces of equipment. They ripped open his shirt. I stood and gaped. This was happening to somebody else, like something in a TV hospital drama.

One of the paramedics said 'Let's shock him'

His partner nodded agreement and they attached two large stickers to his chest then pressed a button on the defibrillator; the machine made a loud charging sound before they pressed another button, unleashing a jolt to his chest. One started chest compressions again whilst another placed a tube in his mouth attached to a bag. After a few minutes, which felt like hours, they repeated the process again; his body convulsed again. I looked on, stunned.

The paramedics stared at the screen on the equipment. 'We've got an output.'

'Let's get him to the hospital.' His partner spoke as though we weren't there. They quickly placed him onto a stretcher while one of them squeezed the bag every now and again to support Papa's breathing.

It felt like my own heart had stopped. We followed them out to the ambulance. I held Mamma's hand tightly. Once the paramedics had Papa safely into the rear of the ambulance they closed the door. One of them turned to us as the other headed for the driver's side. 'Make your own way to the hospital. And don't try and follow us as we'll be driving quickly.'

I nodded and ushered Mamma back into the house. She looked dazed, fussing around finding her handbag and her coat. 'He'll need a wash bag and pyjamas.'

I was tempted to tell her not to bother but I knew it was something that would stay on her mind, trouble her unnecessarily so I dashed upstairs. In the bathroom, I gathered a razor, some shaving gel and I heard my mother rifling through a cupboard. Underneath the sink, I found a wash bag and stuffed everything inside. She had come to a standstill, trying to choose a pair of pyjamas, so I grabbed the nearest and we went back downstairs. I pushed everything into a carrier bag from the kitchen and locked the door carefully behind us.

'He's been complaining about chest pains,' Mamma announced as we were halfway to the hospital.

'I noticed him the other day complaining about pins and needles in his arm.'

'I told him to see the doctor. All this stress hasn't been good for him.'

Papa had a business to run and Uncle Gino and Jez had got themselves involved with the Walsh family. I cursed silently. I was heading for the hospital in the certain knowledge Papa had had a heart attack. Martin Kendall and Jimmy Walsh were to blame.

I tightened my grip on the steering wheel and found my jaw clenching. I didn't want to look at Mamma; I couldn't bear to think what she was going through. Once we'd parked I took her arm as we walked over to the accident and emergency department where a riot seemed to be in progress. Children were running around the place thumping each other, kicking the furniture and screaming at the top of their voices, their mothers unable to keep control.

I stood by the reception desk asking if we could go see Papa. A nurse appeared moments later and ushered us to a small room. 'Would you like some tea?'

Mamma looked at her blankly.

'I'll get someone to bring you some tea. Someone will be along shortly to speak to you.'

Time dragged until a young doctor came bustling into the room. He spoke in a matter-of-fact tone. 'We think he's had a heart attack and that's why his heart stopped – the paramedics did an excellent job in restarting it. We're going to take him for an emergency procedure to open the blood vessel in his heart that's blocked, we'll then be moving him to intensive care overnight.'

My mouth felt too dry to say anything and then I heard Mamma's voice. 'Can we see him?'

'Yes, but only briefly I'm afraid as we're about to move him.'

It was a short walk through to a room with a bank of monitors and equipment with leads and tubes all leading to Papa. A machine was breathing for him. Nurses and doctors ignored us as they gathered equipment around Papa. A nurse beckoned us to his bedside and Mamma grasped

Papa's hand before a raised voice asked us to step aside. Then they whisked him down the corridor.

We sat and waited. There was activity all around us with the staff bustling to and fro, occasionally giving us a kindly smile. Mamma's mobile rang but she ignored it until I persuaded her to dig it out of her bag. She thrust it at me – Uncle Gino.

'We're at the hospital.'

'I just heard. It's terrible. How is he?' I gazed over at Papa, relieved by his regular breathing. 'The doctor says he's stable.'

'We'll be there. We're on our way.'

'There's no need. I'll call you if anything changes.'

Despite all our differences Papa was still Uncle Gino's brother, and it reminded me there was nothing stronger than a family bond. I was determined that Martin Kendall spent the rest of his life behind bars, preferably sharing a cell with Jimmy Walsh.

Another nurse arrived. 'A bed has been made available in the cardiac ward. I'll show you the way.' She led us through the corridors until we reached the right ward and she left us waiting until eventually they wheeled Papa into a space near a window and an orderly drew the curtain around him with a flourish. Mamma sat perched on one of the high-backed rigid plastic chairs.

Minutes stretched into hours. Afternoon changed into early evening.

A nurse bought Mamma a sandwich, which she didn't touch although she sipped on some tea. My stomach rumbled reminding me how hungry I felt. To my surprise I saw Jackie walking into the ward and it took me aback for a moment.

'I've just heard, John. I'm so sorry.'

Mamma gave Jackie a feeble smile.

'Dean is with my mother. I had a last-minute interview this afternoon for a job in the Bay.'

I found a chair and she sat talking with Mamma, finding the right words, the sort of words that escaped me. Sitting there with Jackie took me right back to months earlier when Dean had been hospitalised.

A nurse arrived and turned to me. 'I'm sure your father will be much better in the morning. You should go home and rest.' She fussed over Mamma, organising for her to stay the night in one of the family rooms.

I hugged Mamma. 'Call me if there's any change.'

She drew a hand over my cheek. 'Of course.' Outside the chill autumn evening had given way to persistent drizzle, the sort that soaks you to the skin without you realising it.

'Have you eaten?' I asked Jackie.

She shook her head. 'Fancy a takeaway?'

I ran to my car and followed Jackie to a takeaway restaurant she knew. It was an odd sensation watching Jackie organise our meal in the kitchen of her mother's house. She found two trays, heaped food onto two plates and we each took one through into the sitting room.

It was warm and comfortable and for the first time that day I relaxed as I listened to Jackie telling me about her interview, complaining about some of the questions one of the men had asked about her childcare arrangements. Jackie finished a bottle of German lager with the last of her curry.

'Has your father been under a lot of stress?'

I could see the sincerity from the warmth of her eyes.

'There are some problems with the property the family owns in Pontypridd.'

She moved towards me along the sofa and held my

arm. It sent a spasm of warm recognition through my body. 'I'm sure he's going to be fine.' She took her hand away but I wanted her to keep it there; it felt right, reassuring, consoling even. I caught her gaze. I touched her hand and our fingers intertwined and my heart started a familiar beat that years ago I recognised every time I looked at her.

I curled a hand around her face and pushed back the hair from her face.

'John, I ...'

Then I kissed her. Softly at first without the rawness of that first night years ago. Now, we were both older and maybe wiser. But the passion returned and soon hungry lips consumed each other and I fumbled with her blouse and reached to unfasten her bra. She unbuckled my belt and opened my fly but then she leant back.

'Do you really...?

'Of course.'

Chapter 34

A little after eight the following morning my mobile rang. I had already spoken to Mamma who sounded tired but relieved that Papa seemed out of danger. I sat eating a breakfast prepared by Jackie and it felt natural, as though the years of arguments and ill feeling had withered away.

'How's your father?' Wyn said.

'Over the worst.'

'I'm very pleased to hear it, sir. I've traced that final woman we spoke about yesterday. I've got an address in Abercynon. I thought as you were in Aberdare it might be on your way in.'

I glanced at Jackie. Wyn had obviously assumed I was staying with my mother. 'Send me the details. I'll meet you there in half an hour.'

Jackie held my embrace for a long time that morning. I left the house and headed north along the A470. From Wyn's directions I found the car park and waited until he arrived. I didn't have to wait long and he joined me in the car laboriously explaining how he had established the identities of all the women Yelland had dated. I listened, with a growing admiration for his ingenuity and resourcefulness. All this social media stuff had passed me by but it got me thinking that perhaps I was missing out.

We left the car and walked over to a block of flats. A glazed wooden entrance door badly needed several coats of paint. No intercom, just a bank of bell pushes with numbers.

'It's number six,' Wyn said.

I pushed the right button. We waited. It felt like several minutes had passed before a diminutive figure appeared in the hallway. She peered at us; we pressed our warrant cards to the glass and she frowned before opening the door.

'Florence Mulholland?' I said. 'Detective Inspector John Marco and Detective Constable Nuttall.'

'Yes. What do you want?'

'We need to speak to you about Brian Yelland. Can we come in?'

She hesitated but then pulled the door open.

Florence walked ahead of us up the stairs. She was short, with a high forehead and a thin, narrow mouth. I tried to guess her age, mid-thirties at least, with the air of a thwarted spinster.

The sitting room was comfortable and tidy with the occasional ornament. A television and a surround-sound system dominated one corner but there were no photographs of family or personal touches. It all felt sterile.

'I understand you had a relationship with Brian Yelland.'

Her bottom lip quivered. 'We met through an internet dating site.' She glanced over at me, daring me to look critical.

'How often did you meet him?' I studiously sought a neutral tone to my voice.

'I don't remember, exactly. A few times. We got on really well. I have had lots of dates through various sites and when I met Brian it was one of the more successful.'

She made it sound like choosing the right shade of paint for a domestic makeover.

'After a while I suspected things weren't right. He didn't seem keen.' She paused, looking down at her intertwined fingers. 'Things had developed quite quickly.' She looked up at me, the pain of sharing personal secrets with a stranger obvious.

'How much did you know about him?'

'I knew he was a prison officer. And he was having some disciplinary problems.'

'Were you aware he was attending Alcoholics Anonymous meetings?'

She flicked back some hair that had fallen over her face. 'Yes. And I knew he had problems with managing a gambling habit. But you see, Inspector, I thought I could help him. He was the first man for years who … paid me any attention. And my father had a gambling problem. I really did think I could help.'

'So what happened between you?'

'I suspected he was seeing somebody else. He cancelled a date and I was angry. So I went to his place.' She paused.

'Did you follow him?'

'Yes, he drove down into the middle of Cardiff and I followed him to this pub. It was an enormous old place. He didn't see me, he kept staring at the door and after a few minutes another man walked in. I saw them talking, the other man gave Brian an envelope.'

'Could you describe this man?'

'I can do better than that. I've got his photograph.'

Her disappointment seemed tempered by the discovery Yelland wasn't seeing another woman. Perhaps she had thought there was still a chance for her? She reached for her bag and fumbled through its contents. Expectation almost got the better of me; I was tempted to suggest she simply tip out the contents onto the coffee table. She pulled a mobile from the bottom and scrolled through the images.

She thrust it over at me. 'There, that's the man he was meeting. It all looks very underhand to me.'

I gazed at the image. My throat tightened and I let out a long shallow breath. 'Did you ever see him with this man again?'

She stared over at me and blinked. 'They met one

other time. They had a blazing argument.'

I handed the phone over to Wyn who looked at the image and opened his eyes wide.

I parked behind two marked police cars full of officers not even Martin Kendall would pick a fight with. It had all taken some planning and in the rush I had forgotten to call the hospital. So I rang Mamma, her reassurance Papa was improving assuaging my guilt that I had not been to see him.

A casual drive past his block of apartments in the marina in Penarth had confirmed Kendall's Porsche was parked in its reserved spot. After speaking to Florence we had established the exact date and time Yelland had met Kendall. Now it was time to get his explanation.

'Let's go,' I said, and I gave the instructions. Two officers joined me as I walked over to the entrance. At the top of the stairs to the first floor I paused, checking that the two officers were behind me. We strolled down the corridor and knocked on his door. I had been rehearsing what I would say to him since I had seen the images that morning. The door opened and he filled the space in front of me. 'Martin Kendall, I'm arresting you on suspicion of the murder of Brian Yelland.'

He shook his head scornfully and walked back into the flat, reaching for his coat. 'You're making a big mistake.' He reached over for his mobile. 'I'll call my solicitor.'

Kendall left a brief message and tossed the handset onto the coffee table. The two officers snapped on a pair of handcuffs and escorted Kendall downstairs. The custody sergeant was expecting me when I strolled into the custody suite.

'Glanville Tront has already arrived,' he said.

Martin Kendall and the Walsh family could afford

the best lawyers in Cardiff. I heard the familiar sound of Lydia's voice as she spoke with one of the uniformed officers.

Lydia raised a questioning eyebrow as I explained how I had justified Kendall's arrest. 'There could be a very good reason for both meetings.'

Now it was my turn to raise an eyebrow. 'Yelland was taking money from Kendall and Walsh. Perhaps he made one demand too many?'

We sat in the custody suite waiting for Glanville Tront to finish his discussion with Kendall. Lydia organised two rancid-looking coffees in thin plastic cups. A uniformed officer notified us that Glanville Tront and Martin Kendall were ready and we walked through into one of the other cork-lined interview rooms. A tape recorder sat on the table thrust against a wall. The smell of dead skin and old clothes hung in the air. Within five minutes my nostrils would become accustomed to the stale odour and my hearing familiar with the droning of the air conditioning.

Glanville Tront swept into the room. He had fine, thin, silvering hair grown in long strands drawn over his head. It gave him a bohemian appearance. Whenever I met him I recalled the first time he had cross-examined me – it had been a demeaning, unsettling experience that left me heading straight for the pub. Glanville wore an immaculate navy suit, white shirt and glistening pink silk tie.

Martin Kendall followed and both men sat down.

'Good to see you, Glanville.'

'Good afternoon to you too, Inspector. Let's get on with this.'

After we got the formalities completed, I stared over at Martin Kendall.

'Do you know Brian Yelland?'

'He was murdered recently.'

Good start, at least he was answering my questions.

'Did you know him?'

'Can't say that I did.'

'So you've never met him?'

'No.'

'Brian Yelland was a prison officer. And he was one of the officers responsible for the billet where Jimmy Walsh had his cell at Grange Hall.'

Kendall nodded. 'If you say so.'

'Can you tell me what your relationship is to Jimmy Walsh?'

'You know full well I work closely with Jimmy in his various businesses.'

'And what sort of businesses does he have?'

Glanville Tront interrupted. 'Do you *really* want a list of Mr Walsh's businesses?'

For the time being I didn't pursue my question.

I scanned the visitor log from Grange Hall. 'Can you confirm how often you went to see Jimmy Walsh at Grange Hall?'

'Quite a few times. We are mates.'

'Did Jimmy Walsh ever mention Brian Yelland?'

Kendall shook his head. 'Not that I remember.'

'I want to show you a photograph taken at the time you met Brian Yelland.'

I watched with undiluted pleasure the blood draining from his face. Even Glanville Tront made an odd sort of gurgling sound.

'The photograph was taken by Brian Yelland's girlfriend.' I pushed over a printed version of the photograph.

'Is that you?'

Glanville Tront reached for the photograph, peered at it and then leant over, whispering something in Kendall's ear.

'No comment.'

His Scottish accent couldn't hide the minute tremor in his voice.

'You handed him an envelope. A large Jiffy bag type envelope. Can you confirm what was inside?'

'Really, Inspector have we got to spend all afternoon talking about envelopes being passed in a public house,' Glanville purred.

I gave Glanville a patronising smile. 'Does your client wish to reply? I'm sure you advised him about the implications of not replying during this interview.'

Glanville parted his lips as though he wanted to reproach me but thought the better of it.

I continued, getting into my stride. 'A week before Jimmy Walsh's release you met Brian Yelland for a second time.' I pushed over a second photograph. By the lifeless colour of Kendall's lips I'd need to call the medics soon. 'You had a blazing row with Yelland that day. What did you argue about?'

'No comment.'

I looked straight over at Kendall and used my most reasonable voice. 'Now is your opportunity to explain why you lied to me about meeting Brian Yelland.'

Kendall folded his arms, drawing them closer to his body.

Glanville adjusted his tie and scribbled his notes obviously warming up for another interruption. 'Murder is a very serious offence. What possible motive is there?'

I ignored him.

'Is it true you were paying Brian Yelland in exchange for favours he could provide Jimmy Walsh with in prison?'

'No comment.'

'Brian Yelland got greedy. He wanted more money.

But you refused and when he threatened you and Jimmy Walsh, it was the final straw.'

'Really, Inspector. This is utter conjecture. You're making this up as you're going along. You have no motive. Please tell me which senior officer authorised my client's arrest.'

I could have cheerfully throttled Glanville Tront, using his expensive silk tie. But I didn't reply and gave him a businesslike nod that suggested I wasn't finished.

'On the night of Brian Yelland's death where were you?'

'No comment.'

I could see the anger bubbling up his eyes, in the way his shoulders seemed to swell. And I wanted to tell him never to approach Uncle Gino and my father or anybody else in our family ever again.

'A man was seen leaving Brian Yelland's home in the early hours. An eyewitness confirms the man had a prominent nose, rather like yours Mr Kendall. Although it was dark, there was enough street lighting.'

I leant on the desk, peered over at Kendall and watched his eyes darting around. His arms twitched. 'Why did you visit Brian Yelland on the night he was killed?'

'Fuck off.'

I steepled my arms and propped my chin on both hands. 'Did you kill Brian Yelland?'

Chapter 35

Lydia sat next to me, in the reception at the production company's offices in West London, tapping out a message on her mobile telephone, something she had done a lot of on the journey from Cardiff that morning. The reception was full of well-watered indoor plants that glistened under the artificial lights. Marble lined the floor and the sound of muffled conversation spun around the stairwell that curved its way to the upper floors.

I stared over at the girls on reception.

One of them looked similar to Tracy. Tracy and I had spoken tentatively yesterday, and I had made excuses about visiting my father when she had suggested we meet for dinner. By early evening I had left the hospital. Papa was still breathing with an oxygen mask and more colour had returned to his cheeks. Mamma seemed more settled and some friends had arrived and fussed over him so I had left.

I should have gone home but I had headed to the Incident Room.

I had sat staring at photographs of Jimmy Walsh and Martin Kendall.

My unbridled abhorrence for both men was replaced by a determination that nothing would stand in my way of seeing them both spend the rest of their lives behind bars. Kendall's detention meant he was languishing in the cells and the chances he'd make bail were zero, knowing the attitude of the district judge in the magistrates' court to a person facing a murder charge.

The sound of someone calling my name interrupted my thoughts. It also interrupted Lydia's texting. A woman with long hair down her back waved over at us. 'They'll see you now.'

We followed her and stopped by a door that

needed a security code. She tapped it in and led us through various corridors, the air conditioning cool against my skin. She pushed open the door with *Editing Suite* in large letters on a stainless steel notice and pointed towards two men sitting by a long table in front of three large monitors.

Both men wore faded and expensive-looking denims. 'Stephen Gate,' the older man said. He had more hair than his colleague but both had three days' worth of stubble. 'And this is Justin Leigh.' After the usual pleasantries, we sat down.

'I appreciate information was given to the police that filming had stopped by six.' Leigh had a broad West Country accent. 'It was a filthy day. We knew the forecast was for rain but the producer continued. We got a lot of filming done in the afternoon and there was a break.'

Another woman walked in with a tray of coffee and fancy-looking pastries.

'I am interested in any filming that took place after six pm,' I said.

Gate replied. 'Of course, of course. Justin was giving you some background.'

It sounded like an excuse but I let it pass.

'We've put together all the filming recorded that day. As you can appreciate there is a lot. I'm not certain where you want to start. There were half a dozen cameras. When we're filming something like *Doctor Who* we shoot hours and hours of material that might never be used.'

I knew from my checking the night before that Ben Evans had told us he left before ten pm. 'When did you actually finish?'

Gate glanced over at Leigh. 'It was near eleven o'clock actually. The rain had abated so the producer continued. We were working to some tight deadlines.'

'It still doesn't explain why you misled us,' I said

flatly. 'You do realise a man has been killed.'

Gate blinked, Leigh swallowed self-consciously.

'I want to work back for each camera from eleven o'clock.'

'We had better get started then,' Gate said.

Leigh went over to the second monitor and adjusted the screen so that Lydia could watch the coverage with him. Gate did likewise and for the next two hours we sat watching various clips of scenes that would never make it onto the screen. Gate explained that each minute of a finished programme meant hours of recordings. This was turning into a very long day.

He clarified each camera angle and explained how a recording like this was organised. By lunchtime, we had watched the recordings from three of the cameras from eleven pm to seven pm. I couldn't see Jimmy Walsh and Kendall taking the risk of being in Roath Park much earlier.

The same woman returned with sandwiches and bottles of sparkling water.

We ate as we watched the disjointed coverage. My back was aching, so I stood up and stretched.

Gate was staring at his screen when more tea and coffee arrived. 'A camera crew was sent around the opposite side of the lake.'

'What, nearer the café?' I said, sitting down and pulling my chair nearer to the table.

Gate glanced at his watch. 'The production assistant will be back later this afternoon, but she told me she was hoping to get some shots across the lake, something atmospheric. Is this something you want to see?'

I stared at the screen. 'I want to see everything.'

The camera panned across, taking in the Scott Memorial before zooming in towards the opposite bank.

'I don't know why she did this. It is a complete

waste of time.' Gate let the coverage run on until eventually the camera seemed to jump up and down. 'Obviously she's not stopped filming,' he said, clicking the forward button, running the film on quickly.

And then suddenly something flashed across the screen.

'You've missed something.' After a morning of watching disjointed video clips my pulse accelerated.

Gate made the necessary adjustments.

'Run it after the recording of the Captain Scott Memorial,' I said. 'And can you slow down?'

Lydia and Leigh had stopped watching their screen and Lydia had moved her chair so she could sit behind me.

I peered at the monitor. I could see the drizzle hanging in the branches of the trees, the camera dancing around. Then I saw the outline of three men. 'Stop,' I shouted.

Gate paused the coverage and we stared at three ghostly silhouettes.

'Can we enhance those images somehow?' I stared at the screen again.

'I'll see what I can do,' Gate replied.

He clicked and fiddled with various controls until a grainy image emerged of the three men.

'That's Felix Bevard,' Lydia said behind me.

I stared at the image. Even a poor-quality image like this couldn't hide the swagger of the man next to Bevard. Jimmy Walsh's swagger. And between him and Felix Bevard the outline of a man with a ponytail was clear enough. Jack Ledley. It meant he was inextricably linked to the original murder of Robin Oakley. I wondered if he really had been prepared to give evidence against Walsh. Ledley had seen Bevard on his last afternoon so if Ledley was working for Walsh he could be another suspect.

My mind spun into overdrive as I thought about the fake police officers in Pontypool, and if Walsh was looking for Ledley then it wasn't to buy him a round of drinks. It meant that Ledley was his next victim. And it meant we had to find Ledley first.

Desmond Joplin, the Crown Prosecutor, ran a hand over his bald patch for the tenth time that evening. Alongside him by the conference table Acting Detective Chief Inspector Hobbs alternated a pained expression of alarm with confusion. He was out of his depth. This was past his pay grade.

'We've got direct evidence Jimmy Walsh's alibi is suspect,' I turned to look at Hobbs.

I knew he had been the sergeant on the Oakley case. It meant someone hadn't done a thorough job. It meant fingers would wag. It meant blame was to be apportioned. The confusion in his eyes turned to a scheming edge I had seen so often when he drew on his Teflon suit.

'Let's run through this again,' Desmond said.

'We know Walsh could have left the restaurant and travelled to Roath Park. He could have been there and back within half an hour. The restaurant was packed with guests. We spoke to a staff member whose evidence wasn't taken at the time.' I glanced over at Hobbs and raised a critical eye brow. 'He remembers quite specifically Bryant, one of Jimmy Walsh's associates, hadn't arrived until much later in the evening. And it was Bryant's evidence that strengthened Walsh's alibi.'

'I see,' Desmond said. 'It looks as though the original investigation wasn't as thorough as it might have been.'

Sharpening the knife, excellent.

I nodded sagely.

'We know Bevard was going to give direct evidence against Walsh.' I dipped my head towards the computer screen of the laptop on the table. 'This is it.'

'So who is the third man in these images?'

'It's Jack Ledley. And he's the man Bevard met the afternoon he was killed. DI Ackroyd from the dedicated source unit was aware of Ledley. It was possible he would be a supergrass witness as well.'

'None of this implicates Martin Kendall?' Hobbs managed a mean edge to his voice. But he wasn't going to deflect me that easily. He knew the original Oakley enquiry was a mess and I was picking up the pieces.

'Martin Kendall was up to his neck in it, no doubt about it. Let me remind you, sir, it was a routine search of one of Bevard's taxis that found traces of Oakley's blood. If the original investigating team had viewed all the filming we might already have Walsh behind bars.'

Hobbs sulked back into a guilty silence.

Desmond interrupted. 'How far did the dedicated source unit get with Jack Ledley?'

'Not far at all.'

'Do we know how to contact him?'

'There's a team looking for him now.'

'Really?' Desmond sounded surprised.

'And there are others posing as police officers looking for him as well.'

Desmond and Hobbs gaped at me together, realising another life was at stake.

'I'll increase the resources available to track down Jack Ledley. We need to identify whether he will give evidence against Walsh,' Hobbs said.

Hobbs and I turned to Joplin who replied after a brief pause. 'I originally reviewed all the evidence in the

Oakley case. It was all most frustrating. Everything pointed to Jimmy Walsh. As I recall Martin Kendall was a most unpleasant character.'

My enthusiasm got the better of me. 'This video is a game changer. We need to arrest and charge Walsh. And we arrest Bryant for perverting the course of justice. We arrest them both, then interview them separately. And then refuse bail.'

I could imagine the reception Jimmy Walsh would get from the custody sergeant and especially from the prison officers.

'Let me review all the evidence again.' Desmond said. 'But you still have the murder of Felix Bevard unsolved.'

I didn't reply.

'Is it possible Kendall killed them? Shot them on orders from Jimmy Walsh?'

'Kendall has a solid alibi for the Bevard murder.'

'Has it been *thoroughly* checked?' He shot a glance at Hobbs who looked very uncomfortable.

'We've taken it apart. And Mrs Walsh had an alibi too. Both carefully planned.'

'Then there is someone else, perhaps a contract killer from outside the area. I know it sounds dramatic but it's not unheard of. I'll call you later, Inspector,' Desmond said.

I closed the laptop and left. The possibility that some professional assassin had killed Felix Bevard was an option I wanted to ignore. It meant we might never find the killer and more importantly Jimmy Walsh might escape justice.

By ten that evening I left and drove home, despairing that Desmond Joplin was taking his time making a decision. I had a ready meal from the freezer and ate without enthusiasm, flicking through the channels on my television.

It was midnight when my telephone rang. 'Desmond Joplin, Inspector. I've authorised an arrest.'

I whooped with delight and punched the air with my fist.

Chapter 36

I returned to the custody suite, relishing the opportunity of confronting Jimmy Walsh. His appearance was very different from the regulation prison clothes he wore for our first meeting. His hair had been neatly trimmed and there was a faint tang of lemon and pine from his cologne. He turned a manicured finger around the gold cufflinks of his double-cuff shirts. The combined value of the bespoke suits worn by Walsh and Glanville Tront, together with the enormous chronograph watches hanging on their wrists, would have amounted to a deposit for a flat in the Bay.

As I tore open the cellophane packaging of the interview tapes Glanville pulled a fountain pen from inside his jacket, one of the expensive varieties with a mottled body. Coffee in white plastic cups sat on the table but Glanville and Jimmy preferred to sip from small bottles of San Pellegrino.

Once I had organised the formalities I pressed the switch on the tape recorder.

I looked up at Jimmy. I had evidence, now I had something concrete. And my eagerness to challenge him meant my heart rate was off the scale.

'One of my colleagues interviewed you several years ago about the murder of Robin Oakley in Roath Park.' I paused; it wasn't a question but I half expected a reaction. I didn't get one. 'You were arrested as a suspect. Do you remember being interviewed?'

'Of course.'

No point in denying the obvious. At least Glanville had told him to cooperate.

'At the time my colleague Detective Inspector Webster asked you to confirm your whereabouts for the night Mr Oakley was killed. Is it correct you told the officer you had been in an Italian restaurant all evening?'

'Yeah, I seem to remember being at a party. A place off Albany Road, nice Italian restaurant with a disco and lots of grub.'

'The party was very busy.'

Glanville interjected. 'And what is your question, Inspector?'

'Did you leave the restaurant at any time?'

'I've got an alibi. I was there all night, you know that.'

'Of course, Philip Bryant.' Lydia had Bryant's original statement. 'Philip Bryant confirmed he recalls you being there throughout the evening. Were you sitting with him all night?'

'I don't remember.'

'You must have mingled, spoken to the other guests. Did you step outside for a cigarette? It's difficult to believe Philip Bryant would have seen you for every minute of every hour.'

'Are we going to go over what was discussed all those years ago?' Glanville managed an inquisitorial edge to his voice. 'Because it seems to me unless you have something new this interview is a *complete* waste of time.'

I was sorely tempted to butt in and tell Glanville I would conduct the interview however I wanted. I gave Lydia an encouraging nod to continue.

'So, Mr Walsh can you confirm whether you left the restaurant any time?'

Jimmy let out an exasperated sigh. 'I was there all night. How often do I have to tell you people the same thing.'

'What time did you arrive?'

'It was early.'

'But was it between six and six-thirty?'

He shrugged.

'Between six-thirty and seven?'

Another shrug.

'And when did Philip Bryant arrive?'

'He was there when I arrived.'

Lydia replaced the statement on the table. I saw the exhilaration in her eyes at the casual lie from Walsh.

I spent half an hour, much to the irritation of Walsh and Glanville, getting Walsh to confirm the details he had provided in his original statement. The truth is easy, lying is difficult: it needs a good memory to recall every detail of the falsehood. Glanville occasionally interrupted, making certain Walsh felt he was getting value for money. Eventually he butted in. 'I really do think this has gone on long enough, Inspector.'

And I still had the photographs from the *Doctor Who* production company.

'I want to be absolutely clear. Did you go to Roath Park on the evening Robin Oakley was killed?'

'I think Mr Walsh has dealt with that.' Glanville made the whole thing sound very tiresome.

'I was in the La Scala all night.'

I pulled the photograph from underneath the file of papers in front of me. I glanced at them and then up at Jimmy. For the first time there was a genuinely worried frown on his face and glee swept through my body. Glanville maintained a businesslike approach by tapping his fountain pen on the papers.

'Can you take a look at this photograph?' I pushed it over the table at Jimmy.

I was trying to keep my breathing flat, but my pulse hammered in my neck. I could hear it in my ears. Glanville moved nearer to Jimmy, staring at the photograph.

'It's quite grainy,' Glanville said. 'Where was it

taken?'

I kept my voice low but firm. 'I believe this is you in the picture. You're the man at the end.'

'Once again, Inspector. Where was this photograph taken?'

I ignored Glanville, and stared straight at Jimmy. I could see the recognition on his face. Now he knew I had evidence. Evidence enough to charge. Fear perspired from every pore on his face.

'Jimmy, can you tell me if this is you?'

Glanville leant over, and whispered something in his ear.

'No comment.'

'This photograph was taken by a camera in Roath Park on the night Robin Oakley was killed. It is a photograph of you and two accomplices.'

Jimmy Walsh folded his arms tightly and closed his eyes. He then opened them and stared at me unblinkingly. His silence was as good as an admission. My pulse slowed but the exhilaration built with the certainty of his guilt and that I had enough evidence to prove it.

The inside of a magistrates' court must be the same all over the country: a dock where the defendants stand, with stairs leading to the cells downstairs, a raised area where the judge sits and below him or her, a court clerk. Normally the seats reserved for the press would have been empty but that afternoon the press were out in force, every seat taken. I recognised the regular reporters from the television news programmes.

Bernie Walsh sat at the back, her clothes immaculate and the make-up millimetre perfect. The girl sitting by her side must have been her daughter as the resemblance was unmistakable. Next to her was a man in a suit who I guessed was David Shaw from Goldstar Properties.

'Nobody here to hold Martin Kendall's hand?' Lydia whispered.

We sat in seats reserved for police officers. The court usher, a former constable I knew from years ago, sat at the end of our row.

'He doesn't have any family.'

Glanville Tront swept into the courtroom wearing a sombre red pinstripe suit, a cutaway collar shirt and a tie knotted flamboyantly. He ignored me, but then I hadn't exactly expected him to shake me by the hand. He exchanged pleasantries with Desmond Joplin who looked rather shabby alongside him. Who says crime doesn't pay?

I had attended court many times in the past but that afternoon lifted my spirits. My elation at the prospect of Walsh being remanded in custody was tempered by the knowledge we had no evidence to link Walsh to the murder of Bevard. It must have been the same frustration Detective Chief Inspector Webster felt when he knew Walsh had killed Oakley but had no evidence. If only his team had been more competent … and as I held that thought, Dave Hobbs walked in and sat next to Lydia. He nodded, I nodded back.

Walsh appeared in the dock flanked by two security guards. Glanville scurried over. There were angry pouts, jabbing fingers and Glanville's palm being waved, calming Walsh's temper.

We stood up as the district judge entered. He surveyed the packed courtroom, a brief smile passing his lips. Desmond was the first to his feet once the court clerk had read out the various formalities. Despite everything, I felt nervous. Once we had decided to prosecute there was no going back, we had to trust the system. Desmond laboured his objection to bail, reminding the judge that murder was the most serious offence. Then it was Glanville's turn. He performed at his most theatrical best, challenging the logic of the prosecution's case, emphasising Jimmy had strong family ties, was a successful businessman and pointed out that the case was based on a grainy, indistinct and unconvincing photograph. Even I felt queasy once he'd finished.

As the district judge announced his decision to deny bail I wanted to slump back in my seat, to shout with delight, dance on the spot. Walsh disappeared back into the safe environment of the cells at the court building.

Lydia looked pleased; it was another step towards making certain Walsh and Kendall were behind bars. Hobbs leant forward, attracting my attention. 'Good result. Keep me posted with the forensics results from Kendall's property.' Then he left. I followed Lydia out of the court building and we headed towards Queen Street. Our success called for a celebration and years ago it would have meant hours touring the pubs favoured by the detectives of Southern Division where the publicans turned a blind eye to our indiscretions.

'Call Wyn and Jane and tell them to meet us at Lefties.'

Lydia smiled, one of those warm contented curl of her lips, as she found her mobile and relayed a message to the Incident Room. Alex Leftrowski had left Russia for a better life in the West and when I first knew him, he regularly reminded me how lucky he was to live in Cardiff. It had usually been when I was staring at the bottom of an empty glass of beer, my eyes floating in various directions and my brain unconnected. Since those early days the bar had broadened its appeal, away from the hardened drinkers to fashionable sofas and an expensive Italian coffee machine.

'John Marco,' Alex said as though it had been yesterday when we last met. 'It good to see you after much time.'

'How are the boys, Alex?' Both his sons were his pride and joy, his reason for working twelve-hour days.

'They are growing big. Too big. You look happy. Do you want to celebrate? No champagne for you.' I accepted the good-natured reproach with a smile. I ordered for Lydia and me, telling Alex to expect two more. Wyn and Jane must have run over from Queen Street in their eagerness because they arrived in time for me to order on their behalf. When I returned to the sofa Lydia had started giving Wyn and Jane a detailed account of what happened in court.

'Thanks boss,' Wyn said, reaching for his pint glass. Jane had a tall glass with a white wine spritzer, which she tipped towards me in thanks. Lydia had been particular about the variety of continental lager she enjoyed and I left the half-empty bottle on the tray as reassurance. My bottled water looked lonely by comparison.

'Well done everyone,' I said.

Wyn relaxed after two large mouthfuls of his beer. 'Forensics are going through Kendall's property. Hopefully there will be evidence we can use. He had every video box set imaginable, *Breaking Bad*, *The Sopranos* and all the *Godfather* films.'

Jane looked surprised by Wyn's loquaciousness.

'And Alvine will go through all the evidence from the Robin Oakley inquiry,' Wyn continued.

'You should have seen the look on Walsh's face,' Lydia said, her voice deadly serious.

It stunned us all into a momentary silence until I replied. 'Well, he'll have an even longer face by the end of tonight once he's been processed in Cardiff jail.'

I no longer needed alcohol to help me relax. The comfort of knowing Martin Kendall and Jimmy Walsh were safely behind bars was reassurance enough. As Wyn drank more Brains best bitter he even cracked the occasional joke. I saw a new side to Jane who dropped the jaded, tired-of-life halo with simple small talk.

Two hours flew by before we left the bar.

It was a cloudless night and for once I noticed the stars.

Chapter 37

When I sat in the Incident Room gazing up at the fuzzy image of Jack Ledley the euphoria from the night before seemed a distant memory. He was a direct link to Jimmy Walsh's presence in Roath Park the night Bevard was killed. Years of policing allowed a dark veil of uncertainty to drag itself across my mind as I considered the strength of the evidence against Walsh. It reinforced the need to trace Jack Ledley. And now Walsh knew we had the video evidence it made it all the more imperative for him to find Ledley first. After all, if Ledley did become a supergrass then Walsh really was facing the rest of his life behind bars.

The sound of muffled conversation on the stairwell beyond the door broke my concentration and I turned and saw Lydia sharing a joke with Jane. They each gave me a smile of acknowledgement.

'Morning, boss,' Lydia said, shrugging off a thick fleece.

Jane perched a tall takeaway coffee beaker on her desk, and tossed her bag under it.

'We've got the uniformed officers who led the search teams in Pontypool arriving soon,' Lydia said, looking at her watch.

The computers on their desks hummed into life. The monitors flickered as Wyn entered the Incident Room. 'Did you see the news last night? I've never seen so much coverage.'

'It was only the preliminary remand hearing.' I wanted to sound authoritative but I could hear the earlier uncertainty creeping into my voice.

Before anyone could reply two uniformed officers barged into the Incident Room. The older one's shaven head glistened in the artificial light and the younger had a close-trimmed short back and sides. I waved them towards two chairs. They sat down, placed hands on their knees and clenched their jaws.

'Bring us up to date.' I couldn't remember the names of either officer so I spoke to the room. Luckily, Lydia saved my embarrassment.

'Constable Williams led the team that searched the northern part of the town, sir.' She nodded at the bald officer who adjusted his position on the plastic office chair.

He took his cue. 'We went into every shop and pub and bed and breakfast. But we couldn't find anyone who had seen anyone resembling either Bevard or Ledley.'

'How many hours have you put into this search so far?' I could hear the bean counters in headquarters squealing in pain at the overtime. Thankfully, it would be Acting Detective Chief Inspector Hobbs's problem.

He shook his head slowly. 'A lot, sir, and I've had some of the officers' team leaders complaining they need them back.'

With police resources scarce and the public demanding value for money, I didn't blame them. Constable Barclay, who had led the second team, had a similar story. Standing by the board he gave us a guided tour of the town as he glided a hand over the map. We listened for an hour as the officers gave us the details of where they had searched and who they had spoken to. Several of their team had spoken to the same people more than once and a local councillor had grilled two officers about the inquiry. I made a mental note to email Dave Hobbs warning him to tell the public relations department they could expect some disgruntled politicians complaining police time wasn't being utilised effectively.

'How much longer do you want us to search, sir?' Barclay returned to his seat.

Now it was my turn to step towards the board.

I gazed at the map. Pontypool was one of the many post-industrial towns in the eastern valleys still suffering from the recession before last. I stuffed my hands into the pockets of my trousers and pondered.

Barclay continued. 'It could take us days, maybe even weeks, to find him and we don't even know for certain he's there.'

The look of ice-cold anger on Walsh's face when he was taken down into the cell at the magistrates' court came to mind. Bernie Walsh would have instructions to find Ledley. She'd have the same person tracking him down that killed Bevard and the reality that I had no idea who was responsible filled me with a sick feeling. I looked over at the photograph of Norcross. I couldn't ignore his long association with Walsh. I recalled our interview at the start of the inquiry when he denied any involvement in killing Bevard: he needed to be watched. Perhaps I could get Hobbs to authorise a surveillance team. I bowed my head for a moment, anticipating how he might react.

'We carry on. A man's life is at risk. At least we know Jimmy Walsh is out of the way so that might make it harder for Bernie Walsh to find Ledley.'

I scanned the team in front of me and read on their faces their determination and agreement with my decision. Other policing priorities would have to wait.

'I'll be up there later today.'

I mentally calculated when I might arrive once I had seen my father in hospital. I left Williams and Barclay to finalise the details with Lydia and strode back to my office already composing the emails to Dave Hobbs and the public relations department.

Papa was sitting up in bed when I arrived and Mamma sat on the tall visitor chair by his side. She beamed when she saw me. I found a chair and sat down.

'We've been told Papa can go home,' she said as though he wasn't there.

Papa rolled his eyes. He still looked pale and I stared over at him. His cheeks were more sunken and the skin around his mouth was tight. I wanted to say – *are they sure?* Instead, I smiled and said, 'That's great news. Is there going to be any follow-up treatment?'

'He needs to take things easy for a few weeks.' I could see her relishing the possibility of having him home where she could keep an eye on him. 'Then he has to start some exercise – walking and swimming is good.'

A few weeks at home would drive Papa mad, and what would happen to the business in the meantime? There was a resigned look on his face that implied he was agreeing to humour his wife for now.

Small talk filled another twenty minutes before an agitation gnawed at my mind that I needed to be in Pontypool.

'Hello, John.'

I recognised Jackie's voice immediately.

I stood up and kissed her briefly on the cheek. This time I lingered. Her perfume was delicate, full of warmth; it reminded me of our recent night together. As I went to find another chair, I noticed the grin on my mother's face.

'I had the second interview this morning, John.' She sat down and gave my mother a smile of acknowledgement. 'I start next month.'

'That's good news,' I said.

'Congratulations,' Papa said.

Jackie turned to me. 'I heard all about that man Walsh on the TV. Does it mean the case is over?'

I glanced at my parents in turn, knowing the answer they wanted to hear.

'Of course.' I hoped I sounded convincing. Then I wondered if Lydia, Williams, and Barclay were making progress.

An odd uncomfortable feeling overcame me as we sat there discussing hospital food and the television from the night before. Jackie was my ex and although we appeared to have rekindled something I wasn't certain if I wanted it to. Mamma certainly did but she had never really liked Tracy. 'I need to get back to work.'

Mamma smiled again. 'Papa will be discharged tomorrow, John.'

'I'll call tomorrow night.'

Jackie got up too. 'I'll walk out with you. I've got to drive back to Basingstoke today.'

We walked out of the ward and headed for the lifts. 'John.' Jackie touched my arm. 'I wanted to tell you that it was really special the other night.'

We reached the open landing by the lifts where visitors were waiting.

There was a fondness in her eyes I hadn't seen for years. It made me wonder what I had missed in those wasted years when I spoke to the bottom of a pint glass more often than to her. A message arrived on my mobile as I wondered how to reply.

Get back to QS – Walsh has been released.

Chapter 38

'What the fuck happened?'

I grasped the top of the chair tightly. Desmond Joplin sat opposite me at the conference table, avoiding my gaze. Hobbs balled his fingers into a tight fist. As he sat down he waved me to a chair but I couldn't sit so I paced around the room.

Joplin gave a dry cough and then cleared his throat. 'A judge released him on bail. Walsh's lawyers argued that the quality of the recording was so poor it could not be relied upon.'

My mind raced. Only a circuit judge could have considered an appeal from the district judge in the magistrates' court.

'Who was the judge?'

'Does it matter?' Hobbs said.

'It was one of those part-time judges.' Desmond sounded despondent. 'Walsh's lawyers managed to get him to hear their appeal because he was finalising something else in court this morning.'

'He needs to be taken out and shot.' Both men looked up at me startled. 'You know what I mean … This is so wrong.'

I stood by the window and stared out into the dull grey afternoon. Forecasters promised rain later and in the last week the temperatures had dropped a few degrees. Soon enough the investigation was going to get much colder too. 'Walsh killed Oakley – no doubt.'

'We know that, John.' Hobbs managed to sound supportive.

'And he was responsible for the death of Bevard …'

Joplin piped up. 'But there is no evidence.'

The sky darkened and the first drops of rain fell.

'Walsh is subject to a night-time curfew,' Joplin said. It sounded conciliatory.

'It means he has all day, every day to find Ledley.'

I walked over to the table and stared over at Hobbs. 'I'll need another team of officers for the search in Pontypool. And a team keeping tabs on Walsh.'

Hobbs parted his lips but said nothing, realising his contribution would be unwelcome.

'And a team following Norcross.' I didn't wait for Hobbs to object and I left.

Lydia, Jane and Wyn all stood up when I entered the Incident Room and gave me troubled looks.

I marched over to the board. 'I've got more officers for the Pontypool search.'

There were grudging nods of approval. 'We need to find Ledley.'

I listened as Wyn recounted his exploration into Ledley's family background. It had been a fruitless search so far. We knew he had been born in Lowestoft on the east coast of England but then nobody knew why he had arrived in Cardiff. Wyn had called the police in the Suffolk town and they'd reported that he had no family there and nothing was known about him.

'What brought him to Cardiff?' I said.

Nobody answered.

'Lydia, you're with me – let's go back to Pontypool.' I looked over at Wyn and Jane again. 'I need you both to be going over everything about Ledley. If he's a likely supergrass then Bevard's death has got to be the biggest motivation possible for him to come forward and implicate Walsh.'

I reached for my car keys, found my jacket and headed out for Pontypool.

Lydia settled into the passenger seat but although it

was her turn to choose a CD she must have realised it wasn't the time for opera. I powered the car along Newport Road and on towards the motorway.

On the motorway, I switched on the police lights and accelerated into the outside lane. Traffic cleared out of our way and soon I reached the junction for Cwmbran. I indicated left and as we slowed for the increasing traffic, my impatience grew. The journey along the A4042 dragged. Lydia commented about the vagaries of the judicial system but I said little. Eventually I pulled into the car park of the police station in Pontypool and we hurried into a conference room. I recognised Williams and Barclay but none of the dozen or so others were standing around the room. They stiffened from their relaxed postures as I strode in. A map with large circles drawn on various parts had been pinned to the board against a wall with an image of Ledley pinned to one side.

'The original teams are still out there,' Williams said. 'There is a new team of lads from Eastern Division. And there might be more arriving later.'

The young faces in front of me looked to be straight out of the training academy.

'We're looking for a man called Jack Ledley.' I pointed at his image. 'He's a person of special interest in an ongoing murder inquiry.' Several intense stares bored into me. 'His life is at risk and we need to find him.' I turned to Lydia and she gave me a photograph of Jimmy Walsh. I pinned it under the image of Ledley. 'And if you see Jimmy Walsh around call me at once. He is dangerous. And if anyone tells you that someone else has been asking for Ledley then call me.'

There was nervous blinking now and clenching of jaw muscles. Once the officers left I walked outside and put a cigarette to my lips. The police station in Pontypool had survived the modernisation programme of the Wales Police Service and I guessed that it was a political decision more than operational imperatives from the cramped and old-fashioned premises I had seen that morning.

Smoke scoured my windpipe and I pulled my jacket collar nearer my face. Winter was around the corner but for now I could still smoke outside. The citizens of Pontypool paid me little attention as they wandered past the police station. A pair of elderly women were deep in conversation outside a charity shop and several men walked past me with dogs on leashes. I ground the butt of the cigarette under my shoe and walked back inside.

Lydia was alone now in the conference room making notes and staring at the board. 'I think we might extend the scope of the search. We've been focusing on Pontypool because Bevard bought stuff in that shop. But we could extend the search south to Griffithstown.'

'How far do we go? We'll have reached Cwmbran and then Newport before we know it.'

We stared in silence at the settlements marked on the map knowing that Ledley was sitting somewhere watching the television or reading the newspaper. 'I need to see these places.'

'There are teams all over the town,' Lydia said. 'I don't think that we could add anything.'

She was right but I wanted to be on the ground banging on doors.

My mobile rang: I snatched at the handset. It was an unfamiliar number. 'Detective Inspector Marco. Area control. Your mother has been involved in a road traffic accident.'

Chapter 39

The satnav offered me two routes to Nantgarw where Mamma had crashed. Instinct made me choose the longer route that skirted to the south of Caerphilly rather than retracing my route to the motorway and its jams. Half an hour later I pulled up near a marked police car parked behind Mamma's Ford Focus.

In front of it was an ambulance and I saw her sitting inside, a blanket wrapped around her shoulders.

'We called an ambulance, sir,' the road traffic officer said once I'd carded him. 'But I don't think she's hurt.'

I strode over to the paramedics and Mamma's face lit up when she saw me.

'John, it all happened so fast.'

'Your mother should be seen by a doctor,' a green-cladded paramedic said.

Mamma shook her head. 'No hospital.'

'It really would be for the best ...'

'I need to speak to John.'

The paramedic left us alone.

'The black van followed me,' she whispered.

An icy finger ran up my spine.

'It followed me from the hospital. How did they know where I was, John?'

'I ...'

'It got very close so I pulled off the road. I wasn't driving fast.'

'Did you see any of the men inside?'

'It all happened so quickly.'

She pulled the blanket closer to her face. 'He started to bump the car.'

I scarcely believed what she was telling me.

'The van hit me lots of times. Back and forth. I was really frightened. Then he pulled away and he overtook me and made me stop. He was in front of me and I was scared. He came over to the car.'

'He started shouting.'

'What did he say?'

'That we had once last chance to sell. Friday, he kept saying that Friday was the end of it.'

I grasped her hand.

'Can you describe the man?'

She shook her head. 'He was wearing a mask.'

'I think you should go to the hospital – get them to check you out.'

She shook her head again. 'Papa is coming home tomorrow.'

I jumped out of the ambulance and spoke to one of the paramedics. 'She wants to go home.'

He started to protest but I raised a hand. 'I'll make certain she sees a doctor.'

I turned to the traffic officer standing by his patrol car. 'I'm calling a CSI team. I need the car examined so stay here until they arrive.'

The ambulance drove off, heading for Aberdare and my parents' home. I sat in my car dictating specific instructions for Alvine Dix. She mumbled a complaint about it being late and that her shift was finishing soon and did I know what the overtime bill had been like last month. My patience finally snapped. 'It's my mother, for Christ's sake. Just do it. Now.'

I tossed the mobile into the passenger seat and drove after the ambulance. I pulled onto the drive as one of the paramedics helped Mamma into the house. She looked relieved to see me as she flopped onto the sofa. After the paramedics left I made coffee but when I returned to the living room she was fast asleep.

I called one of my parents' neighbours who came round immediately. Jan East had been friends with Mamma for over twenty years and listened with open-mouthed disbelief as I gave her a redacted version of the hit-and-run.

'I'll be back later and in the meantime any problems give me a call.'

I left the house. My anger with Walsh was turning into something much darker. I drove down into Cardiff. I clenched my fingers around the steering wheel and powered the car on to Cyncoed.

I pulled in by the kerb and looked over at The Glades.

It was pathetically unimaginative name for a house.

Walsh's Range Rover Sport was parked next to a BMW Series 4 coupe. I thought of my father, and the image of my mother sitting in the ambulance came to mind. I had no choice. I got out of the car and marched over the road.

Jimmy Walsh emerged from the house with an empty bottle of champagne and walked towards the rear of his double garage. He hadn't seen me until I almost reached the tailgate of his 4x4. My blood was already at boiling point.

'Stay the fuck away from my family, Jimmy.'

He stopped in his tracks and looked over at me, a narrow grin creasing his face. I stepped towards him.

'This is private property.'

'I know what you did to my mother, you bastard. And if you ever—'

'And what are you going to do, John Marco? Fuck all, that's what.'

'There'll be evidence.'

'Like the evidence you've got for the Bevard case? Nothing, that's what you've got. And as for that pathetic film. Well Glanville thinks we'll have it thrown out before you even get to court.'

He took two quick paces towards me and he jabbed the bottle in my direction. 'Now this is private property. You're trespassing.'

I clenched my fists. I could almost touch him.

'If you ever go near my mother again—'

'Fuck off policeman. This is private property.'

I seriously contemplated launching myself at him. And kicking the shit out of him. There were no witnesses in the drive, but Bernie Walsh was probably inside, an empty champagne glass in hand waiting for a refill. I unclenched my fist. I had to make it legal. I had to make certain he went down for the rest of his days. I could see now why the senior management of the WPS wanted him convicted so badly.

I backed away and retreated down the drive.

'Next time I'll report you.' Walsh shouted after me.

I got back to my car, the sweat dripping down from my armpits. I tapped the steering wheel with a clenched fist and sat there for a few minutes. By now, the curfew restrictions had started and not even Walsh would venture outside. In the morning, a team would follow his every movement. My mouth felt dry and exhaustion swept over me.

It was an odd sensation waking up in my parents' home in the room I had used as a child. The curtains were the same although the wallpaper had been changed in favour of a neutral off-white colour that matched the shining gloss of the woodwork. Everything I had to do that day swam around my mind: every CCTV camera covering the route from the hospital to the scene of the hit-and-run would need to be viewed. Then forensics pressurised to produce a report. And I needed to coordinate every available officer to be looking for Jack Ledley.

I heard the sound of Mamma on the staircase downstairs, realising the twelve hours' sleep she had last night must have been beneficial. It was just after eight so I padded downstairs. Mamma sat by the kitchen table waiting for the kettle to boil.

'How are you feeling this morning?' I said.

'Tired.'

'There'll be a policeman here later to keep an eye on you.'

'I'll be all right. Don't fuss.'

Boiling water made a thumping sound in the kettle which switched itself off but Mamma stayed put. I made her coffee; she had never liked tea. Then I organised cereal and toast which she ate without enthusiasm.

'Papa will be okay you know.'

'Don't tell him what happened.'

I could tell there was little conviction in her voice. I shook my head slowly. 'Not today maybe but ...'

There was a knock at the door and Mamma's neighbour Jan bustled in. Once I had showered, I kissed Mamma and left her, with her neighbour mouthing confirmation that everything would be fine.

I stood on the front door step and lit my first cigarette of the day. I rang the forensics department and was pleased to hear Tracy's voice. I had rung her last night to tell her about my mother before she had heard it from Alvine. 'I'm really sorry, John.' Tracy sounded too formal and detached somehow. 'How is she?'

'Tired. Is there any news on the forensics?'

'Alvine has made it a priority. Maybe later this morning.'

I rang the Incident Room and dictated instructions for Wyn to find the right CCTV coverage and for Jane to review Walsh's known associates. I heard a shout in the background and thought I heard Lydia's voice. Then a scuffle as the handset was passed to her.

'Good morning, boss. We've got a name for Ledley's girlfriend.'

Chapter 40

It should have taken me forty-five minutes to reach Pontypool but I managed it in thirty-five although I expected several other road users to complain about my driving from the gesticulating that followed me as I overtook erratically and cut inside cars.

Donna Wilkinson, Jack Ledley's girlfriend, had an address in Pontypool and I had to hope Jimmy Walsh didn't have the same information.

I parked alongside Lydia's car. As I left the car my mobile rang.

'Inspector Marco? I was asked to call you if Jimmy Walsh left his house.'

Tightness returned to my chest. The officer responsible for following Walsh continued. 'He's travelling towards the motorway in a Range Rover Sport.'

'Keep me informed.'

I headed to the main entrance of the police station and found Lydia deep in discussion with a uniformed sergeant.

'This is Sergeant Tom White – he knows the family.'

White had an eighteen-inch collar, at least, and more flab than was healthy for him. He looked world-weary as though a lifetime of policing had taken its toll. 'The Wilkinson family are well known. Donna has two brothers that have been in trouble before. One of them did a stretch for aggravated burglary and the other has been involved in some low-level drug dealing. We had a tip-off a while back that the younger brother was growing cannabis in a disused railway tunnel. It turned out he was growing mushrooms and selling them in the local markets for cash. He was fiddling his income support. We reported him to the government department but nothing happened. Nothing ever does but—'

I didn't want to be here all morning. 'Where does she live?'

Lydia pointed at the map and ran her finger to a street in Griffithstown.

'It's in the middle of a terrace, boss.'

'And there's a back lane?' I looked over at White who nodded.

'Let's go.'

I ran back to my car, Lydia by my side. My mobile rang again and I took the call as I jumped into the car. 'Norcross is on the move, sir. I was to notify you if he left the house.'

'Where is he going?'

'He's going down towards Newport Road.'

I raised my voice. 'Follow him and make sure you don't lose him.'

Norcross was heading in the same direction as Walsh.

All the mistakes made in the previous Oakley inquiry came to mind. Ledley might well be implicated in a murder so as of right now we should have been arresting him. Maybe that was the right thing to do. Maybe the right thing didn't matter any more when all that mattered was getting enough evidence against Walsh to put him behind bars for ever.

Lydia turned up her nose when she got into the car and then powered down the window, making an exaggerated gesture of wafting away the smell of stale smoke. We followed the unmarked car from the police station on the short journey to Griffithstown. I parked with one set of wheels on the pavement near a junction. I spotted the right street name on the gable of the end terrace. My mobile rang. 'It's one of the houses halfway down.' I recognised White's voice.

'Call me once you've got the back lane covered.'

I watched as White and a young constable left their car and walked down the rear lane.

My mobile rang. It was the officer following Walsh. 'We've lost him, sir.'

I shouted. 'What the hell do you mean?'

'There was a lot of traffic on the Newport Road. We lost him near the Cardiff Gate park.'

'Well bloody well go and find him.'

I called the officer following Norcross. 'Where is he?'

'I think he knows he's being followed, sir.'

'What the fuck do you mean?' I knew I sounded desperate.

'He slows then accelerates as though he wants us to do the same. And there's a lot of traffic.'

'Keep me informed.' I looked over at Lydia who had guessed what had happened judging by her frown.

My mobile rang seconds later. 'Looks quiet,' White said.

I drove down the street until I reached number twelve.

With the rear covered, there was nowhere for Ledley or Donna to go. I marched up to the front door and rang the bell. It didn't work. I rapped my knuckles on the door. Nothing. Then I formed a fist and knocked. The neighbour's front door squeaked open.

'You after Danny, love?' A woman with a flour-dusted apron stood on the threshold. 'Only he works nights.'

'Who lives with him?'

'Hard to tell. It's a big family, mind. Who are you? Council?'

'Does his daughter live here?' I smiled at the woman.

'Donna? Haven't seen her for a while. She used to hang around with my Hayley. Thick as thieves they were. Always in trouble. Tell me your name and I'll tell Danny.'

I banged on the door again. 'Thanks for your help.'

The woman sulked back into the house.

Lydia was talking into her mobile and I guessed White was outside the rear door. I leant down, pushed open the letterbox and shouted. 'Danny, wake up.'

I heard movement upstairs and then a telephone rang, three times, until a muffled voice answered. It might even have been the neighbour calling. Then the sound of urgent footsteps before a staircase creaked.

'What do you want?' A man's voice shouted from inside the house. A key turned in the lock. A bleary-eyed face appeared, the door kept on a chain. I flashed my warrant card. 'For fuck's sake, what have they done now?'

'Can we come in?'

He closed the door, let the chain fall clear and eased it open.

Danny Wilkinson wore a thin dressing gown over red pyjamas. A large paunch hung over his waistband and his hair needed a decent comb.

He led us through into the kitchen where he stopped abruptly when he noticed White and the other officer standing in the back yard. 'What the fuck is going on?'

'We need to speak to your daughter, Donna.'

Lydia opened the back door and White and the other officer entered.

'You people are always picking on my lads even when they've done nothing wrong.'

'Does she live here? Danny, we need to speak to

her.'

'Why do want to speak to her?'

I turned up my nose; his breath could strip paint.

Lydia raised her voice, her patience wearing thinner than mine. 'Is she with Jack Ledley?'

'I kicked him out long ago. Useless piece of shit he was.'

'Where could she be?'

Another call reached my mobile from the officer following Norcross. 'Sorry, sir, we lost him. He jumped a light and we couldn't follow him because of the traffic.'

Now we really had to find Ledley.

My mobile rang again but I didn't recognise the number so I sent it to voicemail.

Danny looked at Lydia and me with distrustful eyes.

'Her life may be at risk,' I said.

He squinted, calculating whether we were telling him the truth.

'She works in the Big Pit Museum up in Blaenavon. Some days she'll stay with a friend of hers in Forge Side.'

'What's the address?' I said

'How the fuck would I know.'

I jabbed a finger at Danny's arm. 'This is really important. What is the name of her friend?'

He blinked in surprise. 'Bridget something.'

We left Danny Wilkinson boiling a kettle, complaining he'd never get back to sleep. We strode back to our cars. I could hear White talking into his mobile telephone – obviously with somebody in the office at the Big Pit Museum, demanding to know the name of any employee called Bridget.

I remembered the call to my mobile so I reached for the handset in my pocket. I listened with increasing alarm to the elderly voice.

279

'Damn,' I almost shouted. Lydia gave me a puzzled look. I looked over at White. 'You go to the Big Pit. I need to call in one of the local shops.'

I ran back to the car, waving at Lydia to join me. I reversed clumsily before flooring the accelerator. 'The owner of that ironmongery shop we visited just called me. She's seen Ledley.'

'At least we know he's still alive.'

I flashed my lights at a dawdling car but it had little effect so I pressed the horn. The noise seemed to reverberate through the car and around the narrow streets. I waved an encouragement for the driver to accelerate but it had the opposite effect and he slowed down. So I pulled out and overtook the vehicle racing away from Griffithstown. Eventually I pulled up outside the shop.

Before I got out of the car I called the officers following Walsh. 'What's happening?'

'We found the Range Rover parked in the services. No sign of him.' The news set my teeth on edge. 'And there are two other officers here, sir.'

'What the ...?'

I heard voices and muffled conversation. 'The Range Rover is parked next to a Ford Focus that the other two officers followed.'

My heart raced. Walsh had switched cars but now he was with Norcross.

Lydia followed me to the shop; I almost kicked the door open in my haste. A man in his mid-seventies was talking to a man standing behind one of the counters. They stared over at us. Boxes of candles and paraffin lamps stacked on the countertop caught my attention.

I flashed my warrant card. 'I spoke to the owner last week about a man we're looking for.'

The man behind the counter turned his head and

shouted, 'Mam.'

It was only seconds but time seemed to drag. The door from the shop area into what I guessed was the owner's house opened and the woman I'd seen the previous week strode out. She gave me a brief nod of acknowledgement.

'After you called the first time I've been looking out for him. He came in looking for two paraffin lamps. He had a cheek. He wanted to know if there was a discount. We don't do discounts here. That's for all them supermarkets. He had long hair with a ponytail. Like a young girl. And I could see tattoos on his arms.'

'Did he say anything else?' Knowing Ledley had called was useless without knowing where he was going.

'He paid and left.'

'Was there anyone with him?'

She shook her head. I felt desperate. 'Is there nothing else you can tell me?'

'I saw his car.'

'What make and model was it?'

She gave me a patronising nod of her head. Her son piped up from the other side of the shop. 'Mam doesn't drive. She wouldn't know one car from another.'

She smiled at me again.

'What direction did he go in?'

'He went into town of course.'

I made for the door, fearing I had wasted another twenty minutes.

'I saw the number plate.'

I peered over at her.

'The car had the same letters as my late husband – NLO – Norman Lawrence Owen. Never forget that.'

I looked over at her son instinctively for reassurance.

'Nothing wrong with Mam's eyesight.'

I ran back to the car. Lydia was already on the telephone calling the Incident Room, requesting a full search of all vehicles with NLO in their registration details. She called White as I started the engine. Even from listening to one side of the conversation, I could tell he was nearing the Big Pit Museum.

I didn't need the satnav. There were signposts. I was driving north up the valley. Fast.

Lydia's mobile rang and she switched on the loudspeaker setting.

'I've spoken to someone in the office at the museum. There's a Bridget who lives in G Row in Forge Side,' White said.

'G Row?' I said.

'The terraces up there have still got names from the original rows when they were built for the ironworkers.'

It sounded like something out of a dystopian movie. Maybe each worker had a number too.

'We're looking for a car with a registration NLO,' Lydia said.

'I'll get onto it. Forge Side is on your way towards the museum. You can't miss it.'

'On our way,' I shouted. Lydia finished the call and I flattened the accelerator. My mind turned to Jimmy Walsh. An ominous foreboding made me glance at every vehicle coming in the opposite direction. I dreaded the possibility he had found Ledley before us. The traffic was light, just the occasional delivery lorry and white van.

We headed left from the main road towards the closely packed terraces of Forge Side. The houses clung to each other. Narrow, with tiled roofs and plastic windows, they perched over each other and the pavement. My stomach churned. We passed Row A and then B before reaching Row G.

A battered old Ford Fiesta – NLO 452J – was parked halfway down. On the opposite side was White's marked police car. I parked in the middle of the road, jumped out of the car and raced over to the open door of number ten.

Two tan leather sofas dominated the small sitting room. Stuffed into one corner was an enormous television and surround-sound speakers screwed high up on the wall. I heard the crackling of police radios and the young police officer who had accompanied White emerged from the kitchen ashen faced.

'Through there,' he said.

I stepped into the kitchen and straight into the worst nightmare possible.

Chapter 41

Jack Ledley lay sprawled under the kitchen table. Blood was splattered all over the floor, the walls and then I noticed the bloodied footprints. Sergeant White knelt over Ledley, his fingers feeling for a pulse on his wrist. He looked up at me and shook his head slowly. I stood rigid to the spot, sensing Lydia behind me.

'We'll need a CSI team,' I said through gritted teeth.

White stood up. 'I've already notified area control.'

'Did you see anything?' I said.

'The door was open when we arrived.'

In the distance, I heard the sound of an ambulance siren. Looking down at Ledley I doubted the paramedics could do anything. We retraced our steps to the front door. Anger and despair were a dangerous combination. Another man was dead and this time I could point the finger of blame directly at the incompetence of the dedicated source unit and Inspector Ackroyd. The noise of the approaching ambulance grew louder until it pulled into the street, stopping in front of my car. I barked instructions at the paramedics to check for life signs and make certain they contaminated the crime scene as little as possible.

White joined Lydia and me on the pavement. 'Do you want me to start some house-to-house enquiries?'

On the opposite side of the street half a dozen residents had gathered in small groups occasionally giving us anxious glances.

I drew deeply on a cigarette. I sensed Lydia staring at me. I wanted to get back to Queen Street and give Dave Hobbs and Inspector Ackroyd a piece of my mind. But I knew I had to wait until the crime scene investigators arrived. I surveyed Row G. There were a dozen houses on both sides. We had little time to waste.

'Of course, let's get on with it.'

I told White and the uniformed constable to take the opposite side of the street. Lydia headed down to the bottom of the terrace just as the paramedics emerged. They confirmed what I already knew, packed their bags and reversed their ambulance up the street. Two marked police cars arrived and more young officers emerged. When I explained the circumstances their mouths fell open and they listened intently to my instructions to secure the crime scene. I headed up to the end of the terrace and hammered on the door. I had spoken to two residents of Row G by the time the scientific support vehicle from Eastern Division pulled into the street. A white-coated CSI emerged with three others.

'Jack Ledley's been murdered.' I jerked my head towards the open door behind me. 'His body is in the kitchen.'

'Who else has been inside?' One of the CSIs asked.

'Only the officers who found the body and myself and the two paramedics.'

The CSIs left me standing on the pavement as they filed into number ten, Row G.

I hurried down the street to join Lydia. She gave me one of her disappointed troubled looks. 'Nobody saw anything, and nobody heard anything.'

Despair gripped my throat again; I had to swallow heavily.

'They must have used a silencer,' Lydia continued.

A professional, somebody with a clear cold-blooded approach. I fisted my right hand and tapped it onto my left palm.

The young constable walked over the road and stood by White. 'One of the neighbours says she saw two men by Ledley's front door. They were only there for a second. Then they went in as though they had a key.'

'Can she give us a description?'

'They were both about my sort of height – five ten. And they both had black jackets. They were in a small silver car. She thought it was a Ford but she can't be certain.'

It had to be Walsh and Bevard's assassin.

'Take her down to Queen Street. I'll organise for an artist to do a photofit.'

'What, now?' White said.

I scowled at him. 'Right now. And I need every available officer from your division doing house-to-house. Circulate the descriptions we've got.'

I went back into the house. Alvine was in the kitchen; the place felt cramped with three investigators working together. 'Let me have the report soon as you can.' I didn't wait for a reply. I headed for my car.

I should have gone straight to the Incident Room, caught up with Jane and Wyn, monitored progress. But the red mist that had descended around me as I peered at Ledley's bloodied corpse hadn't disappeared. I strode towards Cornock's office. I refused to contemplate the possibility he would not return or that Hobbs's promotion would be permanent. Now we had another murder on our hands. It might not be the death of an innocent man, but Ledley didn't deserve to die. After telling Hobbs exactly what I felt I would demand a meeting with Inspector Ackroyd. I was already rehearsing the sort of comments I'd make.

I reached Cornock's office where common sense and politeness got the better of me so I knocked, but I didn't wait for a reply before barging straight in.

Hobbs sat by the conference table, a plate of sandwiches placed in the middle alongside expensive-looking potato crisps, the sort with a trace of skin around the edge. He had opened a red bottle of Ty Nant water and poured two glasses. He wasn't waiting for me to join him for lunch because Inspector Malcolm Ackroyd sat opposite him.

'Inspector Marco.' He managed a formality I wasn't going to reciprocate.

'I've just driven down from Blaenavon.'

Both men stared over at me. Ackroyd chewed on a mouthful of sandwich.

'Jack Ledley was killed this morning.' I let the announcement hang in the air. Ackroyd stopped chewing; I hoped the food would stick in his craw. 'He was shot in the house where he was living. Several times actually. It looked exactly like the crime scene in the café in Roath Park when Felix Bevard was killed.'

'I had no idea,' Hobbs said.

'If the original investigation into Oakley's death had been handled properly we would have put Walsh behind bars years ago.'

Hobbs averted his gaze, settling it on the pile of sandwiches. It was about time he realised the reality and lost whatever appetite he possessed.

I turned to Ackroyd. 'If you had shared information with me about Ledley earlier we might have found him sooner.'

'Calm down, John,' Ackroyd said.

'Don't you tell me to fucking calm down. I'm not the one responsible for Ledley's death.'

'Now you've really gone over the top.'

'Have I?'

Ackroyd snorted, reaching for the glass of water and I noticed the slight trembling of his hand.

'Let me remind you that until you unearthed film footage from Roath Park we had no idea Ledley was implicated in Oakley's death.' Ackroyd was right of course but I wasn't going to give him the satisfaction of seeing me agree with him. Ackroyd's confidence grew. 'You know full well he kept bad company.'

I guffawed. 'Bad company. A man is dead.'

Hobbs interjected. 'We need to find who killed him.'

'I know full well who killed him.'

'Evidence, John.' Hobbs managed his condescending best. 'You'll need evidence. Gold-plated, bombproof evidence.'

I looked back at Ackroyd. 'I'll need to interview all the officers on your dedicated source unit.'

Ackroyd, shaking his head, goaded me.

'If you stand in my way again I'll take this investigation straight to the chief constable. I've got a murderer to catch. I don't give a fuck about the niceties of your dedicated source unit.'

Ackroyd glanced at Hobbs. I turned to look at him. 'And Acting Detective Chief Inspector Hobbs, I expect your complete support ... sir.'

I left Superintendent Cornock's room praying I'd ruined their cosy lunch.

Alvine stood by the board in the Incident Room staring at the images of Walsh and Kendall when I marched in.

'The forensic report on the property we recovered from Kendall's home makes interesting reading.' She held up a sheath of papers in her right hand.

I nodded towards my office. Inside I shrugged off my jacket, draped it over the coat stand and sat down, gazing at the report Alvine dropped onto the middle of my desk.

'Page five,' she said.

I flicked through to the right page as she made

herself comfortable. Once I finished reading and the significance had sunk in, I looked over at Alvine. 'Are you certain?'

'Of course. It seems that your friend Martin Kendall has a collection of glass paperweights. Personally I wouldn't have thought that master criminals like him would have collected anything.'

'And you're certain that Yelland's fingerprints are on one of them.'

'It's quite a collectable item apparently. I did a quick Google search on it.'

'So we've got another link between Yelland and Martin Kendall.'

Alvine stood up.

I heard movement in the Incident Room and shouted for Lydia. She passed Alvine on her way out.

'Alvine's got a smile on her face,' Lydia said, vaguely surprised.

'Don't take your coat off,' I said.

It was after eight that evening when Lydia and I had finished speaking to Sharon Yelland. She had confirmed that her late husband's godparents had given him a valuable paperweight as a graduation gift. The only explanation was that Kendall had stolen it as some macabre memento. I had called Cardiff jail and arranged to interview him the following morning.

The message from Cornock suggesting we meet that evening was unusual and unexpected. There was something on his mind, but he had a friendly enough demeanour when he settled into one of the leather sofas in a quiet corner of Lefties, cradling a pint of Brains best bitter. 'I haven't been here for years.'

Colour had returned to his cheeks, and it struck me he had put on weight. His eyes had a contented, relaxed appearance.

'How are things going, sir?'

He took a mouthful of beer. 'This job can take over your life. You live and breathe policing until you can't enjoy anything else. And it takes its toll on family.'

'Are you likely to be returning to work?'

'I've got another meeting with the medics next week. But I feel much better.'

'And how is your wife?'

'She's enjoyed having me around but I think she's getting bored of seeing me all day. And our daughter is back on an even keel.' He paused, taking another swig. 'You probably know that she got herself involved with a bad crowd. She was treated for drug addiction. She came back to live at home and in the past month she's been working with a charity. And it's all going very well.'

'Glad to hear it.' I sipped my orange juice.

'I hear you had an exchange of views with Dave Hobbs and Malcolm Ackroyd.'

Now I realised a reprimand was likely.

'I appreciate this case has been very difficult with your family getting involved. But you need to keep perspective. Other people can do the finger wagging. If Hobbs or Ackroyd are at fault the WPS will deal with it. In our own time and in our own way.'

I wasn't about to contradict Cornock. But the WPS had a habit of doing very little, and knowing that Hobbs and Ackroyd would still be around didn't fill me with confidence for the future of policing in Cardiff.

'Tell me about the investigation.'

I explained about the paperweight that meant Kendall had been inside Yelland's property. Then I summarised Chris Taylor's eyewitness evidence and told Cornock we had images of Kendall and Yelland together. Cornock nodded at the relevant times and made approving noises. 'I'm going to interview him again in the morning.'

'And have you made any progress with the Bevard inquiry?'

I paused. 'We have no idea who pulled the trigger. But Jimmy Walsh was responsible for directing the murder – I know it.'

'How did Walsh know that Bevard was going to grass him up?'

'Yelland and Roger Stockes, the prosecutor involved in the supergrass deal, knew each other. We suspect Yelland may have got information from him. He then shares details with Walsh in return for generous contributions.'

Cornock shook his head.

A silence filled the space between us although behind me the bar was getting busy. Men with expensive-looking suits and open-necked shirts mingled with women in pencil skirts and high heels.

'Are you certain it was Stockes and Yelland?'

I shrugged and held out both palms.

'So what was the motive?' Cornock finished his beer, stood up and made for the bar, returning with a second pint and more orange juice. It gave me time to dwell on my answer.

'I believe Brian Yelland got greedy and demanded more money from Walsh.'

'Perhaps, but it doesn't help with the Bevard case. Would Walsh have killed Yelland just because he was blackmailing him?'

It surprised me Cornock sounded so certain.

'Walsh is a sociopath, sir,'

Cornock finished his second pint by the time I had

rehearsed all the evidence we had accumulated.

'You've missed something straightforward, something obvious.'

'And in the meantime I've got Jimmy Walsh running around on bail.'

'With the possibility the case against him might collapse.'

Every time that possibility entered my mind I tried to dispel it into a dark recess but it kept coming back to haunt me. I offered to buy Cornock another drink but he shook his head, gathered up his jacket and left. I left the rest of my orange juice and headed for home.

Chapter 42

A prison officer with hands the size of shovels escorted Lydia and me to one of the interview suites at Cardiff prison. Like so many of the Victorian jails, the twentieth and twenty-first centuries had developed around it until it stood next to one of the biggest shopping malls in the United Kingdom.

Lydia dragged over two chairs to one side of a table; a tape recorder sat at the other end safely screwed to the wall. I sat down and opened my papers.

I slipped the photograph of the paperweight under some papers when I heard footsteps approach. A prison officer opened the door and Martin Kendall strode in with a young solicitor from Glanville Tront's legal firm in tow. The officer joined his colleague outside and they stood, expressionless, looking in at us through the thick Perspex of the window.

'Mark Doyle,' the lawyer said, reaching out a hand.

Once the pleasantries were dispensed with, I opened the cassette tapes and popped them into the machine. I cast a glance at everybody present. 'Let's get started. This is a supplementary interview as part of our investigation into the murder of Brian Yelland.'

Martin Kendall had lost that well-fed muscle-pumped aura. He looked paler, unshaven. Prison clothes didn't suit either; I could imagine him complaining like hell about his badly sized shirt and ill-fitting jeans.

'Brian Yelland was a prison officer at HMP Grange Hall. He was responsible for the billet where your boss Jimmy Walsh had his cell.'

Kendall narrowed his eyes.

'Did you pay Brian Yelland to provide favours to Jimmy Walsh whilst he was in prison?'

'Don't know what you're talking about.'

'I would remind you that we have photographs of you meeting Brian Yelland.' I flicked through my papers and pushed over a photograph.

Kendall kept staring at me. He said nothing.

Doyle scribbled in a legal notebook. I couldn't understand what he could possibly be writing.

'Now is your opportunity to explain to me why you had a meeting with Brian Yelland.'

More silence.

'You know from our first interview that an eyewitness describes a person matching your description being present at Yelland's home in the early hours of the morning he was killed.'

'Haven't you covered all this before, Inspector?' Doyle said. There was a hint of West Wales to his accent, maybe Pembrokeshire.

I gave him a smile without parting my lips.

'How long have you been collecting paperweights?'

He frowned at me, obviously puzzled.

I flicked through some of my papers. 'You have thirty different paperweights. The crime scene investigators who finalised the search of your home made a list of them. And photographed each one.' I placed an image of one paperweight after another in front of him.

'If these are not your property now is the time to tell me.'

I put one hand on top of another and placed them on my papers giving him a kindly, I-am-here-to-help look. It didn't work, he didn't reply. He looked through me. So I sorted through my papers until I found the important photograph.

'I'd like you to look at this.' I pushed over an image of Yelland's paperweight. 'It was found in your home when we conducted a search after your arrest. Does this belong to you?'

I could see the arrogance draining from his eyes like an iceberg under a midday sun.

He stared at the image carefully, obviously calculating whether he could answer. Did he know we had fingerprints? I waited. He lifted his gaze from the photograph, glanced at Doyle and then over at me and shook his head.

'Is that a no, Mr Kendall?' No reply. 'This paperweight belonged to Brian Yelland. It was given to him when he graduated.'

Doyle reached over and fingered the photograph.

Kendall remained completely impassive.

'How did this paperweight come into your possession?'

I paused, and sat back in my chair. He knew that I was talking to a murderer. And to a man responsible for stalking my father and who probably enjoyed planning my mother's hit-and-run.

'I believe that you stole it from Brian Yelland's home. It proves conclusively that you were in his home. Now is the time to explain. Tell me if there was anyone else involved. Because I believe that Jimmy Walsh wanted Brian Yelland dead, as he wanted Felix Bevard dead. And you're part of the conspiracy to kill both men. There's a big difference between one life sentence and three. How old are you now?'

Kendall was making an odd scratching sound in his throat.

'Three life sentences? You won't be released until you're in your seventies. The world will have changed a lot by then. Now is your opportunity to cooperate. Why don't you tell us what you know?'

Kendall folded his arms, propped them on the table and leant over towards me. 'You have no fucking idea.'

I found a quiet table at Mario's and ordered an all-day breakfast before spreading the newspaper on the table. The sports pages of the *Western Mail* had a large piece about Cardiff City's game against Nottingham Forest the following evening. It profiled all the players, ranking them against their opposite numbers. Last weekend's victory had taken Cardiff City into the promotion play-off places. There was a buoyant positive mood about the quality of the players and the article was full of complimentary comments about the quality of the football played that season.

I turned to the inside sports pages. With Wales playing in the European cup for the first time the newspaper had been running a series of interviews with some of the famous footballing heroes of previous Welsh teams. The face of Walter Underwood, Gloria Bevard's father, peered out of the pages and it took my attention immediately. I had scanned the article before my meal arrived and pushed the newspaper to one side so that I could eat my bacon and eggs. After I'd finished I returned to reading the article a second time. It was odd seeing his picture. He made comments about how lucky he had been to play for Wales; he gave a detailed description of the goal he had scored. It brought back all the old memories of going to football with Papa. Underwood must have told the reporter about his family and how his daughters and grandchildren were so important and that he was blessed to have them living so close.

I finished my Americano, left enough change for the bill and headed for Queen Street.

It was difficult to imagine Gloria Bevard living an

anonymous existence in a suburb somewhere. She wouldn't have fitted in. She would have missed her sister, her nieces, her mum and dad. I was only now starting to realise how much I had missed being a proper father to Dean. I reached the entrance of Queen Street and punched in my security code.

How would Bevard have reacted when he was interviewed by the officers from the dedicated source unit? He had to be sure that Gloria would have gone with him. Taken their children from their home, from their extended family.

'Good morning, sir.' I didn't recognise the voice. It was a uniformed officer. 'I need to punch in my code.' I looked over at him, puzzled, before realising I was still standing outside the rear door.

Something wasn't right.

I had to think clearly. I had assumed that some casual drunken comment between Stockes and Yelland had been the source of Walsh's information about Bevard. But I had nothing to substantiate it. How else would he have found the information? Then it struck me that everything about Gloria Bevard suggested she would have refused to move. Her parents, her sister and all her family lived in South Wales.

'Of course.' I stood to one side as the officer punched in his number and the door buzzed open.

I walked up to the Incident Room in a haze. What would Gloria Bevard have said had Felix Bevard told her? She would have refused. Inspector Ackroyd had told me that Bevard had not discussed the supergrass deal with his wife. But what if he had?

I heard the greetings from Jane and Wyn and Lydia but I paid little attention as I walked over to my room. After booting up my computer I glanced over at the folded

Western Mail perched on the edge of my desk and thought again about Walter Underwood. Gloria Bevard filled my thoughts. I reread all the preliminary statements. She had been out with her friends on the night her husband had been killed. Quickly I found a record of what her friends had said. Gloria and Felix had a troubled relationship. The more I read the more unease crept into my mind like the start of flu; you know something isn't right but until you start sneezing and coughing you don't know what's wrong.

And then Cornock's reminder that I might have missed something really simple came to mind.

We had been looking in the wrong place for Jimmy Walsh's source of information about Bevard's supergrass agreement. I shouted at Lydia. She appeared in the doorway of my room moments later.

'Shut the door.'

She grimaced, clicked the door closed and sat down.

'Gloria Bevard might have told Jimmy Walsh about her husband.'

Lydia grimaced. 'Are you suggesting she was involved in his murder?'

I squeezed my eyes closed. 'I should have seen this sooner. Gloria Bevard would never have left South Wales. She's a Valleys girl.'

'But that means she'd be implicated in Bevard's death.' Lydia shook her head slowly. 'I can't believe it.'

'I've read the statements from the girlfriends she was with on the night of Bevard's death. A couple make reference to how she and Felix had argued a lot.'

I leant over the desk and thumped an open palm on top of the papers. 'They've all got perfect alibis, Bernie Walsh, Martin Kendall, Gloria Bevard and above all Jimmy Walsh. It doesn't make sense.'

'I suppose we could requisition her telephone log.'

'Make it a priority.' A telephone call reminded me that I had to attend Jack Ledley's post mortem. I hurried over to the hospital. I wasn't in the mood for small talk from the assistant or the sound of classical music thundering through the mortuary as Paddy McVeigh got to work. It set my nerves on edge and I couldn't stop thinking about Gloria Bevard. I remembered the look on her face when I mentioned Kendall's name. At the time, I was uncomfortable with her reaction. I cursed silently that I had not seen it at the time but death can play games with the emotions.

Back in Queen Street I ploughed my way through the preliminary results from the house-to-house enquiries around Forge Side. Wyn and Jane had given me a summary but it wasn't good enough; I had to read them for myself. They managed to persuade me not to view the CCTV coverage from the middle of Blaenavon, telling me in clear terms there was nothing to help us.

I left Queen Street at the end of the afternoon and headed out to the hospital to collect my father. Papa was sitting on the high-backed chair next to his bed, Mamma by his side. His impatience disappeared when he saw me and he smiled broadly. We gathered all his belongings together and after thanking the staff profusely left the hospital.

Back home, an hour later, Papa sank into a chair and started watching recordings of various television programmes he'd missed whilst in hospital. I sent Lydia a message enquiring about progress with Gloria Bevard's telephone records. The answer was the same – still waiting.

I decided to stay a little longer. The doorbell rang and I assumed it to be a neighbour but once Mamma had opened the door I recognised the dull flat sound of Uncle Gino's voice.

'Is he back?'

'Come in.' Mamma sounded tentative.

Uncle Gino came into the sitting room. He still had his trademark tie pulled down a couple of inches from a loosened shirt collar. The tufts of hair around his ears needed trimming.

'How are you?' He shook Papa's hand vigorously.

Mamma gave him a cool, brittle gaze as she sat down beside me on the sofa. She didn't offer tea or coffee and soon enough Gino got the message but as he left he jerked his head at me indicating that he wanted to talk to me.

'I'll see Uncle Gino to the door,' I said.

I walked with him to his car and he turned towards me.

'I didn't want any of this to happen. You know that.'

'I told you to stay clear of Walsh and Goldstar Properties.'

He rolled his shoulders. 'They were offering the best price.' He lowered his voice. 'They came to see us yesterday.'

'Who?'

He looked down at his feet, and kicked some pebbles off the tarmac surface. 'Mr Shaw and a man called Norcross—'

'What the hell did they want?'

'They …' He gazed up at me. 'They gave us until Friday. After that the deal is off.'

I couldn't believe it. Jimmy Walsh had the audacity to stalk my family in the middle of the court case against him. He must have felt confident, arrogant enough to believe his prosecution for the Oakley killing would collapse.

'We could lose everything,' Gino said.

My anger boiled over. 'Papa has had a heart attack and my mother was involved in a hit-and-run because of you and Jez. At this moment I don't give a fuck if you lose everything.'

I turned my back on Uncle Gino. As I walked to the front door I heard his voice. 'You be sure to tell your father.'

Mamma was standing in the hallway when I entered and she gave me a quizzical look that said I needed to explain. We joined Papa and I gave them a word-by-word breakdown of what Uncle Gino said.

'After what's happened I'm going to keep the old place,' Papa said, turning his attention to the recording of a football game.

I left my parents and headed back into Cardiff, my thoughts immediately focusing on Jimmy Walsh. A part of me wanted to be pleased that Walsh's property ambitions would be thwarted but I was worried, too, knowing how vicious Walsh could be. A yawn gripped my jaw as I passed Quakers Yard and I drove home in a blur hoping I could sleep.

Chapter 43

I slept soundly, hardly moving all night. That morning I chose my navy suit, a powder-blue shirt and tie that Tracy had given me as a birthday present. In Queen Street I walked over to Lydia's desk. 'Have we had Gloria Bevard's call logs?'

'It's just arrived, we're working on it now.'

'Send it to my machine. I'll print it out.'

An optimism that I hoped was not unfounded filled my mind. I reached my desk, fiddled with the mouse and within minutes was reading the printed version of Gloria Bevard's mobile telephone log. I called Lydia's name. I had found a blue and a pink highlighter by the time she appeared at my door.

She was clutching the same printed sheet that was in front of me.

'For now I want to look at the telephone calls she made the day her husband died.'

Lydia's eyes had a steely determination. 'Wyn is putting together a spreadsheet.'

'Okay.' I took the blue highlighter and drew a box around all the calls Gloria Bevard had made that day. Then I highlighted in blue the calls she had made between four in the afternoon and eleven in the evening. It amazed me how many she'd made. There were dozens. I was hoping for inspiration quickly but the volume daunted me.

I could hear the activity from the Incident Room when Wyn and Jane were tracing the identity of the owners of various numbers. The words *pay-as-you-go* were spoken too often for my liking. After two hours Wyn stood in my doorway and announced that they had made some progress. He was pinning an A4 sheet to the board of the Incident Room with one eleven-digit mobile number printed on it.

'Mrs Bevard telephoned this number at four-thirty on the afternoon Bevard was killed. It lasted forty-eight seconds.'

Wyn turned to look at the rest of us. Sensing our impatience, he quickly added, 'She doesn't call the number again until after eight o'clock. Then she calls the number three times within a few minutes. The calls don't last more than ten seconds.'

Jane butted in. 'Which suggests they weren't answered.'

'But she made calls to dozens of other people.'

'That's right boss,' Wyn said. 'But this is a number she had never rung before.'

'I want all the other numbers she called that day traced.'

'There are quite a few pay-as-you-go,' Jane said. 'But most of them are monthly contracts.'

I stared over at the mobile number.

'The number is dead, boss. I tried it,' Wyn said.

'Where was that number sold?'

'A shop in Southampton.'

'There might be CCTV. Call them. Now. And get as much detail about the numbers that were called from that mobile.'

The waiting seemed interminable. I reread reports and doodled more mind maps. After a mid-morning coffee I walked through into the Incident Room and over to the board. Jane had a picture of a young boy and girl in a small frame by her telephone. I knew they weren't hers so I assumed they were a nephew and niece. I didn't even have a photograph of Dean in my wallet. Wyn's desk was characteristically tidy, and knowing the way he worked there was probably order to the pencils and highlighters neatly stacked in the large brightly coloured mug.

I stared at the photographs. Knowing that we had enough to make a case against Martin Kendall brought a smile to my face. Peering into the eyes of Jimmy Walsh made me shiver; he had eyes like a shark, black and impenetrable.

Back in my room I flicked through the entries in Walsh's file from HMP Grange Hall. I read the family background – no siblings although an identical twin had died in hospital as a baby. His mother had been in her forties giving birth and she had a history of abusive and violent relationships. The probation reports made sober reading so I was pleased to see Wyn standing in my doorway.

'I've sent you an email from the shop in Southampton, sir.'

I turned to the screen, clicking until I opened the attachment. The coverage started at eight am and, guessing that the shop would be open until late that same afternoon, I decided to fast-forward sections. After half an hour I got into the routine of spotting when customers arrived so I glared at them and then pressed fast-forward to the next new customer.

After two hours I regretted embarking on the exercise. The small of my back ached, and my eyes felt smudged, so I got up, stretched, went to the bathroom and splashed hot water over my face. I returned to my office with a double strength instant coffee from the kitchen.

I ploughed on for another hour, this time fast-forwarding more frequently.

The time said 3.30 pm when I stopped, realising that I had missed something. The shop was full, all the assistants were busy, some demonstrating mobile phones to various customers, others processing orders.

I rewound the recording.

The back of a man's head caught my attention as he walked into the shop and up to the counter. I squinted. A troubled thought crossed my mind that I recognised him. I double-checked the date on the recording. It was a Saturday, several weeks earlier.

I fast-forwarded the recording for a few minutes and then pressed play. The order was finalised, the assistant beaming at the customer, bundling the mobile phone box into a carrier bag. I wanted him to turn around. I wanted to look at his face.

Seconds later he duly obliged. I clicked pause. I sensed the skin on my forehead furrowing and tightening. I was staring at the image of Jimmy Walsh. I pushed my chair back and it crashed against the radiator behind me. I gazed at Walsh. It felt like minutes as everything about the investigation ran through my mind.

'Lydia ...' I called out but Wyn must have reached the same stage in the recordings as I had because he shouted his surprise.

I reached for Walsh's prison file on my desk and flicked through until I found the information I needed. Then I checked the date on my monitor. Lydia appeared in my doorway as I marched out to the Incident Room.

'On the date this recording was made Jimmy Walsh hadn't been released from jail. But he was on a weekend release. The prisoners in those open jails get weekend releases before their actual release dates, usually Friday to Monday. And that weekend Jimmy Walsh was in Southampton buying a telephone.'

Wyn nodded enthusiastically. I reached the board and tapped on the image of Gloria Bevard. 'So why was she calling Jimmy Walsh on the afternoon Felix was killed?'

There were three sets of eyes gazing at me intently

when I turned around.

'We need to be certain it was Jimmy Walsh and not a doppelganger,' Wyn said.

'And I know how we can check.' Lydia said before reaching for her mouse. 'We have the recording from the billet where Jimmy Walsh had his cell in Grange Hall. We can compare the images.'

'Of course, good work,' I said. 'Find it.'

It was vaguely voyeuristic watching prisoners walking up and down the corridor, talking to each other without hearing voices. Lydia found the coverage from the billet on the day Bevard was murdered. We had watched once before just to make certain that he really was locked up. That morning Walsh stood by the door of the billet waiting for it to be unlocked. Lydia ran the recording on and recognised him as he returned before lunch. A prison officer made the rounds, counting the prisoners.

He returned later that afternoon, a beanie pulled over his head, coughing into a fisted hand.

Other prisoners walked up and down the corridor, visiting the toilets, taking a shower, but for the rest of the day Walsh was in his cell. It confirmed what we already knew – that he had been ill. The following morning one of the prisoners knocked at Walsh's door. Then Yelland appeared and words were exchanged with another prisoner, who stood in the doorway of Walsh's cell before letting Yelland into Walsh's cell. It was late that afternoon when Walsh emerged coughing and spluttering, still wearing his beanie. He must have been going back to work, no nursing or medical support for Walsh.

I went back to the images of Walsh in the mobile phone shop in Southampton and watched the coverage repeatedly until my eyes burned. Then I clicked back to the images from the billet at HMP Grange Hall. It was the same man, no doubt.

Suddenly I was back in Walsh's cell staring at one of his books about tracing your family tree. It struck me then that the answer had been in front of me all the time.

'There was more than one,' I whispered.

I strode back to my office and clicked onto a Google search. Within minutes I had found a website that provided details of birth certificates.

'What exactly are you doing, boss?' Lydia stood with Wyn and Jane by my door.

I pushed Walsh's file towards her. 'Dictate his personal details.'

I punched in his first and last name and his year of birth and finally the month of his birth. I left blank the relevant county. Seconds later I had twenty results. It surprised me so many children had been born in the same three-month period and christened James Walsh. I was getting into my stride now and I read the results, jotting down onto a pad the details of the births that had the name of the mother in common.

I stopped and let out a long slow breath as I saw the three names I'd written.

'There were triplets.' My voice made a squeaking sound.

Lydia's mouth fell open, her fingers touched parted lips. 'They did a switch.'

'We've seen Grange Hall, there are no walls or fences. It would be easy to change places with a prisoner. The only problem is, they have to be identical.'

'But not all twins are identical.'

I turned back to the monitor and after another few minutes I had the birth certificates of Andrew and Henry. Down the margin of Andrew's the word *adopted* had been printed. 'The probation officer said a sibling died in hospital.

So it must have been Henry.'

'We need to find the adoption records for Andrew,' Lydia said slowly.

If I was right then I was looking at the name of Walsh's triplet who had switched places with him in Grange Hall. My eagerness was weighed down by apprehension that I might be wrong. I'd have a long and tense wait until the morning for the answer.

Chapter 44

I mingled with the prisoners in Jimmy Walsh's billet; some smiled at me, and another offered me a coffee. I walked to the end and saw Walsh's cell door open. There was no one inside; I looked around the billet. The other cell doors were all closed now. So I went inside. It was as I remembered the first time. The same books on the shelf. The same CDs although this time I spotted a CD player – it must have been under the bed the first time.

I woke up with a start, the duvet curled around my legs, my forehead and shoulders damp with sweat. I sat on the side of my bed. I drew a hand through my hair, rubbed my palms over my face and headed out for the shower hoping I could wash Jimmy Walsh from my mind. But it wasn't that easy and I kept thinking about him as I drove into Queen Street.

It was a little before eight when I walked into the Incident Room.

Lydia had already arrived and looked up from her monitor. 'Good morning, boss. What do you think DCI Hobbs will say? Will he authorise the arrest of Jimmy Walsh?'

'Let's wait until we get the adoption records.' In reality I knew Hobbs would want certainty. Evidence that not even the most expensive lawyers in Cardiff could challenge.

The record of the telephone calls made on the mobile Jimmy Walsh had bought arrived later that morning. None of them were traceable. Within an hour the team established they were all pay-as-you-go mobiles. They'd been sold months earlier, enough time for any CCTV record of their purchase in the shops to have been erased.

'I wonder who Jimmy called?' Lydia said.

I stared at the list wondering exactly the same. 'Family and maybe his *associates*. Mrs Walsh, of course.' I spat out her name. I reached into the inside pocket of my jacket draped over my chair and pulled out my wallet. It always seemed full of till receipts I didn't need to keep. I found the business card Bernie Walsh had given me. I scanned the details. I looked over at Lydia. I read the number aloud. 'Is that one of the numbers from Jimmy Walsh's mobile?'

She reached over for the printed sheet and then nodded her head.

'I wonder what DCI Hobbs will make of that,' I said.

Lydia didn't have time to reply as my telephone rang. 'There's a courier waiting for you in reception, Inspector.'

A leather-clad man sat in reception, a helmet on the bench by his side. 'I have a personal delivery for Inspector John Marco. I need to see identification before I can deliver these documents.'

So my threats and cajoling yesterday had done the trick with the civil servant at the General Register Office. I showed him my warrant card, he jotted down the details and I signed his form and took the envelope back to my office.

Nicolas Ackerman and his wife Jennifer had adopted Andrew Walsh by an order of the Southampton County Court. I showed it to Lydia who must have seen the relief on my face as a small piece of the jigsaw fell into place. Then I punched in the name Andrew Ackerman into the Police National Computer and stared at the monitor. It was a long shot. When the screen filled with his image I wanted to jump up and down on the spot, but I looked over at Lydia and thrust a fist into the air. 'Yes.'

Lydia looked over at the screen and her mouth

widened into a broad smile.

I rang central operations in Hampshire police and traced the SIO in charge of the case when Andrew had been sent down for ten months. It took me another six telephone calls to speak to an Inspector Hammond.

'I'm looking at an image of Andrew Ackerman from the PNC,' I said, but before I could continue he cut in.

'Doesn't look anything like that now. He's lost all his hair and he lost a big chunk of his left ear in a fight.'

It explained the beanie I had seen on the CCTV coverage from HMP Grange Hall.

Hammond gave me a summary of Andrew Ackerman's career. Criminality must run in the genes. I thanked him and rang off. There had been something troubling me ever since my last conversation with Cornock when he had challenged me about the motive for Yelland's murder. It had never been about Yelland demanding money for more favours in jail.

I gazed over at Lydia.

'Yelland must have worked out what had happened. We saw him earlier on the CCTV from the billet. He must have realised that Jimmy Walsh had switched places with his identical triplet.'

'Of course.' Realisation dawned on Lydia. 'Sharon Yelland said he thought things were getting better. So he threatens to tell the authorities.'

The triangulation reports we requested for Bernie and Jimmy Walsh's mobile telephones reached my computer sooner than had ever been possible in the past. They could be notoriously unreliable but I sat at the edge of my chair as I read them. The telephone Jimmy Walsh had purchased in Southampton was active between four and eight pm in the

Roath Park area of Cardiff on the night Bevard was killed. And Bernie Walsh couldn't escape the power of tracking her calls which placed her within a convenient radius of HMP Grange Hall late that afternoon. It completed the picture we needed to take everything to Acting Detective Chief Inspector Dave Hobbs. Lydia raised an eyebrow when I suggested she accompany me to see him. She opened her mouth to say something but thought better of it.

We walked through Queen Street; my mind felt settled. Cornock had been right, it had been something obvious. I knew that Walsh had killed Bevard. We reached the door to Cornock's office. I gave it a confident tap with my fingers. There was muffled shout and we entered and sat down by the conference table where I outlined the case in detail.

Eventually Hobbs cast his gaze towards Cornock's fish tank. It looked as though some of the tropical fish had died. He poked a tongue lightly into his cheek and inhaled a long breath.

'First the triangulation evidence is pretty unreliable. There was the case in North Wales a few years ago when we were tracing a missing person and his mobile signal suggested he was miles from where his body was eventually found.

'But—'

Hobbs raised a hand. 'I'm only anticipating how his defence lawyers will react.'

'We can place him in Southampton when he bought the mobile telephone. He was tracing his family. He's got an identical triplet. We arrest Andrew Ackerman and—'

'On what grounds?'

'Conspiracy to murder.' I knew I sounded desperate.

Hobbs shook his head. 'On the basis that we think he might have swapped places with Jimmy Walsh. Get real,

John. The Crown Prosecution Service won't let you run with that. We need evidence, eyewitness evidence. And from what you tell me Jimmy Walsh has already disposed of the only witnesses.'

'But we have Gloria Bevard calling Jimmy Walsh's number on the night her husband is killed.'

I sensed Hobbs struggling to find the right words. 'I grant you that is ... interesting.'

Interesting.

'But without being able to prove Jimmy Walsh had temporarily absconded from HMP Grange Hall you can't make a connection.'

'It all builds a picture. Add all the pieces together. We should interview all the prisoners on the billet. And all the prison officers.'

Hobbs leant over the desk. 'Don't you think one of the prison officers would have come forward by now if he knew anything? And as for the other prisoners – after what happened to Bevard and Yelland. They'll all be scared witless.'

I slumped back into my chair, glancing over at Lydia. Determination and despair filled her eyes.

'I'll do what I can.' Hobbs stood up, announcing that our meeting was over.

I couldn't abide staying in Queen Street so I left and headed to my car. It was on a whim that I decided to drive up to see my parents. I didn't spend time often enough with them. At least we had Walsh facing a charge of murder and I dismissed the prospect a jury might acquit him.

I arrived in Aberdare and Mamma hugged me tightly, reprimanding me for not having called.

I sat with Papa who looked better. He was sleeping well, he had started to follow the exercise regime the hospital had given him and he was looking forward to his next out-patient appointment.

'I've been thinking, John,' he said towards the end of the evening. 'I haven't got the stomach to fight Gino and Jez any longer. There's nothing more important than my health. And now it's time to let go of the past. I'm going to tell Gino we'll agree to sell.'

The pounding in my ears increased until all I could focus on was my father's face. It meant another victory for Jimmy Walsh.

Chapter 45

From the first day of the investigation, Jimmy Walsh had been a part of my life. The discovery of the recording from Roath Park on the night of Robin Oakley's murder meant the prosecution against Walsh had a reasonable prospect of success. But juries can be fickle and the possibility of his acquittal had weighed heavily in my thoughts as I arrived at Queen Street that morning.

It was reassuring that Kendall was in custody with enough compelling evidence to ensure a conviction. As a 'lifer' he'd spend years in a high security category A jail moving around the prison estate until a transfer to a category B jail and years down the track to an open prison pending release. He'd be an old man by then. A comforting thought.

Lydia and Jane were both sitting by their desks, monitors flickering into life. Wyn appeared with mugs of coffee. 'Boss?' he said, glancing at the tray.

I nodded confirmation and he returned to the kitchen.

I sat down in the Incident Room and stared at the board and the faces pinned to it. Hobbs had left me in no doubt yesterday what he thought of the prospect of charging Walsh with the murder of Bevard on the evidence we had. Grudgingly I acknowledged to myself that he was right. But I kept thinking about the images of Kendall and Mrs Walsh on the CCTV coverage in the pubs and clubs of Cardiff.

Wyn returned with my coffee.

'What happens now, boss?' Jane said.

Three pairs of eyes stared over at me. I glanced at my watch. Would Hobbs get me an answer this morning? I sipped my drink. I knew that the rest of the team wanted to see Walsh charged too.

I stood up and paced over to the board. There was evidence. And we had to find it.

My thoughts turned to Ledley and I stared at the map of Pontypool and the various circles and annotations that had been added to it.

'I want the footage from every CCTV camera from Cardiff Gate services to Forge Side collected and examined for a silver car. I want the registration number. And then I want enhanced images of the driver. Then I want all the owners of every house in every one of the streets in Forge Side spoken to again.'

I paused. The door to the Incident Room squeaked open behind me.

'I want artists' impressions from anyone who thinks they might have seen a driver of a silver car. And then I want a public appeal for witnesses. And get leaflets drafted for circulation around Cardiff Gate services. Somebody must have seen something.'

I heard chairs and bodies moving. I looked around and saw Assistant Chief Constable Neary standing behind me. Wyn, Jane and Lydia were already on their feet. I straightened.

'Ma'am,' we said in unison.

Neary's uniform was newly ironed with immaculate creases, and her service cravat perched neatly below her face. If there was a Mr Neary he probably thought she was attractive. A broad fringe of blonde hair draped over thick eyelashes. I hadn't noticed her intense stare before.

'Detective Inspector Marco, I need a word.'

I made for my office and she followed me. Inside I scooped up the papers that had been left from the night before and tried a makeshift exercise in tidying. Neary ignored me and sat down after closing the door firmly.

'I've spoken to Detective Chief Inspector Hobbs last night about the Walsh case.'

'Ma'am.'

She crossed one leg over the other knee and placed both hands on top of each other. If they had decided not to proceed then why had ACC Neary arrived to break the news?

'You and the team have done a lot of good work.'

'Thank you, ma'am.'

'And if you're right and Walsh did do a swap with his triplet then it's quite remarkable.'

'There's no other explanation.'

'Walsh is dangerous and we want him locked up for the rest of his days. I've been reviewing the evidence in the Oakley case. The recording from Roath Park is very grainy.'

A lump developed in my throat.

'We can see the approach the defence will take. They'll challenge the quality of the film. And the other two in the video are of course no longer with us. Is the video strong enough to persuade a jury beyond all reasonable doubt?' Her eyebrows disappeared behind her fringe now.

'And then we have Mr Bryant who provided Walsh with his alibi. The defence will challenge everything on the basis that the waiter was motivated by revenge as Bryant was sleeping with his girlfriend.'

I opened my mouth but realised that she had more to add.

'And we have nothing but circumstantial evidence for Walsh killing Felix Bevard. Even if we arrested Mrs Bevard and Walsh's triplet they would deny everything. It would mean no case and no hope of securing a conviction.'

I could see that the decision had already been made not to prosecute Walsh for killing Bevard and my heart sank. He might even be acquitted and then he'd be free. I felt sick at the thought.

'We could at least arrest Mrs Bevard and Andrew Ackerman.'

'I understand your strong views, Inspector. Especially bearing in mind what has happened with your parents. But they'd have anticipated an arrest and planned their reply.'

'Even Mrs Bevard's telephone calls?'

My doubt had sounded like a criticism. Neary paused.

'A decision was made last night that we had to secure a conviction against Walsh.'

Relief washed over me and I found myself slipping back in my chair.

'But we want to be certain that he goes down for life. And that he serves several life sentences. A decision was made last night to offer Martin Kendall a supergrass deal in exchange for evidence to convict James Walsh.'

I frowned, scarcely believing what she had told me.

'Steps have been taken to begin the process.'

Kendall would walk *free*. The realisation started to poison my mind. My whole body tensed. He had terrorised my family. He was a murderer.

'But he's a killer.' I must have sounded pathetic.

'I know, John, and I know what he did to your family.'

Kendall's image came to mind and I heard that Scottish accent ringing in my ears.

'There really is no other way. We want Walsh behind bars for ever. It's been a very difficult decision I can assure you. But we had to consider the public interest in securing a conviction against Walsh. And Kendall has no family. No ties.'

I looked down at the papers for a moment and then

whispered. 'Where will Kendall go?'

Neary paused. 'We'll never know. US maybe or Australia – somewhere where they speak English. He'll be given a new identity and they'll find him employment. The unit dealing with informants in these situations are very efficient.'

After a few seconds that felt like minutes Neary stood up. 'None of us are happy with this situation but it is for the best. I suggest you keep this between you and your sergeant for now.'

I got to my feet and she reached out a hand and firmly shook mine.

After she left I fell back into my chair trying to unscramble my emotions.

Lydia appeared at my door. 'What was that all about, boss?'

Chapter 46

My anger with Assistant Chief Constable Neary was short lived when I savoured the prospect of interviewing Jimmy Walsh and watching his blood run cold as he realised he was going down for multiple life sentences. I had spent the afternoon after my conversation with her walking along the barrage in Cardiff Bay. The wind had whipped around my face but I had ploughed on hoping I could see the decision had been correct.

The next three days passed in a blur of activity.

There were meetings with Dave Hobbs and emails with complex memoranda from the Crown Prosecution lawyers. They used the words 'public interest' a lot and everyone seemed to be contemplating criticisms from the trial judge. Hobbs even suggested someone would have a quiet word with the Crown court administration staff to ensure the trial judge would be sympathetic to the supergrass deal with Martin Kendall. I expected operational reasons to be cited as a reason to move the trial to a Crown court away from Cardiff and the prying eyes of the press.

I had the team scouring the CCTV for any image of the silver car driving to Forge Side. And coordinating the house-to-house took two full days for Wyn and Jane. I spent one afternoon in Cardiff Gate services asking all the staff if they recognised the Range Rover. It was a thankless task. The appeal for witnesses produced the usual crank calls and hoaxes that Lydia dealt with. It gave me time to prepare for the arrest of Jimmy Walsh. A dedicated source unit headed by a detective chief inspector from Western Division in Swansea had the dubious distinction of interviewing Martin Kendall. It would have made me sick to hear his confession to murdering Brian Yelland and admitting his part in the killing of Oakley.

I had to appear uncooperative when Uncle Gino and Jez wanted to meet once they knew Papa had decided to sell. They complained like mad, presumably because they had told Goldstar Properties that the sale could go ahead and that meant Walsh and his family felt they had another victory.

A cryptic email from Hobbs on a Monday afternoon told me that that evening *'matters would be concluded'*. So later I parked a discreet distance away from Walsh's home. The detached house in Cyncoed was lit up like a Christmas tree and I recognised his daughter and son-in-law arrive in their 4x4. They could pass as respectable upstanding members of the community. They had no idea what had been happening in the interview suites of HMP Cardiff.

I cowered to one side when I saw Walsh and his family drive away. After a few seconds, I followed them into the middle of town. They parked outside one of the expensive restaurants and walked in. Obviously, something to celebrate; after all, they thought they had a new development in Pontypridd that would make them a pile of cash.

Did Walsh ever think about Kendall?

I smiled to myself as I imagined the look on Walsh's face when I'd tell him about Kendall's evidence.

It was after eight that evening when I returned to my flat. I had barely seen Tracy in the past week and she had returned from a long weekend with her parents. She kept her coat on and avoided my attempt to kiss her. She sat on a sofa and put her set of keys on the coffee table.

'I've been thinking a lot recently, John. About us, I mean.' I sensed Tracy had more to tell me. 'Things happened so quickly at the start. I mean, not that I regret it.

But we didn't have time to get to know each other. And with Mum and Dad living away and not in good health ...'

I could see where this conversation was leading. Years ago it would have been the sort of conversation where a beer would have been welcome.

'I can't see how things will work out. Do you?' She looked up and stared deep into my eyes.

I averted my gaze; she must have realised from my reticence that I didn't know the answer. Our relationship had been on cruise control for the past few months and a part of me was relieved she felt the same way.

'I had an interview today for an investigators role with the Hampshire force.'

'I want to be nearer Mum and Dad. They're getting on and we aren't. So I think it's for the best.'

She brushed away a tear and she left soon afterwards.

Chapter 47

The following morning I had the team ready early.

Hobbs joined us in the Incident Room and stood to one side of the board.

'We're going to arrest Jimmy Walsh this morning,' I said.

There were quizzical troubled looks.

'Martin Kendall is going to give evidence against Jimmy Walsh in exchange for immunity from prosecution.'

Jane gasped, and Wyn stood rigid to the spot, his body tense.

'Detective Sergeant Flint and Detective Constable Thorne will arrest Mrs Gloria Bevard and Detective Constable Wyn Nuttall will accompany me to arrest Jimmy Walsh. A team from Hampshire constabulary is going to arrest Andrew Ackerman. We'll get him transferred here later.'

'But that means Kendall gets away with the murder of Yelland,' Jane said.

Hobbs cleared his throat. 'A decision was made in the public interest that we had to secure a conviction of Jimmy Walsh.'

'But Kendall's evidence is tainted,' Wyn said, voicing the obvious. 'He'll say anything to get off a murder charge.'

Hobbs again. 'It's the excellent work you've all done to build a picture of what really happened that has made this all happen.'

'What do we say to Sharon Yelland?' Jane said.

I glanced at Hobbs. The impact on her had probably been ignored 'in the public interest'. Images of her and her children came to mind. At least she knew who had killed her husband. Would that be a comfort? 'I'll see her,' I said.

It wasn't an answer. I could have added – *And I*

hope she'll understand but I didn't think she would. I had trouble with Martin Kendall leading a new life in some warm country.

'We considered her position very carefully,' Hobbs added, but he didn't convince anyone. 'The public interest can often be unsatisfactory.'

It was management speak I hoped I'd never get accustomed to.

I parked on Lake Road East and walked down to the entrance of Roath Park. The air was still; decaying leaves from the sycamores littered the pavement edge. Autumn colours of russet and gold made the park look warm and welcoming. On the tarmacked paths I spotted walkers with dogs and mothers with prams and the occasional jogger. My mobile vibrated in my fleece pocket and I fished it out to answer Lydia's call.

'We should be arriving at Gloria Bevard's place in the next ten minutes.'

'Thanks. Text me when you're outside.'

I counted half a dozen enthusiastic couples out on the lake in rowing boats. We passed the Scott monument and I read the time. Almost eleven. A young mother shouted after a child on a bike and I wondered if any of the visitors that morning knew that a grisly murder had taken place in the café. And that the man responsible was inside drinking coffee, exchanging a joke with Bernie, planning for his eventual acquittal.

A faint smell of stale fat drifted from the café as we neared it. I told Wyn to stand and wait by the entrance. . I spotted Walsh sitting by the window with Bernie. He chewed a mouthful of cake while Bernie sipped on a drink. No fancy cakes where he was going. Losing weight might do him some good. Lydia's text reached my mobile.

I pushed open the door and strode towards him.

He glanced up and did a double take. Then he frowned and looked over at me puzzled.

I sat down at his table.

'This is police harassment,' Walsh said.

Bernie looked at me as though she wanted to stab me.

'Somebody told me you liked Roath Park,' I smiled.

He said nothing.

'Get lost. Leave us in peace,' Bernie said.

'It's the changing seasons I like.'

'What the fuck do you want?' Walsh hissed.

'And being able to walk in the park whenever I want and see my family and know they won't be stalked in the future.'

Another frown. 'It's a good deal; you and your family are getting a good price.'

'And somebody told me you know the storeroom in this café very well.'

'I'm going to call my solicitor.'

You're going to need his help right enough.

'Of course you can. And you won't even have to pay for the call.'

Walsh threw the pastry fork onto the plate.

'Somebody told me you killed Felix Bevard. And that same person told me you killed Robin Oakley.'

'You can't be serious.'

I noticed movement by the front door and saw Wyn standing with two uniformed officers. I turned to Walsh and said the words I had given up believing anyone would say.

'James Walsh, I'm arresting you for murder. You don't have to say ....'

Chapter 48

Sharon Yelland returned from the kitchen with a tray of biscuits and mugs of tea.

'I've got some news,' I said as she handed me a drink.

'I thought there was a reason for the visit.'

She sat down on one of the sofas in the sitting room. Despite everything that had happened she had managed to make the house into a home. There were pictures of the children on the mantel and magazines on the coffee table, which suggested that she had moved on with her life. I spotted some holiday brochures near the television.

'A man has admitted to killing Brian.'

I looked over at her but there was little emotion. 'I see.'

'He was linked to a Jimmy Walsh who was on a billet in Grange Hall where Brian worked.'

She kept looking at me between small mouthfuls of tea.

'However, it's not as simple as it first appears. This man was able to provide us with detailed evidence of Walsh being involved in several murders.'

She raised an eyebrow and now there was sadness in her eyes.

'It was decided that he would be offered a deal – it's called a supergrass deal – so that we could prosecute Jimmy Walsh.'

'What will happen to him?'

'Walsh will most likely face the rest of his days in jail.'

'No, I meant the other man – the one who killed Brian.'

I gathered my thoughts about the best way to tell her. 'He'll be taken into witness protection. He'll be given a new identity and a new life.'

'And his family?'

'He doesn't have any.'

'That was convenient.' She started on a digestive biscuit.

'It wasn't my decision and I know how you must feel about Brian's killer getting away without punishment.'

I wasn't certain how she might react and I felt better having shared with her my misgivings that Kendall was offered a deal.

'I can't get Brian back and even if I could I don't know that I would. He had chosen a life that I didn't want to share and he hadn't listened to me for a long time.'

'What will you tell the children?'

'That they should miss their father and that he wanted to be a good man but ...'

'Sometimes things never work out as you hope.'

Another half an hour passed as we talked and she told me about her hopes for the future. She never sounded aggrieved, accepting that having Walsh behind bars for the rest of his life was reward enough.

Superintendent Cornock had been back in charge for three weeks when the case against Walsh finally got to court. Conveniently, a free morning one Friday appeared in the list of a judge sitting in Carmarthen. It meant a trip out west. Coincidentally the visit by a European head of state to the Welsh Parliament – a recent name change from Assembly having earned howls of derision from some corners of the press – made reporting the events in the Crown court a sideshow.

Lydia and I settled into a seat at the back of the old court building.

Prosecution and defence lawyers drifted into court carrying piles of paperwork.

Walsh had the good sense to accept the inevitable and pleaded guilty to the murders of Oakley and Bevard. We had to accept that Ledley's killer would never face the court although I knew that I was staring at him when Walsh entered the dock. A visiting judge from London who had been a high profile prosecutor at one time with a well-known dislike of organised crime groups seemed the perfect choice. Another apt coincidence. He asked the occasional question as the prosecution outlined the basis of the supergrass deal. By now the defence had given up and Walsh's lawyers pleaded that the court should be lenient.

It didn't help. Nobody thought it would.

The judge imposed a minimum tariff of thirty years, which really meant thirty-five once the parole system had been exhausted. Walsh would be well into his eighties by then. He might even die in prison.

Gloria Bevard burst into tears when she was given a life sentence with a minimum tariff of fifteen years. Without her involvement in telling Walsh about Felix Bevard's proposed supergrass deal her husband might still be alive. Then she slumped to the floor and had to be helped up back to her seat. Bernie Walsh curled her mouth in disgust when the judge gave her the same sentence as Gloria. I had expected to see Andrew Ackerman in the dock as well but he had denied any knowledge of what Jimmy Walsh intended to do on his brief night of freedom. Once the prosecutors and the senior management of the Wales Police Service realised we had enough evidence against Walsh, Ackerman became unimportant.

I got back to Queen Street as the last of the day

shift were leaving.

Cornock bellowed for me to enter when I knocked on the door of his office.

'I've heard.' He beamed. 'I'm sure you're very pleased.'

'Walsh is behind bars. That's the best result possible.'

The fish tank glistened and I noticed a new red striped tropical fish swimming around.

'I waited until you got back,' he said, checking his watch. 'I'm taking my wife to a concert tonight.'

It was the first time I had heard him talking about his social life and for a second it surprised me.

'I thought you should know about Dave Hobbs.'

I held my breath.

'His appointment to chief inspector wasn't confirmed.'

I let out a long slow breath of relief.

'He's accepted a transfer into one of those dedicated source units based in Eastern Division. So your paths are unlikely to cross in the future.'

The prospect filled me with hope.

At low tide North Beach in Tenby leaves the old lifeboat station and its launching ramp stranded high above the white clean sand. Dean, Papa and I wandered around the barnacle-encrusted supports and then on to the edge of the water before looking up at the new lifeboat installation, a modern wooden-clad building. We retraced our steps to the town and then down onto South Beach. Sand in the wind scratched our faces and Dean complained. I fastened the collar of his jacket high up to his chin and we set off along the beach. I held Dean's hand tightly but we only managed to make it halfway along the beach before Papa slowed. I sensed him struggling.

'You go on if you want,' Papa said.

I decided that Dean would probably prefer an ice cream to an extended walk on a windswept beach so we tramped back into town. Out of season the town had a gentle charm that the summer tourists choke. We passed small shops and cafés all anxious for our trade and settled for an ice cream parlour.

We sat in the window and Dean cleared a bowl full of chocolate and vanilla ice cream.

'I'm glad you could make it,' Papa said. 'Has everything finished with that case?'

I nodded. 'They are all safely locked up.'

'We've had an offer for the property.'

I raised an eyebrow.

'It's from a reputable company this time. Tell me what happened to that man Kendall?'

I gave him my I-wish-I-could-tell-you look. I thought about how badly I had wanted him imprisoned. And that it had been an all-consuming objective once he had stalked the family. Did we get justice? Was it all really in the public interest?

We finished our ice creams and headed back for the caravan.

Printed in Great Britain
by Amazon

81704637R00190